SCRIBNER
CANADA

THE
AFRICAN
SAMURAI

A Novel

CRAIG SHREVE

PUBLISHED BY SCRIBNER CANADA

New York   London   Toronto   Sydney   New Delhi

SCRIBNER
CANADA

Scribner Canada
An Imprint of Simon & Schuster, Inc.
166 King Street East, Suite 300
Toronto, Ontario M5A 1J3
Copyright © 2023 by Craig Shreve

This Scribner Canada edition August 2023

SCRIBNER CANADA and colophon are trademarks of Simon & Schuster, Inc.

For information about special discounts for bulk purchases, please contact Simon & Schuster Special Sales at 1-800-268-3216 or CustomerService@simonandschuster.ca.

Manufactured in the United States of America

10   9   8   7   6   5   4   3   2

Library and Archives Canada Cataloguing in Publication

Title: The African samurai / Craig Shreve.
Names: Shreve, Craig, author.
Identifiers: Canadiana (print) 20220394245 | Canadiana (ebook) 20220394261 | ISBN 9781668002865 (softcover) | ISBN 9781668002872 (ebook)
Classification: LCC PS8637.H735 A77 2023 | DDC C813/.6—dc23

ISBN 978-1-6680-0286-5
ISBN 978-1-6680-0287-2 (ebook)

The map on page vii: © Paul Barker

The images on page xi: Oda standard: © Kamon Japanese Clan Samurai symbol © Shutterstock/Aonaka; Akechi standard: Samurai Clan logo © Shutterstock/Musashi2001; Tokugawa standard: Tokugawa Clan image © Shutterstock/SKart74; Toyotomi standard: Japanese pattern © Shutterstock/Baghost

For Ryan Swayze, who I know would have loved
the history bchind this one

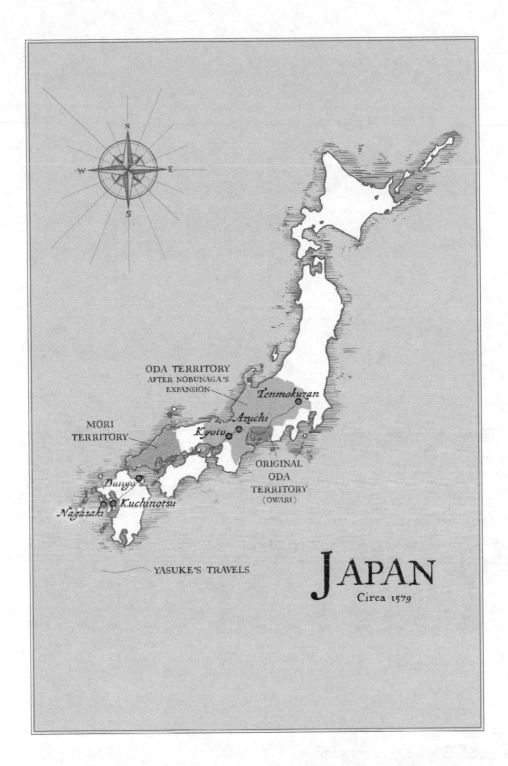

ODA TERRITORY
AFTER NOBUNAGA'S
EXPANSION

Tenmokuzan

MORI
TERRITORY

Azuchi

Kyoto

ORIGINAL
ODA
TERRITORY
(OWARI)

Bungo

Kuchinotsu

Nagasaki

·········· YASUKE'S TRAVELS

JAPAN
Circa 1579

CAST OF CHARACTERS

A note about names: Several key characters in this story changed their names multiple times throughout the course of their lives. For simplicity's sake, I have chosen to use their most historically significant names, even if they were not using those names when the events portrayed here took place.

THE AFRICAN SAMURAI

Yasuke: An East African, taken into slavery as a boy. His original name is unknown. His place of birth is also uncertain, though there is speculation he is of the Makua people in Mozambique.

THE FIRST GREAT UNIFIER OF JAPAN

Oda Nobunaga: A daimyo (warlord) who is viewed historically as the first of the Three Great Unifiers of Japan. Nobunaga was originally the daimyo of Owari Province, before expanding his territory across most of central Japan.

THE JESUITS

Alessandro Valignano: An Italian priest and Jesuit missionary, granted the title Visitor to the Indies, which made his authority in the church second only to the Pope's throughout all of India and Asia.

Brother Ambrosius: A Jesuit missionary in the Nagasaki region

Brother Organtino: A Jesuit missionary long stationed in Japan, one of the earliest of the church's emissaries to arrive in Japan and one of the few priests allowed to remain in the country after the order as a whole was later expelled.

THE GENERALS

Akechi Mitsuhide: First a samurai of the Saitō clan, then a protector of the Wandering Shogun Ashikaga Yoshiaki, before coming into Nobunaga's service

Tokugawa Ieyasu: Daimyo of the Mikawa Province and Nobunaga's most trusted ally

Toyotomi Hideyoshi: Born into peasantry but elevated to the highest role by Oda Nobunaga

ODA NOBUNAGA'S SAMURAI GUARD

Jingorou: Brother of Ogura

Ogura: Brother of Jingorou

Ranmaru: A young samurai and Nobunaga's close attendant

IN THE SERVICE OF ODA NOBUNAGA

Hidemitsu: Akechi Mitsuhide's son-in-law and most trusted lieutenant

Masahide: A trusted samurai in the service of Oda Nobunaga's father. Masahide committed seppuku in an attempt to put Nobunaga on the right path. At Azuchi, Nobunaga built a temple to honor him.

Tomiko: A servant in the house of Oda Nobunaga

THE DAIMYOS

Arima Harunobu: The besieged daimyo who hosted Valignano upon his arrival at Kinchotsu

Hatano Hideharu: Head of the Hatano clan and holder of Yakami castle

Takeda Katsuyori: Daimyo of the Takeda clan after the passing of Takeda Shingen

Takeda Shingen: The legendary "Tiger of Kai," a renowned military leader and longtime rival of Nobunaga's

Ōmura Sumitada: The first daimyo to convert to Christianity

CAST OF CHARACTERS

The Clans

The Mori: A powerful clan holding sway over much of western Japan

The Oda: Traditionally a minor clan, before a young Nobunaga rode a string of victories to national prominence and made the clan Japan's most powerful

The Takeda: A clan with a long-standing rivalry with the Oda clan, once powerful but significantly weakened after the death of their legendary leader, Takeda Shingen

Additional Figures

Ikko-Ikki: Loosely organized groups throughout the country, united under a particular sect of Buddhism. They presented economic, political, and military challenges for Nobunaga and other daimyo.

Murakami: A line of pirates (or sea-lords) who controlled the Seto Inland Sea during the Sengoku period, and who many daimyo feared

All characters mentioned above are real people, except for Tomiko. Any characters not mentioned above are entirely fictional.

ODA

AKECHI

TOKUGAWA

TOYOTOMI

THE
AFRICAN
SAMURAI

I

The Slave and the Daimyo

Make a delicious bowl of tea; lay the charcoal so that it heats the water: arrange the flowers as they are in the field; in summer suggest coolness, in winter, warmth; do everything ahead of time; prepare for rain; and give those with whom you find yourself every consideration. There is no other secret.

—Sen Rikyu, tea master

1

Home is a lost place, more dream to me than memory.

Even the fragments I held on to felt foreign and distant, like things that had happened in another's life. The life of someone who had not been taken away, who had not been severed from his own beginnings. And yet sometimes, a memory would come through so clearly it ached.

As a child, my family and a few others from the tribe made the long hike from our village in the shadow of Mount Namuli to the coast. It was late in the year, the time of the laying of eggs. We set our camps on the edge of the beach and watched the turtles come ashore at night, waves of them, with hard, dark shells and soft, speckled underbellies. They seemed to be moving both independently, and in unison. They used their flippers to create indentations in the sand and rested atop them. We committed the spots to memory, and slept.

In the morning, when the turtles had gone, we dug up the eggs, taking only what we needed. We made the trek back to the village with the eggs carried carefully in baskets. About two months later we would make the long hike to the beach again. We set our camps in the same place on the beach's edge. Under the light of the full moon, the sand began to pucker and shift. One tiny bill poked out from beneath it, then another, then a dozen more, a hundred. A mass of tiny turtles crawling toward the yawning expanse of green froth, drawn there by something we could never understand. I wanted to believe that they were crawling out to sea to find their mothers, to reunite themselves.

The first trip to the sea had been to gather food. The second trip had been to learn why to leave as many as possible, to take only what was needed. I can remember my mother's voice, but not her face. Nor can I remember my father's. I have flashes of reading and writing lessons under a mango tree. Of working alongside the other boys inside the mines, stripping the cave walls for ore; playing with them in the fields, using small pebbles for games of mancala in the dirt of the streets. Of festivals with drums and masks and brightly colored robes, the thrill of seeing visitors from other lands and the wares they brought to trade. And I remember the turtles, rising out of the sand and making their way to the sea.

It was the last time I was free.

"YOU DON'T NEED TO HOVER over me, there is no one on the boat but our own men."

Father Valignano spoke without looking up from his work. The Jesuit looked aged in the thin rays of sun from the porthole, the shadows highlighting the lines on his cheek and forehead and deepening the hollows around his eyes. His head bobbed in and out of the stream of pale light, showing the short gray hair atop it. His equally gray beard, trim and narrow, hung almost down to the paper he scrawled upon. His hand, though, was steady as he dipped the quill and quickly but carefully drew it across the page, and his voice, as ever, held the steadiness of one used to command.

"My job is to protect you from all men. Not just other men," I replied.

"Have you so little trust in our fellow travelers?"

"A bodyguard who relies on trust often fails at his task."

"In Japanese, if you will."

Valignano had still not looked up from his desk. I hesitated, searching for the words. I'd spent many months learning Japanese language and history, both leading up to this voyage and during the long days aboard the ship, but I always struggled to make the switch from Portuguese. After a moment, I repeated my statement in Japanese. Valignano nodded approvingly, and made a few small corrections, then continued on in this language that was new to both of us.

"Why don't you go above, get some air?" Valignano asked, waving me away.

"You know I do not like the sea," I said.

"Yes. For such a large man you are afraid of so many things."

"A man who lacks fear also lacks caution."

"A man who fears too much lacks faith. You must trust in God, my son. He whose faith is strong walks untouched in this world. Unafraid."

I accepted the rebuke silently. I'd learned much from the Jesuits. I could recite large swaths of their Bible in both Portuguese and Latin, and increasing amounts of it in Japanese. I admired the belief of the priests, and I believed it to be genuine, but a small part of me had resisted giving in to it completely. It seemed to me that a man who calls on God to fight his battles quickly forgets how to fight his own. Faith seemed a privilege that could be afforded to the protected, the comfortable, but I would always choose a sword to protect me over a cross.

Though he'd never say it, I suspected Valignano would agree.

The steel-eyed priest looked up from his work, his famously thin patience worn through.

"We will be to port soon, and there will be plenty of opportunities for you to tower behind me and scowl."

I scowled at the comment, then smiled when I realized I was doing it. I bowed and ducked my head beneath the doorframe as I exited.

I had marked my twenty-fourth birthday on this boat, sailing toward Japan. It had been twelve years since I had last seen my village, and I had long since given up hope of seeing it again. I'd been away now for the same length I had lived there. Twelve years free, in Africa; twelve years enslaved, in India, Portugal, China, sold to mercenaries, to an army, to a church. Half my life amongst family, half my life amongst strangers. Half my life a child, half my life a soldier.

I loathed the deck, but I climbed up to it regardless. I had observed the captain carefully and had picked up the basic working of his tools and calculations, but I still could not fathom how men could navigate when there was nothing but water to be seen in all directions. I had tried to read the stars the way I had seen the captain sometimes do, but it was something I had little aptitude for. It frustrated me. In all other things I had proven a fast learner, whether the weapons and strategies of the mercenaries or the books and languages of the priests, but the ways of the sea remained a mystery to me.

I stood at the rail on the leeward side and avoided looking at the sea by watching the ruffle of the sails instead. A handful of men wrestled with ropes and knots while others scrubbed the accumulated salt from the ship's forward deckboards. The decks, the masts, and the entire ship had been blackened with pitch, and the glittering white stain from the seawater showed the evidence of how far aboard the previous day's waves had reached.

Most of the men were belowdecks, and while they had invited me to join them on a few occasions, they trusted me even less than I did them. I had sat alongside them while they told stories, and I had wagered a few coins against them while they threw lots, but it was my duty to remain vigilant at all times, so I did not drink with them, and that made them suspicious of me. Besides that, we had reached the point in the voyage where violence was just below the surface, ready to emerge over the slightest squabble, or the most innocent of slights. Valignano's route to Japan had included stops in India and China, and though we had switched boats and crews at points along the way, this crew had still been close to a month at sea. I had no desire to play peacemaker, and had no patience to listen to the complaints of the men. Their cramped quarters and stale rations were luxuries compared to my own experience on ships.

One crewman, heavily bearded and probably heavily drunk, was berating another while standing over a crate that had been dropped and cracked. At their feet, vibrantly colored silks from China spilled out from the breach onto the salt-scrubbed deck.

In the cargo holds below us, an impossible number of crates held Bibles and crosses and European weaving, jewelry, and other fine items. But mostly guns. Crate after crate of matchlock pistols and long rifles and, Valignano's prize, three powerful new cannons capable of tearing down a fortress wall, or laying waste to a row of cavalry.

The weapons would be offered to the Japanese if they proved pious enough. If they let the Jesuits build their churches. If they let them teach their religion to their Japanese sons and daughters. If they converted, and ordered their clans to convert as well, then they would have powerful European weapons to use against their rivals, and Valignano would have his foothold in Asia. Guns in exchange for souls.

There were parts of the Jesuits' religion that still remained unclear to me, but trade was something I understood all too well. I had been given to Jesuits. In their schools I learned to read and write, was taught the white man's history, the white man's religion.

The stern-looking Jesuit priest who received me clucked his tongue in disgust upon hearing my name and gave me a Christian one instead. They named me after the son of Abraham. They told me the story of God asking Abraham to prove his belief by killing his only son. How Abraham built an altar and tied his son upon it and sharpened his blade, but God told him to hold fast. That he was pleased.

The Portuguese had named me well. Isaac. A man to be sacrificed. A thing to be offered.

2

My first glimpse of Japan was disappointing. We were to dock at Nagasaki, in Hizen Province, where the Portuguese traders had established a lucrative outpost. I was expecting a bustling port town, but a thick fog remained over the bay, leaving anything beyond the curving wooden dock too obscured to report on reliably. The dock itself was busy, but not overly so—mostly canoes carrying sacks of rice or bundles of pears and apples. Men in loose, dark clothing balanced gracefully on the edge of the tiny boats and tossed their cargo up to the deck, or steered the long poles on the aft of the boats to bring their stuff closer to shore.

At the call of land from the captain, the men had come above board and the deck was teeming with sailors. The sour moods of the last week turned to smiles and cheers. Beside me, Father Valignano made an almost inaudible grunt. I followed his gaze. One of the canoes was pushing off from the dock, aboard it a man dressed in a familiar black frock. Valignano did not miss much.

"Drop anchor here, Captain," he ordered quietly. "And prepare to assist a visitor aboard."

The captain barked orders. A collective rumble went through the men, followed by a flurry of activity.

Valignano watched the canoe approach as if his doing so was all that drew it toward us. The priest it carried was helped aboard and presented. He clasped his hands in front of him and lowered his head.

"Brother Ambrosius."

"Father Valignano, it is a blessing to see your voyage successful. We are honored to receive such an esteemed visitor from Rome."

"So honored that you receive me here, rather than ashore."

The priest's shoulders tensed as if he'd been physically struck, but he remained silent, kept his head low. Valignano sighed. He closed his eyes and briefly pinched the bridge of his nose. He made no attempt to hide his impatience when he spoke.

"Very well, then. Captain, we'll need your quarters."

ONCE INSIDE THE CAPTAIN'S QUARTERS, Brother Ambrosius allowed himself a moment to stare at me. I was used to it. My skin was a deeper black even than most Africans, dark enough to appear to shine. My hair, once shaved but now grown again on the voyage, twisted in knotty braids down almost to my collar. I stood a head taller than most Europeans, and my training had made my shoulders broad, my body muscular, enough to be apparent despite the billowing pantaloons and loose cotton blouse I wore. The crab sword at my hip would add to what was intended to be an intimidating image, the sword's blade and hilt painted black to resist rusting from the saltwater spray of a long ocean voyage, and to avoid the telltale glint of metal if it had to be drawn in the dark.

This new priest stood unsteadily, his legs unused to even the slight sway of these shallow waters, but he hid his discomfort well. His brown hair curled below his ears but was neatly kept, and his stubbly beard failed to hide a suspicious-looking scar along the left side of his jaw.

Most priests I'd seen fell in one of two categories—the pink, soft-skinned scholars with round faces who had prepared themselves for their task with years of study; and the wiry, bronzed-skin men with sharp eyes who had been hardened by life before finding an ambition within the church. This man was one of the latter. Valignano was as well. There were rumors that Valignano had stabbed a man to death in a street fight in Venice in his youth, and though such things were impossible to learn the truth of, I had not dismissed them. Some men were born to the faith. Others were reformed to it from less savory backgrounds.

Rather than the customary stance of crossing one's hands in front and tucking them into the sleeve of the opposite arm, this priest stood with his arms down and wide, hands clearly visible. Valignano had offered neither food nor drink once we were inside the captain's quarters, and this priest was wise enough to see the warning in that.

"Your voyage has been a long one, Father. I'll not delay you with the customary pleasantries. I've come to ask that you extend your voyage one day further."

"There is trouble at the settlement?"

"No, Father. Not of any serious sort."

Valignano turned toward the lattice of portholes behind the captain's desk and looked out upon the softly lapping waves. Brother Ambrosius continued.

"The lord of this region is a man named Ōmura Sumitada. He has not opposed us here, but we feel he could be . . . friendlier to the church. Our mission in Kuchinotsu tells us the lord there is willing to be more cooperative."

I watched Father Valignano for any sign, but he gave none. His was the first visit to Japanese shores from one of the higher-ranking priests in the Jesuit church. His title as Visitor to the Indies gave him full authority over all church matters in India and Asia. Given that it would take over a year to get a message to Rome and another year to get a response back, he was for all intents and purposes the pope of the region. It would be difficult to underestimate the value and prestige granted to any lord who hosted him. The priest was smart not to attempt to play on Valignano's ego by spelling the matter out for him. Valignano did indeed possess a prodigious ego, but in the months I had grown to know him, I had never once seen him put his own interests ahead of the church. His devotion to his mission was single-minded. I knew him well enough to know what his questions would be.

8

"And this Sumitada, how will he respond to such a slight?"

"Poorly, I'm certain. But he'll take no action against us. The moratorium on trade between China and Japan remains intact, which continues to be lucrative for us. Every second month, one of our ships arrives with goods from China and loads itself up with Japanese goods bound for Macau, and from there, the Chinese markets. Lord Sumitada will not risk that trade with retaliation."

"And the balance between Nagasaki and Kuchinotsu?"

"It will not be affected greatly. Certainly not enough to cause any further . . . instability."

"So, Japan remains divided."

"Yes, but less so than it was when you last received word."

"Tell me."

With the change in topic, the decision had been made. The men would not be happy with the thought of even one more day's sail, nor was I, but Valignano was not one to consult with others prior to making a decision, nor to be swayed from one once it was made. The men were already dreaming of dry land, comfortable beds, and fresh food, but those wishes meant little to Valignano.

He turned back from gazing out of the porthole and gestured toward the rudimentary map of Japan laid out on the captain's desk. Ambrosius cleared his throat and stepped around to the side of the desk.

"Oda Nobunaga continues to be the most prominent of the daimyos, and has consolidated power over central Japan. He defeated the Takeda cavalry at Nagashino, and though Takeda Katsuyori withdrew rather than submit, the clan is too weakened to be a major power in the region. Lord Nobunaga's siege at Ishiyama Hongan-ji continues, but the warrior monks cannot hold out much longer . . ."

Brother Ambrosius pointed out locations on the map as he spoke, and I yearned to ask of tactics, numbers, weaponry, but knew Valignano would not tolerate my speaking out of turn. I was familiar with Nobunaga's name, the leader of the Oda clan who had overthrown the shogunate some twenty years prior, signaling to the daimyos—the warlords of Japan's shattered territories—that he meant to rule them all. After over one hundred years of a fractured Japan, with each local lord battling anew each spring with their neighbors to either secure territory or extend it, Nobunaga meant to reunite Japan under a single leader once more, regardless of what force was required to do so. Ages-old alliances were broken and new ones were formed, as minor lords sought the protection of an alliance with more powerful ones, and the powerful lords eyed a reunification of Japan under their own banner. I swallowed my questions and listened, absorbing as much as I could.

"There is resistance in the Iga Province. The old ones say that Iga has never been conquered and never will, but Nobunaga will turn his attention there soon enough. His son, Nobutada, was defeated there despite having superior numbers, and Nobunaga will not allow that humiliation to go unaddressed," Brother Ambrosius explained. "The Takeda, while severely weakened, do still hold the region around Mount Fuji, and Nobunaga cannot allow Fuji to remain outside of his control either, if he means to rule Japan."

Valignano stabbed a finger toward me, shocking Ambrosius into silence.

"Speak," Valignano ordered.

"I've said nothing," I protested mildly.

"Precisely. We've traveled together long enough that I know when your tongue is restless. It's a tiring thing to try to ignore. Speak."

"Brother Ambrosius," I began, ignoring the slight sneer across his face and the clear disgust he felt that Valignano was allowing me to address him. "What value does Mount Fuji have? It doesn't look to be strategically placed."

Ambrosius clenched his jaw, but answered.

"Mount Fuji holds no strategic value, but it has immense cultural significance. It is important to the people as a symbol."

"Then he doesn't just seek to conquer," I mused out loud, "he wants the people to accept his rule willingly."

Brother Ambrosius brushed off the comment and continued.

10

"Nobunaga is close to his goal of unifying Japan. He already holds the key cities of Kyoto and Sakai. He will likely march against Iga within months, and, if successful there, would move to finish off the Takeda clan."

He paused to look up from the map. He waved a hand at it as if it were pointless to study because of how often it had changed.

"The only real resistance remaining is the Mori clan in the west. No one else is strong enough, organized enough, and well-funded enough to mount a viable defense. War between the Oda and the Mori is inevitable. A victory there, and nothing stands between Nobunaga and a unified Japan."

Father Valignano looked coolly at the map, listened without reaction, but I knew he was absorbing all of this as well, evaluating the landscape, calculating opportunities for the church.

"How is his disposition toward our mission?"

The priest glanced at me briefly to see if I would be dismissed.

"Perhaps church matters should be discussed—"

"Matters of the church will be discussed where and when I have questions regarding them," Valignano said coolly, never lifting his head to look at Ambrosius.

I fought the urge to smile. The priest became even more cautious.

"I would say he is . . . tolerant. He has refused to convert or be baptized, but we wrote to you of the Shinto priest, Nichijo?"

"Yes. Has he continued to be troublesome?"

"No more. He had convinced the emperor to ban Christianity, but Nobunaga intervened. He ordered Nichijo to debate our own Father Frois on the matter of religion. I was sadly unable to attend, but Father Frois, by all accounts, conducted himself splendidly. Nobunaga overturned the emperor's decree and Nichijo was . . . punished. It should also be noted that Nobunaga has been particularly harsh to the Buddhist monks who have opposed him in the regions. He burned their temple at Mount Hiei and slaughtered everyone there without exception."

"I shall not weep over the lost lives of the unfaithful."

The priest cleared his throat. "Of course, Father. I do not know Nobunaga's feelings for the church, but he does have a strong appreciation of foreign delicacies and ornaments, as well as some of our other offerings."

This time the priest did not glance at me, and didn't need to. I thought of the crates of guns beneath my feet, and the cannons. Enough to make a warring man embrace whatever religion he was asked to.

The priest leaned over the map once more. He looked unsteady in the gentle bob and sway. His face had turned slightly paler, and he clenched the sides of the table too tightly.

"Are you comfortable, Brother Ambrosius?" I asked.

He glared at me, and I hid my smirk. Valignano tilted his head, gave me a look that I understood meant *I'll allow this, but nothing further.* I took one step backward to show Valignano I had received his message, and he continued his questioning.

"The emperor no longer opposes us, then?"

"Not officially, no. The emperor prefers the old ways—"

"As discarded leaders are wont to do, no doubt."

Ambrosius paused at the interruption. I had no idea how long the priest had been in Japan, but no doubt he had grown accustomed to hearing the emperor spoken of with careful reverence. With a simple remark, Valignano had made clear that he would pay homage to no man, and I was certain the remark was made precisely for that effect.

Ambrosius gathered himself and stumbled on.

"The emperor still sides with the Shinto and the Buddhists, but if Nobunaga accepts us, the emperor will comply with his wishes."

"And with his army. What contact do we have with this Nobunaga?"

"Father Frois has met with him several times, and Brother Organtino is well placed with him. The church in Kyoto has appealed to him regularly. Nobunaga is currently in the capital. He is soon to be at Honno-ji temple, just outside of Kyoto. He has organized a festival in the emperor's honor, as a show of gratitude for the emperor's intervention with the Ikko-ikki."

"These so-called warrior monks?" Valignano asked derisively. "So they will no longer stand in Nobunaga's way?"

"These things are not certain. But there are strong signs that the imperial court will advise the Ikko-ikki to lay down their arms, and that they will comply. The emperor has little choice, really, and Nobunaga's visit to the capital will all but assure that the emperor issues this favorable edict. After that, Nobunaga will likely return to his new castle at Azuchi to begin planning his spring campaigns."

"Then it seems, as in all things, the Lord has blessed the timing of my arrival. How far is Kyoto?"

Ambrosius rubbed his scarred jaw and studied the map.

"That depends on how much you are willing to risk. If you can secure safe passage, the fastest route is along the Seto Inland Sea, then overland to Kyoto. That would take about two weeks from Kuchinotsu. Safe passage can be hard to come by, though. The water there is controlled by pirates. Even our own ships we've not dared send through."

Valignano rolled up the map, indicating with little subtlety that the conversation was finished. He smiled, a rare thing that generally inspired more fear than comfort.

"I'll inform the captain of our new destination. We'll dock in Kuchinotsu tomorrow, and once our affairs are concluded there, I will personally carry on to Kyoto. Nothing must stand in the way of our mission. We will bring the word of Christ to every corner. I will not be deterred by pirates. Besides, I have protection."

He patted me on the arm, then turned toward the door. He called out over his shoulder.

"And I have God."

3

The men were indeed unhappy with the new destination, and none more so than the captain. He'd studied the charts for the waters around Nagasaki, not this new port. We inched into the harbor of Kuchinotsu under minimal sail, men at forward positions dropping their plumb lines into the water and calling out the readings. When the captain decided we'd gone as far as we safely could, he ordered the anchor dropped and the sails folded. The great black ship loomed massive in the bay and the commotion it created on the shore was evident from afar.

A small crowd had already gathered on the dock and others could be seen streaming in that direction, picking their way along narrow, rutted roads and jostling past merchants of varying wares. The trade ships that the Nagasaki priest had spoken of would have certainly made their way to this harbor as well, but perhaps not so regularly, and certainly never a ship of this size. The Europeans would still be something of a novelty here. I would be something altogether new.

The first of the longboats was dropped into the water. I climbed down a shaky rope ladder to board it, followed by Father Valignano (who refused the sailors' assistance), then Brother Ambrosius, and a small retinue of lower-ranking priests. We joined the half dozen oarsmen who had already descended, lined up three to each side. The unloading of the cargo would come later, and the sailors would come ashore last, likely not until later that evening or possibly the morning.

The priests were dressed in long black robes despite the heat, their beads and crucifixes worn about their necks. Father Valignano took position, standing at the prow of the longboat while the oarsmen leaned into their work. I stood behind, in loose pantaloons that rustled in the breeze and a flowing white shirt cut to expose the muscles in my arms, a white turban that added the appearance of even greater height. A sash worn around my waist held a long black crab sword and in my right hand I held an imposing-looking spear, the blade on it long and curving. The surest way to win a battle was to discourage it, and though I expected no trouble ashore, I wanted to give pause to anyone considering it. As we reached closer to shore, the minor priests began rhythmically chanting a hymn in Portuguese. We all had our appearances to make.

Ashore waited the young lord of the region surrounding Kuchinotsu. There were tents set up beyond the dock and flags planted into the ground bearing what must be the Arima family emblem. Arima Harunobu and his retinue were dressed in light kimonos, their two swords scabbarded and sashed.

"Do they know they are not to be armed when they receive you?"

Valignano brushed the question off with a wave of his hand, not bothering to turn toward me to address it.

"We must make some allowance for local custom."

Lord Arima, just a teenager, entered the water to greet the boat, a sign of respect. Father Valignano offered his hand and Arima dutifully kissed the ring upon it. Valignano offered a blessing to all ashore, his priests standing behind with their heads bowed solemnly. The silence was broken only by the hushed whispers of the merchants, pointing at me and gesturing to one another of my size. Valignano stood a good head taller than any man ashore, and I was a head and a shoulder above that.

I scanned the crowd and saw no indication of threat. I turned my attention to the men lined up behind Arima. I knew that only samurai were allowed to wear the two swords tucked in a sash at their waist, the longer katana and the shorter wakizashi.

As Valignano's protector, I had paid particular attention to the lessons we received about the samurai—elite warriors trained not just in sword but also in bows, spears, and a variety of other weapons. Men and sometimes women as well, who pledged their complete loyalty, willing to die without question for their lords. Under the shogunate, they were Japan's de facto ruling class. All commoners were expected to bow in their presence. According to the rules of the land, failure to do so, or any other perceived show of disrespect, allowed a samurai to cut a commoner down without repercussion.

These samurai standing behind Arima were short and looked to weigh no more than a few cannonballs, but in even the simplest of movements I could see their control. They'd be no easy opponent in a battle, and I was keenly aware of how few of us had yet come ashore.

While Father Valignano and Lord Arima exchanged pleasantries, I assessed the town—just a few dozen homes with thatched roofs; a temple, also wood but with the roof tiled and decorated for Valignano's arrival; dirt streets snaking amongst the tightly packed homes, a handful of street merchants clogging the way with carts, though the majority of the merchants were here, at the dock.

We were led toward the temple for a formal reception, and up close the buildings were even more susceptible to breach than I had suspected. The wooden walls were thin enough for a strong man to punch through them and the windows and doorways were covered with simple rolls of paper, hung from the frame.

The road leading out of town and winding up the hill was also dirt, turning to pebble, then to stone. Arima's castle would be somewhere along that road, maybe hours away, maybe days, but I could see already that this region was unsuited to the scope of Valignano's ambition. We would not be here long, and Brother Ambrosius would find himself regretting having urged us here from Nagasaki. One of the junior priests would be left behind to implement Valignano's instructions, and we would be on our way as quickly as courtesy allowed.

THE ROAD TO LORD ARIMA's castle was held by his enemies. He and his men had traversed a mostly overgrown trail through a mountainside jungle, then rafted downriver under cover of night in order to reach the port to greet Valignano. We had no choice but to take the same route back. The bulk of the Jesuit party were sent ahead to the port city in Bungo, a slight that Arima couldn't have missed, and which Valignano had likely not meant him to.

We rafted the river in near-total darkness. Arima's men stood at the front of the rafts and moved their poles tentatively through the water, steering from memory.

"The passage is safe?" I asked one of the polers.

"For small groups, yes. It is still our territory, we know it better than any. We can get a few people in and out past the enemy barricades, just not sup-plies of any significant quantity."

The sounds of the surrounding jungle were a cacophony to our foreign ears, but Arima's men listened for the sound that was out of place, and any time they reacted, I tried to identify which noise had caused them to do so.

We slept on the rafts when we could, our rest brief and fitful, and we woke with the backs of our robes soaked with water that had seeped through the raft's planks or sloshed over its edges. In the morning, the heat wrapped itself around us and squeezed tightly. The heavy wool robes stuck to the skin of the few priests who accompanied Valignano, and if any of them pulled back a sleeve or rolled the hem past their ankles to try to get relief, they were savagely attacked by insects.

They scratched and suffered and one priest fainted, his face red and shiny with sweat. I fared better in my blouse and loose pants, but all of us looked jealously at the light silk kimonos of the Japanese, and wondered why they were not swarmed as we were.

Throughout the journey, Valignano remained unaffected, stoically accepting Lord Arima's constant apologies, while at the same time rebuffing any negotiations of trade until we had reached our destination.

"It has been a long siege," Arima mourned, upon our arrival at the castle. "We have little to offer, I am afraid."

"We are not here for food and drink," Valignano assured him, though the others in the company may have disagreed, judging from their haggard looks.

Arima's castle was much like Arima's roads—if they had once been in good repair, they were no longer. There were cracks in the mortar and great chunks of stone missing from the walls, and all had fallen victim to the ravages of overgrown vines. Inside, there were endless drips and leaks, and on days it rained we would lay on our tatami mats on the wet floor, or huddle shivering in our damp robes if the wind turned cold. We ate modestly and slept poorly, the forces gathered outside the walls playing drums throughout the night to prevent Arima's guard from resting.

The negotiations were mercifully brief, unless you were Arima. It was clear to all that he could not hold this region much longer without the much-needed Portuguese arms, and he capitulated completely.

His mistress, barely more than a teenager from the looks of her, was sent away in tears. The Buddhist and Shinto shrines were tied with ropes and pulled down to the ground, and Arima, dressed in a white robe that shone incongruously amongst the gray and grit and dirt that permeated the keep, was baptized in a small pool in the castle courtyard. We were on our way within days, but not before two of Arima's soldiers arrived, escorting a sweaty and half-conscious priest who they had guided up the river and through the jungle.

Father Valignano received the huffing and struggling priest at the castle gate.

"A message," he breathed out heavily. "From Ōmura Sumitada."

I stood beside Valignano, one eye on the suffering priest and one eye on the treeline behind him, watching and listening for any signs of Arima's enemies. I stole a glance sideways at Valignano, wondering if he would offer this priest water or rest, but he did neither.

"Continue."

The priest gulped, nodded. "Lord Sumitada is glad to hear of your arrival in Japan. He was disappointed that he was not given the chance to greet you personally, and he hopes that the esteemed Visitor to the Indies knows that he and his Jesuit priests are always welcome in his domain. As confirmation of Lord Sumitada's continued friendship, he offers the port of Nagasaki to the church of the Jesuits, in perpetuity, to do with as they please."

His message delivered, the priest collapsed to one knee, leaning heavily on the Arima soldier beside him for support. It was a stunning gift. Ownership of the port not only meant unfettered control of trade but also the right to collect taxes on all goods that passed through it. More than just a foothold, it was a veritable chest of gold and a clear declaration of the influence of the Jesuit church.

Beside me, Valignano smiled. Two regional lords, Arima and Sumitada, had submitted to his will, and a critical trading post had been secured. His mission in Japan was off to a very successful start.

4

At Bungo our small party was greeted by a ruddy-faced priest in a wool shirt and trousers. He notified Valignano that a boat had been arranged with a man named Murakami, then bowed and retreated from the tent. I waited a few moments to make sure he was not hovering outside listening, something the priests were unfortunately known to do.

When I was sure we were alone, I turned to Valignano.

"It's hard for me to protect you when you keep me in the dark regarding our travel plans."

Valignano looked at me for a second, deciding whether he would indulge this conversation or simply order me to obey. He sighed.

"Our plans are the kind that you typically disapprove of."

"The dangerous kind, then."

"There is no danger that the Lord cannot protect us from."

"And yet you still bring me to protect you."

"Careful."

Valignano pointed a finger at me and I nodded. He sometimes allowed me to be frank but never to speak without faith. He ladled two cups of water from a bowl in the corner of the tent and handed me one.

"Murakami will be providing us safe passage to Sakai."

"He's a pirate, then?"

"Yes, but a wise one, it seems. The pay being the same, he knows it's easier to transport us than it is to rob us, especially if it leads to future opportunities as well."

"At Kuchinotsu there were sailors, armed men, experienced fighters. Here there is only me. Murakami's men will be quick to recognize that there is only one armed man in the entire traveling party."

"Well then, you shall just have to be exceptionally frightening, won't you?"

Valignano disappeared into the darkness at the back of the tent, then reappeared with a lit candle, which he placed on the table beside the bowl of water. He searched through his things for his paper and quill, and the conversation was over.

The next day we boarded Murakami's ship, thirty men in all. The few that had traveled to Arima's castle alongside Valignano and myself were grateful for the cool sea air, glad to be away from the humidity and the bugs.

Murakami's men were barefoot and wore short kimonos. They had sashes about their waist for daggers and other small weapons, and leather straps wrapped thickly around their foreheads. They eschewed the heavier leather and metal armor and elaborate helmets of the samurai in case they ended up in the water. They'd rather risk themselves in battle than risk themselves being dragged down and drowning.

They stood idly on deck while the Jesuits loaded their things, making no offer to assist. They shifted and stared when I stepped aboard. Murakami, who had been at the front of the boat checking the ropes, whistled and walked toward me. He was unarmed, bare chested, and wearing expensive-looking leather pants.

"I wouldn't want trouble with this one," he said jokingly to his men.

"Then do not give cause for any," I replied.

The pirates were taken aback by my Japanese. Murakami stood his ground, but stared at me open-mouthed, then laughed and clapped me on the arm. The men laughed as well, and Murakami started shouting orders to prepare for departure. Father Valignano gave me the slightest of smiles, then retreated under the cover of one of the canopies the pirates had set up on deck to protect us from the sun.

Our path would take us through the inner islands and to Sakai in three days. There was a shorter path, hugging closer to the coast, but it would pass through waters controlled by the Mori clan, the last clan that offered a true threat to Nobunaga's rule. Nobunaga had already made successful use of the Portuguese firearms against the Takeda clan at the battle of Nagashino, and the Mori would be eager to disrupt the possibility of any furthering of ties between the Jesuits and their enemy. We'd pass through the islands, rather than along the northern coast and Mori territory.

We sailed through the first day and camped ashore at night. Father Valignano stayed mostly belowdecks at sea and in his tent onshore. I checked on him as often as I thought would be tolerated, but was waved away each time. He skipped meals, slept little. Valignano was not one to leave details to others, and every detail of the next leg of our voyage had to be perfect. We were traveling to Kyoto without an invitation to visit the daimyo Oda Nobunaga. Valignano had to find a way to procure an invitation and prepare for it. If Japan could be unified and if the man who did so adopted Christianity openly, then Valignano could convert the whole country in one swoop.

While Valignano worked, the rest of us gathered around a fire in the early evening and ate fish and rice, and the pirates drank sake until their faces flushed. I opened a crate and volunteered a few bottles of Portuguese red wine. They were intended as gifts for Japanese lords and dignitaries, but a few bottles would make no difference, and with the whole of the Jesuit party to protect, I felt more comfortable in the company of grateful pirates than ungrateful ones. The pirates passed the bottles around, drinking, then making sour faces, then drinking again. They offered it back to me but I abstained. I was always on duty, and I preferred it that way.

The pirates shouted and told stories late into the night, and when at last they went silent, they were replaced with a chorus of cicadas. I slept inside the opening flap of Valignano's tent on a tatami mat, my legs extending well past the edges of it no matter how tightly I curled them.

In the morning the pirates moved slowly, heads dulled by drink, but by noon they were recovered. I allowed myself to relax. Though Murakami's men held a reputation as fierce fighters, it was clear that they obeyed Murakami without question, and that Murakami had no interest in trouble. He could have easily adjusted the heading north and sold us all to the Mori for a healthy amount.

When I asked him why he did not, he shrugged and replied, "It's never wise to help the side that will lose."

"The Oda will defeat the Mori, then?" I asked.

He nodded.

"No one knows what will happen. These waters"—he waved one hand toward the sea—"one day they belong to one lord, the next day to another. One day this lord fights alongside that lord, the next day they fight against each other. This is how it has been for as long as any of us has lived. But, maybe not much longer. Maybe soon this will all belong to one man. I know one thing—I will not be the one who angers that man."

"But does it not all belong now, to the emperor?" I asked.

Murakami made a vague gesture.

"We treat the emperor with the utmost reverence, but the emperor's authority is granted by the heavens. Nobunaga's authority is granted by the sword. Even the most pious of men fear the second more than the first, when that sword is pointed at their throat."

Murakami smiled and walked off to check on some of his men, dangling traps over the side of the wooden railing to catch the evening's dinner. I looked out over the coast. The islands were sparsely populated, and what population there was had moved inland from the shore, likely because of the threat from Murakami and others like him. There was the odd shack built from wood blasted gray by the sea and the wind, and often leaning precariously to one side, but mostly there were fields of grass and wildflowers, rolling hills, and a clear view of the mountains in the distance, and with Murakami's men having shown no sign of aggression toward us, I spent time on the rail, merely enjoying the view.

There was still a magic in seeing a place for the first time, breathing new air, hearing new sounds. When I'd first been taken, slavers brought me to India. Despite my terror and my exhaustion, I had been fascinated by the smell when I was led from the dock, shocked by the clamor of voices in the city. I had spent my whole life to that point in a quiet village and never expected to see any more of the world than that, never had need to believe that other places existed, or to spend time wondering about them.

My father had traveled to many cities and villages, and I loved hearing stories of the places he saw and the people he traded with, but they had never sparked any desire in me to see those places myself. It was my mother, always, who was spellbound.

Memories of home came rarely to me, now, and when they did, I shut them off as quickly as I could. For a while I had tried to remember. Each new sight I came across, I would try to describe it in my father's words, try to speak of it to my mother, but I had long since lost the will to do so. I could no longer communicate with my ancestors. Perhaps I had traveled too far from my home.

On a rocky outcropping on the leeward side of the boat, a woman sprawled out in the sun. She wore nothing but a simple cloth wrapped around her hips. Her legs were lean and muscular, her stomach flat, and the water glistened blue and green and yellow on her skin. Beside her was a pile of a half dozen or so clams, a few bits of coral, and a single starfish. She leaned forward to watch us pass and I could see the ragged row of her teeth, chipped from carrying shells up from the bottom of the shallow sea, and her eyes streaked red with blood vessels burst from the pressure of the depths.

The pirates fishing along the rail turned away immediately, and I did as well. I'd been aboard enough boats to recognize the superstitions of sailors, and to understand the lengths to which they would go to remove someone who is seen as bringing misfortune. I heard a soft splash and turned back to see the rippling circles where the woman had entered the water, and I watched that spot until the boat sailed around the bend, but I did not see her resurface.

5

We had barely set foot to land at the port of Sakai before Valignano started barking orders. He'd settled on a march of several days from Sakai to Osaka, then a full night's rest followed by a final march from Osaka into Kyoto. It was not the quickest mode of travel, but the one that would generate the most excitement. Possibly word would reach Nobunaga's ears and pique his interest enough to request an introduction.

Valignano drilled the procession of priests with military precision. He would ride on horseback at the front of the procession in a formal black robe, a bejeweled crucifix about his neck and carrying a box that contained a splinter of the holy cross. I followed behind, spear polished to a mirrorlike clarity, almost as tall on foot as Valignano was on horse.

Next would come the remaining priests in more modest brown robes, and sandals that I doubted would survive the journey. They were instructed to hold books in front of them, but I knew that only a small handful of them could read. The rest would look studiously at the page and chant their hymns from memory. Others carried bells on the end of ropes that they would swing from side to side, in unison. Leading this group was a trio of priests who had the unenviable task of holding upright a carved wooden cross larger than any of them, knowing full well that Valignano would be angered if it were allowed the slightest lean. Trailing at the back of the procession were hired porters Murakami had arranged for, and who were under strict instruction to draw no attention to themselves.

Father Valignano's carefully planned pageantry had precisely the right effect. The sound of bells drew the townfolk into the street, and they stood in rows alongside us as we passed, pointing and clapping and chattering excitedly to one another. A few times I made out words like "giant" or "oxen" or "ink," and knew that the fingers were most often pointed at me.

The first day went smoothly, but problems began to arise as we got closer to Osaka. The port towns had seen Africans before, loading and unloading boats at the dock, or even about town on occasions when foreign sailors spent a night ashore, but in the inland cities, many had never seen a black-skinned man before.

People pushed into the street and held their arms against mine, comparing size and color, sometimes jumping to see if their head could reach mine, then challenging their friends to do the same. When we were able to clear them aside, they fell in behind our procession, as many of the men and women from the smaller towns had as well. Our retinue swelled from a parade of dozens to one of hundreds. We reached Osaka a full half day later than we had expected. We were greeted by seminary students from Kyoto who were eager to join us on our march into the capital. They had brought fresh sandals for the priests, who accepted them gratefully, their feet scabbed and swollen.

In the morning, a crowd waited outside the gate, much larger than the one that we had picked up along the route. Word had gone around during the night, and people were eager for a glimpse of the strangely dressed Europeans and the black-skinned giant.

"It's too dangerous," I told Valignano. "We should separate. We'll travel to Kyoto in small groups, avoid the crowd as much as possible, and meet up there."

"Nonsense. We will march into Kyoto in the full glory of the church, and the more Japanese souls that march in behind us, the better."

Valignano ordered the gates opened, and sent a half dozen horses to clear a path through the crowd. We marched out toward Kyoto in the same formation. The seminary students filed in behind the priests as penitents.

They had stripped their robes to their waists and marched with their heads bowed, chanting and whipping their backs and shoulders bloody with short, knotted ropes and tightly tied bundles of reeds.

The crowd pressed inward but allowed us to pass. By midafternoon we'd reached the outer edge of the city, and the people grew rowdier. The procession had taken on a festival atmosphere. Men drank sake from leather pouches and danced in wild, jerky movements. Professional women slid their kimonos open, revealing a breast or sometimes more to catch the attention of potential customers. The mass of people pushed and jostled. People tore at my clothing, leapt up and tried to hold themselves from my shoulders like children.

The porters were locked in by the crowd and unable to move. The penitents had their lashes taken from them and men from the crowd used them on one another while laughing and shouting. The cross was hauled down and the choir had ceased any attempt at singing. Valignano swiveled, surveying, and for the first time since I'd known him, he looked uncertain.

A surge from the crowd pushed some of us forward, some others backward, separating us further. A man fell beneath the wave of bodies and was trampled underfoot. The crowd heaved outward like a giant lung. Food carts were overturned. A few wealthy patrons being carried in palanquins were pinned hopelessly against the sides of buildings. The beggars and apothecaries and artists and merchants abandoned their wares to look for safety. Pots were shattered, canvases torn. Animals burst free from twisted cages, furthering the commotion. There were fistfights dotted amongst the mass of bodies, the splintering of wood as one man was thrown through a wall.

In front of me, Valignano's horse reared and panicked, and he fought to control it. He pointed to the church, shouted something inaudible, jerked the reins tight. The church was now only a few blocks away, built in the same pagoda style as other buildings surrounding it to make potential Japanese converts feel comfortable, but thankfully built high enough above its neighbors to be clearly visible.

Valignano's words were lost in the chaos, but his gesture was unmistakable—every man for himself.

I pushed men away with the staff of my spear to clear a small opening and ran. I bounced off men and women alike, and the drunken revelers fell into chase, a writhing snake following me through the streets. I tried to keep the church roof in front of me but at times was forced to turn. Through narrow streets and narrower alleyways I lost sight of the church rooftop, then located it again. The crowd had picked up the thrill of the game, cheering each time they sighted me and calling excitedly for the others. My shirt was torn from my back and a man held it above him as a prize before he was overrun by his compatriots.

Lungs and legs burning, I pressed forward as quickly as I could, aiming myself toward my target at every opportunity. A block away, I turned a corner and was met with a dead end, the path ahead of me blocked by a wooden fence. I spun to reverse course, but it was too late. The mouth of the alleyway was already filling with the fastest of the pursuers.

I charged the fence, hoping it would give way. I flung myself forward and heard a satisfying crack. Splinters dug themselves into my forearms, and behind me, the crowd was delighted at the show of strength. Blood dripped down my wrists and fingers, but the gate of the church was now in front of me, a pair of balding men in frocks waving me eagerly inside. I collapsed to the ground in exhaustion and they closed the gate behind me, dropping a thick-looking log across and securing it in place.

"Come."

The two priests grabbed my arms and led me inside. Valignano and a handful of the other priests were already within.

"The others?" I asked.

"Still outside the gates, but they should be safe. The mob mostly followed you."

As if to punctuate Valignano's words, a chant went up from outside the walls, calling for the black giant to be brought out. The wooden posts creaked beneath the weight of the crowd pressed against it. Valignano looked out the doorway.

"Will it hold?"

"It was not built to be a fortress."

The priest that answered had the look of a man who had spent more time in libraries than on ships. He looked almost plump beneath the loose robes, but his face was all angles—the ridges of his cheeks shining almost through his skin, and his nose a sharp, sloping arrow. His face was clean-shaven, and his eyes were a pale, shimmering green that had a strange calming effect. He kissed Father Valignano's hand.

"I am Brother Organtino. I wish we were greeting you under more comfortable circumstances, but we are glad of your safety." He turned to me. "You have wounds that need tending."

I looked at my arms, scraped and bleeding and with bits of wood dug into the cuts. Organtino gestured, and a bowl of water was brought forward. I grimaced while a young priest set about cleaning the wounds.

Valignano busied himself checking on the others. A rock thrown from outside the fence clattered loudly against the tiles of the roof, then another. The chants of the mob turned from drunken to ugly. A few heads bobbed above the line of the gate as men climbed on and over one another to glimpse inside. The gate bowed inward.

The shouts changed again and the heads turned, then dipped out of sight. There was the sound of hooves, and of some kind of rod or staff striking violently against skin, against bone. Screams and panic and chaos of dispersion, then after a few moments, stillness.

"Open the gate."

Organtino spared a moment's glance to Father Valignano, then strode into the courtyard to remove the log and slide the gate open. A dozen men on horseback entered, dressed in black armor and heavily armed. Each carried a long staff, which they had used to quell the riot, and two swords on their waists. The backs of their saddles sported flags with an identical emblem: four petals of a flower, black and trimmed in gold.

The man on the lead horse dismounted. "Lord Nobunaga would see the man responsible for this disturbance."

Brother Organtino bowed slightly. "We serve at Lord Nobunaga's pleasure, but please carry word to your lord that this disturbance is not of our making."

The man brushed past Organtino and stalked up the steps of the church. The chaos of only a few moments before was replaced by silence, broken only by the clink of the man's armor, the snort of one of the horses behind him. His eyes went wide when he saw me. His hand moved closer to the hilt of his sword and he squatted slightly, ready.

Beside me, Valignano stood, smoothed his robes.

"I am Father Alessandro Valignano, Visitor to the Indies and representative of His Holiness, the Pope. I have come from Portugal via Rome. I am in charge of this mission now, and we would be most pleased to meet with your esteemed lord."

What little composure the soldier had lost he regained quickly. He stood straight, removed his hand from his sword.

"Lord Oda Nobunaga has sent for the black-skinned man, no one else. And my lord will see him at once."

6

I was granted time to get fresh clothing and little more. Brother Organtino whispered a few words of advice while helping me dress in a clean shirt and doublet.

"He can be . . . erratic. But he is seldom irrational. If he greets you warmly, do not get too comfortable. If he greets you angrily, do not panic. He will not expect you to know their ways, so there may be some tolerance for error, but very little. He is, above all things, curious. If you can tell him something he does not know, he will value you for it."

I tried to absorb Organtino's words, but he gave them nervously, which only increased my own discomfort. I was trained to deal with threats, not with foreign politics. I had many times been witness to Valignano's smooth and subtle diplomacy, but my role in every such scenario was to stand quietly, look imposing, and watch for danger. It should be he standing before Nobunaga, not I.

Father Valignano was barely able to contain his fury at being left behind. I had thought for a moment that he might attack the Oda soldiers and demand an invitation. After all his careful preparations to draw Nobunaga's attention and gain an audience, it was I who would be brought to the Japanese warlord, with Valignano excluded. In truth, I desperately wished the priest could speak on my behalf. Instead, I would have to stand before Nobunaga after having caused a riot in his capital city. Every button Brother Organtino fastened felt too tight, every word of advice he offered too overwhelming.

Valignano stewed in the corner, unaccustomed to being in a situation that was not completely under his control. He watched us whispering to each other. He'd stepped toward us, hoping to offer his own instruction, but a stern stare from the waiting soldiers held him at bay. There would be no rescue from him.

Outside the gates of the church, a few revelers still remained, but they pressed themselves against walls and into alleys to make way for the Oda clan horses. I trailed along behind on foot. Still, I had not been bound. I hoped that was a good sign, but the most likely scenario remained that I was on the way to my own execution.

The Honno-ji temple was a walled Buddhist compound only a few blocks away from the Jesuit church. It would have been impossible for Nobunaga, or anyone else inside, to have missed the commotion of less than an hour ago. I was suddenly tired, the events of the day settling into my bones, but I had to be at my best. Not only did my life depend on it, but I would now be the first emissary of Father Valignano's mission, and while Brother Organtino had already established relatively friendly relations with Lord Nobunaga, the future of the church in Japan might well depend on this meeting.

Word of the strange man's summons had spread throughout Honno-ji, and a small crowd gathered inside the gates to see me. The crowd was much more subdued than the riotous mob in the street. They kept their distance and examined me with curiosity but otherwise gave nothing away, their expressions blank, no signal I could read as either friendly or unfriendly. I was led past them, into the inner courtyard, and past a row of squat, modestly decorated buildings.

I relied on my training, studied my surroundings. Noticeably absent from the Buddhist temple were any actual representations of the Buddha. I remembered Brother Ambrosius's account of the burning of Mount

Hiei and the recently ended siege against the Ikko-ikki, the warrior monks whose influence over Japanese affairs Nobunaga had broken. The statues had surely been removed, and in fact, Nobunaga's use of the temple as a temporary residence was likely a less-than-subtle jab in the eye of the remaining Buddhist priests. I would have to be careful with the politics. Valignano had trained us all well, but there was still too much I did not know.

I was led up the steps of a large building just off to the side of the main sanctuary. The antechamber was bustling with samurai, merchants, minor lords, and other dignitaries, each bearing gifts both exotic and exquisite. I was pointedly aware that I was about to meet one of Japan's most esteemed men empty-handed, but there was nothing to be done about it.

I was also unarmed for the first time in recent memory. Even in sleep I had always kept my spear close. Standing weaponless now was as uncomfortable as standing naked would be for most. As casually as the horseback samurai had treated me, there was no doubt I was a captive, not a guest. There were murmurs amongst the others in the antechamber. My head grazed the low ceiling and all eyes were upon me, though most were respectful enough to pretend otherwise.

The cavalry leader slipped quietly into the main hall and returned within moments. He was accompanied by a young man with soft, pale skin and charcoal eyes. The man was dressed in an elaborate orange kimono trimmed with green and accented with flecks of silver. One of the waiting lords greeted him as Ranmaru, but the young man merely nodded at him politely.

Ranmaru gestured me forward, and some of the stares of the waiting supplicants turned ugly now that I had been summoned ahead of them.

I was halted at the doorway. The young man who had answered to the name of Ranmaru erroneously introduced me as the "Black Monk," but now was not the time for corrections. I ducked my head under the doorway and entered the main hall. I immediately prostrated myself upon entering, touching my head to the floor and remaining there. Valignano had made certain that all of his traveling party were well prepared. I had been trained for the customs of the Japanese court, and on this occasion at least, was begrudgingly grateful for Valignano's attention to detail. I was tapped on the shoulder, rose again to my full height.

The main hall was a large open space with a high vaulted ceiling. Wooden beams crisscrossed the ceiling, painted in bright colors and some bearing pictographs of Buddhist legends. Whatever decision they had made to remove the statues in the courtyard, they had chosen not to make here. If this were some concession, it would mean Oda Nobunaga accepted that there were limits to his power, but it was too much to assume without knowing more.

The window shutters along the wall were speckled with gold leaf, but the walls were otherwise bare. Along them, men sat in rows on tatami mats in brightly colored kimonos decorated with designs of flowers or fish, mostly motionless but some sparing a sideways glance to where Ranmaru and I stood.

At the far end of the room, a series of elaborate silk screens were displayed on a multi-leveled raised dais. On the lower level of the dais, three men sat turned sideways to the entryway to the chamber, and behind them, on the dais's highest level, Oda Nobunaga.

He had a short triangular beard, jet black, and a neatly trimmed mustache. His hair was pulled back tightly and bound in a knot behind him. Unlike the men seated along the wall in rows, Nobunaga wore a simple forest-green kimono, but one that was obviously of a high quality, the tones of it shimmering in the light of the lanterns. Nobunaga raised his hand and waved us forward.

The doors to the chamber closed behind us on wooden tracks and I allowed Ranmaru to bring me toward the dais. I kneeled and bowed again, touching my forehead to the cold floor.

I heard the rustling of movement. Ranmaru tapped me again on the shoulder and when I looked up, Nobunaga was before me, hands clasped behind his back. Nobunaga tilted his head and studied me. He gestured for me to rise. He looked up at the towering black man before him and there was the faintest smile of amusement on his face. He reached one hand to my neck, pinched the skin between his fingers, then examined his fingertips, looked at the spot on my neck where he had rubbed to see if the skin had lightened. I was unsure if I was allowed to speak, but decided to risk it.

"If it please my lord, I speak some Japanese. I hope my lord will not be displeased at the quality of it."

There was an audible gasp from the men sitting along the walls, followed by hushed muttering. Even the three men on the lower dais, stoic up to this point, glanced upward. The men could not have been more different. The first was small and lean and ugly, his lips curled tight to hide his teeth, his eyes set close. The second was fat and reddening, his features lost in the folds of skin beneath his chin. And the third was older, the pate of his skull mostly bald, the hair on the sides of his head graying and wispy.

There was a look of surprise in Nobunaga's eyes as well, but the smile still held, as if he were sniffing out some trick.

"Would you remove your shirt?" he asked.

I did so, unfastening the doublet, then pulling off the blouse beneath. Nobunaga waved his hand and called for a washbasin. A trio of servant girls appeared within moments, two carrying a wooden bucket filled with water and the third carrying a scrub brush. They kneeled and hid their faces and held the items above their heads.

Nobunaga smiled again at me, dipped the brush in the water, and proceeded to scrub my skin, first the chest, then the arms, then walking around me to scrub at my back. I recalled, for a moment, the humiliation of being prodded and examined by the rough white men who had loaded us into the hold of the ship that would take us away from our home.

Nobunaga's curious probings were more respectful.

I stood as still as possible, chin tight to my chest, the sleeves of my shirt draped around my wrists like loose chains. The brush scraped painfully against my skin, especially where I had already cut my arms bursting through the wooden fence in the alleyway earlier in the evening, or where much older wounds across my back and torso had scarred over with skin that was puckered and ridged. Nobunaga dropped the brush into the water bucket and the servants crab-walked away, not turning their backs or showing their faces.

He examined my skin again, pinching, then checking his fingers for residue, amazed that the color did not come off in his hands.

"What is your name?"

I gave Nobunaga the name the Portuguese had given me. Nobunaga made a tortured attempt to repeat it back to me.

"Yasuke."

I nodded, not willing to counter him.

"This skin. How is this possible?"

"I come from far away, my lord. This is the color of my people."

"And are they all so tall?"

"Yes, my lord, though not all so strong. And none so handsome."

The joke was risky, but paid off. Nobunaga clapped me on the shoulder and laughed loudly. The men along the walls took his cue and joined in, the sound echoing through the chamber.

"Come, sit! You will be my guest for the evening. I am eager to learn more."

I rebuttoned my shirt and doublet. Nobunaga called for food and drink, setting off a flurry of activity. A tatami mat was placed to the right of Nobunaga's and I was urged to sit there. Ranmaru took up position behind me. Servants appeared and disappeared, so many and so quickly that it was hard to track them. Long, flat boards were placed in front of the men on the dais, then in front of the men lining the chamber as well, then cups, then plate after plate of small dishes. There were rice cakes and fish and wild game that could have been pheasant or quail or wild geese, served alongside radishes, beans, a small Japanese potato, tofu, nuts, yams, apricots, peaches, apples, oranges, and sour plums.

A jug of sake was brought forward and Nobunaga poured the first cup for me with his own hand, something I recognized was a great honor. I had avoided alcohol throughout most of the voyage, just a few drinks with some of the ship's officers, and not a drop since setting foot on land. My duty to protect Valignano required me to be always sharp, but I was free from that duty tonight.

I suspected that refusing the cup Nobunaga offered would be a great offense. I raised my cup toward Nobunaga with both hands and drank. It was like fire compared to the smooth Portuguese wine I had occasionally tasted, and I coughed and squinted, but Nobunaga only laughed.

I watched carefully how my hosts ate, and tried my best to imitate. The chopsticks were clumsy in my large hands. Ranmaru whispered in my ear, "You're doing well, Yasuke. Pick the food up with your fingers if you need to, just be discreet about it."

Grateful, I ate quickly, trying to disguise my lack of skill. The flavors had been exquisitely paired, and after months of ship rations, followed by the limited meals Lord Arima could provide while his castle was under siege, then the burnt and smoky meals onshore with the pirates and the tasteless offerings of the pious march to Kyoto, I savored each mouthful.

Nobunaga turned to me excitedly, snapping his fingers.

"Do you think you could lift that girl?" he asked, pointing to one of the servants. She had just picked up Nobunaga's tray to replace it with a fresh one, and froze now. She looked up at her lord and then at me, clearly uncomfortable at being noticed.

I stood and smiled at her in what I hoped was a reassuring way. I looked at her long enough to notice details—her brown eyes circled with black, but highlighted with striking orange flecks; her chin narrow and slightly off-center, as if she were used to chewing her lip; her hair smelling faintly of citrus—then I pushed those thoughts away and fixed the smile to my face. I had only rarely been around women, and each time I was close to one there were emotions I had to guard against. Things I couldn't allow myself to feel.

"You are safe," I said to her, immediately feeling foolish for doing so.

I gestured for her to clasp her hands together, and she put the tray down and did so. I wrapped one hand around her clasped hands, small and soft within mine, and lifted her easily into the air. I turned to wave over another servant and lifted her with my other hand as well.

The men clapped and cheered while I stood holding the two girls above me on the dais. Nobunaga raised his arms excitedly. I had a hard time aligning this amicable individual with the stories I had been told of a man who burned temples, ordered the deaths of women and children. But I had seen enough war to know that some men hold two souls inside them.

"You must show me where you are from!"

Nobunaga barked orders. The girl with the orange-flecked eyes slipped away without a glance before I could say anything more to her. A male servant scurried toward Nobunaga, bringing a canvas scroll.

"Your monk Organtino provided this gift," Nobunaga said, proudly unrolling the canvas. It was a map of the world, beautifully painted, and as detailed as the knowledge of the Portuguese sailors could make it. He looked at me, expectant. I could see the eagerness for new information, the curiosity which Organtino had noted.

I looked at it uncertainly, not wanting to disappoint. I had seen the charts in the ship captain's quarters many times, but they were marked for sea, not land. I tried to recognize how those drawings related to the map unfurled in front of me. I pointed to where I thought Africa was, and Nobunaga traced with his fingers the distance from there to Japan.

I watched, but while he was astounded at how great a distance it was, I was astounded at how short it was. I had little interest in the work of sailors, but I had picked up enough to judge distances off a map, and while I felt a world away from where I had first been taken, Nobunaga had marked that distance with the span of a hand.

"I would like to see this marvel one day!"

I was pleased by his excitement, but I remembered Brother Organtino's advice. Nobunaga could swing from one mood to another in a moment. There was no time for reflection. Things had begun well, but I was still far from safe.

There was more sake, more food. The men sitting on the main floor laughed and joked but remained dignified, aware at all times of Nobunaga's presence. Only the three men sitting on the dais below Nobunaga remained quiet.

I studied them for a moment—the eldest gray-haired and tonsured, the bulkier man with thick black beard and mustache, and the third man wiry, his face ugly and twisted but with sharp eyes. The three of them wore silk kimonos, but atop them, elaborately patterned surcoats, broad at the shoulders and tapering toward the sash about their waist. They knelt comfortably, their heels tucked neatly beneath them. They were mostly still, but every small movement had the formality of ceremony. I noticed that they alone had been permitted to wear their swords in the hall, while the men lined up along the sides sat without theirs.

I thought to ask who they were, but decided against it. When Nobunaga had eaten his fill, he clapped his hands again.

"Bring a storyteller. Let us hear of the Divine Wind."

Ranmaru leaned forward and whispered to me, "Nobunaga favors you. This tale is one of his favorites."

In short order, the sliding doors at the back of the hall were pushed aside once again, and three men marched in unison to the center of the hall. At first glance, I thought they were dressed similarly to the men who had retrieved me from the Jesuit church, in head-to-toe armor. As I looked closer, I noticed that, unlike the horsemen, there was no metal in the armor of the trio of men, other than their helmets. The armor was entirely composed of thick leather, slightly bulkier and clumsier-looking. It seemed like an older version of the armor of the horse-backed samurai, and if this were indeed some costume, there'd been almost no time for these men to have donned it. The only possibility was that there was a small army of entertainers at the ready, waiting to respond to whatever Nobunaga requested.

The three men bowed down to the ground, then leapt up to their feet with a grace belying their heavy-looking costumes. The hall fell silent, and the first of the three men called out in a loud, clear voice.

"Three hundred years ago, the Mongols sent their ships to our shores. The tyrant Kublai Khan had conquered the Chinese empire and had his sights set on what challenge would be next. Japan was not yet known to Kublai, but reports reached his ears of our pirates raiding the sea villages of China and Korea, and thus we became known to him. On the day the Mongol sails were first seen off our coasts, there was a fire at the shrine of Hachiman, the great divinity of archery and war. A most inauspicious omen."

The story had the feel of one that would be well known to all the lords and samurai present, but all men were held rapt nonetheless, and none more so than Nobunaga. I risked a longer look at him in profile. The knot of hair tied tight and low to the back of his head, the flickering lanterns shadowing the line of his cheek and jaw. He was not just watching the actors, he had fixed them with an intent stare, as if he were willing them to perform the story in just such a way. The three actors fanned out in a defensive formation, hands on swords.

"The Mongol ships struck first at Tsushima, and we were unprepared for their barbaric tactics. Never before had a foreign army set foot on our lands, and the Mongols surged across it, cutting us down."

While the lead actor continued, the two behind him fell dramatically, stood, fell again.

"The honored samurai Sukesada drew his sword and struck down twenty-five invaders in one-on-one combat, but the Mongols were too many, and emerged victorious."

The actors drew wooden swords from their scabbards and stepped through their battle poses.

"They moved on to Iki, where they met the same brave resistance, but ultimately, the same result. They sailed into Hakata Bay with the bodies of Japanese warriors nailed to the prow of their boats and hung from the masts, staining the sails purple with our honored blood. Japanese forces gathered on the shore, waiting for the sun to rise, and the attack to come, but in the night, the wind came. At the edges of the forest, trees a hundred years old were felled beneath its strength. The gusts tore tiles off the roofs of the temples and launched them at the enemy ships. The water roiled angrily and rose to strike. The sails bulged, then tore, and the Mongols yelled to be heard by the man beside them. The ships pushed out to sea, and when the morning came and the winds calmed, the Mongols had fled back to safer shores."

The men leaned on their swords in fake-exhaustion and prayed their thanks for the typhoon which had saved them. The lead actor lifted his head.

"It would be seven years before the Mongols returned. The second war played out much like the first. Tsushima, then Iki, then the boats sailing in to Hakata Bay. They boarded the rowboats and poured ashore like fleas. They fell under sheets of our arrows, but they continued ashore regardless. For every Mongol we struck down, another picked up the body and used it as a shield. They pushed their dead toward us and hacked at us from the spaces in behind. A sea of flesh crashing over us, twisted bodies and rotted teeth, and we could not tell the living from the dead but for which eyes had rage within them and which no longer did.

"When they were too close for our arrows we drew our swords and struck at the horror before us but we fell beneath their weight, were pulled down off our horses and slaughtered. The line broke, men retreated into the cover of the woods, abandoning the shore. The bodies of both armies littered the beach, but when all looked lost, the sky darkened once more. The seas turned black and the waters rose and foamed.

"By the time the first lightning struck, the Mongol ships were already tilting, being dangerously pushed far onto one side, then rolling dangerously far back to the other. One ship's captain misread the waters and turned abreast of the waves. We watched from the forest's edge as the back end of the galley was heaved upward and came crashing forward. The thick central mast cracked on impact with the water and the deck splintered. A dozen Mongols spilled screaming from the rupture into the twisting sea, thrown ingloriously from this world into the next one. Another boat rolled quietly over and was pulled under whole, there and then gone, like a dying man's heartbeat.

"The remaining captains were more decisive in their actions, quickly pulling up their anchors and allowing themselves to be pushed out to calmer waters in the deep sea. On the shore, the Mongols panicked. A few dozen ran foolishly toward the ships and launched themselves into the raging waters, swimming a few short strokes before being pulled below, drowning. Others scattered along the beach in either direction. Most just stood still, and remained so while we picked up our bows, calmed our horses. In the coming days we cut the Mongols down on the beaches, in the woods, tracking every last one of them and finishing them. Never again did their ships return to our shores. Once again, the Divine Wind had struck for Japan, and swept away our enemies."

All in the hall stood and cheered. The actors removed their helmets and bowed low, first to the dais, then to either side, then again to the dais before backing out the way they had come. Nobunaga raised his chin, as if the victory the men spoke of had been his own. One of the men in the hall raised his cup toward Nobunaga and shouted, "Tenka fubu!"

The chant was taken up by the others as well, and soon all the men in the chamber were standing, cups held toward Nobunaga, shouting:

"Tenka fubu! Tenka fubu!"

I fumbled for a moment to come up with the translation.

Tenka fubu.

The realm under one sword.

7

The hour was late when I returned to the Jesuit church, escorted by four of Nobunaga's soldiers. Things had turned briefly somber after the story of the Divine Wind, but the mood changed back to one of revel before long. One man seated along the wall had boldly called for the foreigner to grace them with a story and I, with Nobunaga's urging, complied.

I had gathered the sense that it was a room of mostly warriors, much to my relief. I was uneasy with politics, but I was comfortable in the ways of soldiers. I launched into a telling of my defeat of a sultan chief and his two guards, all on camel back. If there was a word in Japanese for "camel" I did not know it, so I described great horses, a head and a half taller than the Japanese steeds, with short shaggy hair and humps on their backs that carried water so they could cross through deserts for days without drinking. I drew amazed whispers as I described the tall horses with humps carrying princes or warriors, detailed the flowing robes and curved blades of my enemy.

I tried to match the actors' dramatic movements while telling of the battle, and when I returned to the tatami mat at Nobunaga's side, the men cheered my victory. They had shouted particularly loudly when I described removing the sultan from his mount by striking the camel in the face with my bare hand. When Nobunaga turned to me and asked quietly if the story was true, I replied, "Not one word of it, my lord," prompting Nobunaga to smile broadly and pour more drink.

When I was released at evening's end, I backed out of the chamber, bowing to all of my hosts, but to Nobunaga most deeply. I thunked the back of my head loudly off the doorframe, earning one final laugh from the assembly before I departed.

Now, at the gate of the church, I breathed deeply of the night air and gathered myself. I was not quite drunk, but I was already tired when the night began, and now my eyes were heavy, my thoughts slow. A soldier knocked on the gate and there was the sound of sandaled feet moving quickly through the courtyard. They had been waiting.

The gate opened and Brother Organtino stood on the other side. His look was first one of relief, then of curiosity. He bowed slightly to the soldiers, who turned and left without a word.

Organtino touched me on the sleeve.

"Have you been drinking?"

"It seemed the polite thing to do."

"Father Valignano will not be pleased. Come." Organtino sighed, but I thought I saw also the hint of a smile.

The gate was swung shut behind me and we went inside. Organtino waved a hand and tea was brought, the steaming cup curled almost completely inside my thick fingers. Valignano was indeed not pleased, the disdain on his face clear. However, after so much time spent in the company of sailors, he had learned to lower his standards of piety, at least for those who were useful to him.

"You were well received, it appears."

I nodded. I wanted nothing more than to lay on my mat and sleep, but that was not to be. I sipped the tea, breathed in its heat.

"There were many people there, bearing gifts, lined up to pay homage. Few were admitted. Inside the hall there were probably two dozen or so men seated on the floor, three others on the dais, then Nobunaga above them."

"What did you learn of him?"

I paused, reviewing what I had observed, and what of it that could be useful. I realized that in truth, Nobunaga had given away very little.

46

"He was friendly. He behaved modestly, though it's clear from the way others watched him that he is feared. He encouraged drink, but drank little himself. As Brother Ambrosius noted, he has a taste for foreign gifts. He was quite proud of the map Brother Organtino had presented him."

Organtino nodded in appreciation. Valignano was impatient.

"Cruel or kind? Wise or foolish? Observant or naïve?"

"I saw little evidence to say."

Valignano snorted. "What of the three men seated below him?"

I described the three as best I could while Organtino nodded. When I finished, he provided further details.

"Nobunaga's generals. The small man with the puckered face is Toyotomi Hideyoshi. He has a reputation as an excellent strategist, and he is quite adept politically as well. When Nobunaga's forces were set in siege around Inabayama Castle, Hideyoshi befriended a local farmer and learned of a goat path that led up to the castle's rear wall. Hideyoshi took a small band of men along the path, scaled the wall at night, set fire to the stores to distract the soldiers inside, and opened the front gate for Nobunaga's army to march in. What would have been a monthslong siege was over in a day.

"The heavy man you saw is Tokugawa Ieyasu. He is a daimyo himself, lord of Mikawa Province, but he has pledged his loyalty to Nobunaga, and so far that pledge has proved unshakable. He is bold, sometimes too much so, but also patient and extremely loyal. He once held a castle against the Takeda clan with only five samurai. He ordered the gates opened and all the braziers lit, then had one of his men play the war drums. Victory for the Takeda would have been as simple as walking through the gate, but instead, they were convinced it was a trap. The Takeda camped out below rather than taking the castle, allowing time for reinforcements to arrive.

"The third general, the oldest of the three, is Akechi Mitsuhide. A man given more to art and philosophy than to war, but dangerous in his own way, nonetheless. He was critical in arranging the politics in support of Nobunaga's overthrow of the Ashikaga shogunate. Before that, he spent years as a ronin, a samurai without a master. He had long served the Saitō clan, and did not immediately join Nobunaga after they were defeated, so he was not sworn to any daimyo. We don't know what changed his mind, but he was quite poor by all accounts. It is often the case with ronin—the loss of their lord also means the loss of their land, and often plunges them into poverty quite quickly. Many resort to banditry to survive, but Akechi by all accounts maintained his moral standard. I was told a story that when he threw a small dinner party for friends, his wife sold her hair to pay for it. When he found out, he was so overwhelmed that he swore an oath to never take a concubine, no matter how high a position he might rise to."

"Hmm. A man of honor, at least."

I recalled Valignano standing stoically while Arima's mistress was sent away in tears. While none of the priests could marry, there were stories of some who were known to frequent brothels, and Valignano had always reacted with disgust to even the mention of those rumors. Infidelity was a sin he had no patience for.

Valignano rubbed his eyes, his own show of fatigue deepening that which I felt. I sipped again from the tea but didn't speak, hoping for a quick end to the conversation and a night's sleep.

"We mustn't judge their honor by our measures, Father Valignano."

"On the contrary, Brother Organtino. That is precisely what we are called to do. We may decorate our churches to look like their temples, learn their languages and their customs, but we must not compromise our morals. We will bring them closer to God, brother, not let them push us further from Him."

"Of course." Organtino lowered his head in apology. "I will work to arrange a meeting for you at once, Father."

The teacup slipped from my hand and clattered along the floor. From the corner of the room, I looked at the two now-frowning priests through bleary eyes.

"I think I need to sleep," I said.

* * *

BROTHER ORGANTINO KEPT HIS WORD, and two days later I was in front of Nobunaga again.

The prior day, Lord Nobunaga's armies had paraded majestically through the streets of Kyoto. Father Valignano questioned me again about the reception at Honno-ji, and I walked him through every detail I could recall—the scrubbing, the mispronunciation of my name, the performance of the actors, and my observances of the men in the hall, the three generals, and Nobunaga himself.

While I spoke, the procession marched through the street below us. The cavalry first, lightly armored warriors on sleek-coated horses, flags bearing the Oda emblem fastened to the saddles and flapping idly as the men trotted by. Following them, the ashigaru, the foot soldiers, in leather helmets and loose-fitting clothing, with metal shoulder protectors and a chest plate composed of a series of leather tabs, covering the chest like scales. They marched behind the Oda standards and bore naginatas, a weapon similar to my own spear but with a thinner-looking pole and a longer, curved blade, probably meant more for hooking and slashing than my own, which was meant for stabbing and, if needed, throwing.

Nobunaga's samurai were not part of the march. They would be waiting in the courtyard of the Imperial Palace, alongside the three generals, the older philosopher Akechi Mitsuhide, the heavy-jowled loyalist Tokugawa Ieyasu, and the wiry strategist Toyotomi Hideyoshi, as well as the emperor, and Nobunaga himself.

We stood on the second story of the Jesuit church while the procession made its way through the streets of Kyoto, toward the Imperial Palace. I watched as a warrior, studying the way they moved, the weapons they carried, the space between men and the precision of their coordination. Valignano, with Organtino at his side, watched as a politician would.

"Why the show of force?" Valignano asked.

"The emperor is still the divine ruler of Japan," Organtino explained, Valignano's brow crinkling at the use of the word "divine." "However, he has no military might. The emperor has always relied on the shogun for defense. Over time, the position of shogun replaced that of emperor as being the de facto ruler of Japan, with his shugo in place as governors of each province. But the control of the shogunate slipped as well, and the provincial shugos started acting independently. They kept the taxes they collected rather than sending them to the capital, and fought their neighboring provinces in attempts to expand their territory. The shugo who had been in place to serve as the shogun's governors became independent daimyos, or warlords, leading to the splintering of Japan and a state of war that has lasted a hundred years."

"But now Nobunaga has removed the shogun altogether, and is uniting the provinces again. The emperor must now lean on him alone."

"Precisely. Politics here are a complicated balance between tradition and reality. The emperor must never lose face. Nobunaga honors him with this parade, while at the same time making it clear to the emperor that he is now the preeminent military might in Japan. At the same time, he shows the remaining daimyo that he controls the emperor, which also makes him Japan's preeminent political might."

"He who controls the crown is stronger than he who wears it."

Organtino nodded, and Valignano went back to watching the parade, the wheels in his head, as always, spinning.

THE HONNO-JI TEMPLE WAS A mass of moving bodies when we were escorted in. Everywhere men and women were pulling down decorations, packing up food and clothing and arms, loading up carts, and feeding, watering, and reshoeing horses. The display for the emperor completed, Nobunaga was clearly eager to be out of Kyoto.

Valignano had brought his own retinue when summoned—beside

Brother Organtino and myself, there were another dozen or so minor priests, hauling carts and boxes. One of the guards at the gate began an inspection, but another quickly waved him off. It seemed Nobunaga had given orders to treat us respectfully. Nevertheless my spear was asked for, and my sword. I entered the antechamber, again unarmed.

Without the two dozen men lined along the walls, the main hall looked much larger. Nobunaga sat on the highest level of the dais with the regality of an emperor himself. The three generals who had sat below him two nights prior were not present. Only the soft-skinned and dark-eyed youth, Ranmaru, who showed us in before taking position at Nobunaga's side.

Organtino began the proceedings.

"Lord Nobunaga, as always it is my great pleasure to see you, and our great honor at having been received. It is also my great honor to introduce you to a man of much esteem and high rank within our church, who has traveled many months by sea for the opportunity to meet you. I present Father Alessandro Valignano, Visitor to the Indies."

Valignano bowed, but not to the depth that the occasion required, and that was certainly not by mistake. Nobunaga nodded toward Valignano, allowed the slight to pass. There was no hint of the looseness and informality of our prior meeting. Nobunaga had not yet even glanced in my direction, or acknowledged me in any way. I stood just off of Valignano's shoulder, a few steps behind him. He stepped forward.

"As Brother Organtino has stated, I have indeed come far, my lord. I bring greetings from the pope himself, who has expressed his gratitude that you have allowed us to bring God's word to your people. I hope that our God blesses you in your works, and that you allow us to continue in ours."

Valignano waved his hand and boxes were brought forward.

"I hope my lord will favor us by accepting these small gifts from us."

Boxes were opened, and items presented. Fine crystal goblets and bottles of the best Portuguese wine, velvet robes and furs and intricate gold necklaces. Nobunaga inspected each gift dutifully, holding the glasses up to the light, rubbing the cloths between his fingers, but there was little other reaction before Ranmaru collected the items and summoned servants to ferry them away. Nobunaga had still not spoken.

Father Valignano had his back to me. I could not see his face, so I could not read whether his next words had been carefully planned, or skillfully improvised, but neither option would have made the words less shocking than the other.

"I offer a final gift, the likes of which exists nowhere else in Japan. If the church is allowed to continue its work here, we will work under the protection of Lord Nobunaga. That means I have no more need of my own protection."

I felt my skin constrict. There were no other crates in the room, nothing to be brought forward. I looked at the back of Valignano's head, as if by doing so I could stop him from speaking. The others in the room had not yet made the connection.

"I offer one of the finest warriors I have ever met, in any land," Valignano continued. The realization of what was to occur started to seep through the room, and I could feel it like a physical wave. Beside me, Organtino's arm twitched.

"Trained from a youth and having spent half his life at arms, he is a young man but an old soldier. Trained in sword, spear, dagger, bow, mace, and arquebus, as well as tactics. I offer my servant, the one you call Yasuke."

The wave crashed, washing over all who were assembled. Valignano and Nobunaga faced each other, unblinking. Only Organtino reacted, looking over at me with a wide expression that indicated he had known nothing of this. Nobunaga smiled, albeit slightly, as if this were the concession he had been waiting for, and I wondered if this exchange had been prearranged. It would not be unlike Valignano to have emissaries discreetly ask which gifts would be most welcome, but he was equally skilled at reading a man on the spot and offering what most interested him.

My chest tightened, as if the air in my lungs had been replaced with ice. There was a single moment in which I thought to speak, but I did not know what I would say. What could I say? I alone in this room held no power. I did not have the church behind me, as Valignano and Organtino did, nor a strong clan at my back like Nobunaga and Ranmaru. I had been taken from my village and my people, separated from those who would support me, and forced to rely on the goodwill and resources of those who would exchange me at the first opportunity for something of greater value.

I was angry at Valignano, but more so at myself for having so foolishly misjudged my place. I had served Valignano and the church long and well, and they had treated me well in return, but I was not kin to them. I was property. All I had been kin to had been left in the streets and soil of the African village, or separated from me on the dock in India.

I stood fast, kept my expression still. There was nothing to be said or done. With just a few words, I had been sold once again.

II

Azuchi Castle

"Who does not know the order that our flesh should serve to repay kindness and life should serve for bonds and moral obligations?"

—From the Noh play *Tomoe*

8

My father was away when the slavers came to our village.

As a child, I'd spend most of my day in the deep black of the caves breaking chunks of rock off the wall and placing them in sacks at my feet. The dust choked my lungs and I knew the proximity of the other boys solely by the sound of their coughing. The older boys would haul the rocks up into the daylight and smash them apart, looking for the streaks of iron, and once or twice during the day they would come back down with bread and bowls of watery stew, both of which we ate by feel.

I was stronger than most of the older boys, though I had not yet reached the age of being cut. After hours in the cave we would emerge, our fingers bleeding and sore, and let the sun force our eyes wide again. If the haul was good, the adults would light a great fire in the center of the village and melt the iron in the hearth, then pour it out to cool and work it into any number of things—tools, jewelry, weapons. We would trade it to visiting Arabs or Indians for cloths and grains, or some of our men would pack as many bags as their mules and horses could carry and leave for days at a time, trading with other tribes around the region and sometimes beyond.

My father was such a trader, and he would return from his trips with fantastical stories of cities with great clay towers, markets filled with strange wares, kings and queens of fabulous wealth with gold chains linking their ear and nose, their hands adorned with rubies and emeralds the size of beetles. He would tell us of libraries with row upon row of books written on parchment and leather, animals racing across the plains or hanging high up in the treetops or lazing indolently by the side of streams and pools, and men who covered themselves in dry ash to appear as ghosts, or who pierced their skin to make pictures upon themselves with the scars.

My mother had asked me once what I would do, when I became a man. Would I follow in my father's footsteps?

I had just caught up with her on the dusty road leading from the shared farmlands to our village. She was with three other women, carrying baskets of yams and millet, and I startled her as I approached.

"You are almost as tall as your father," she exclaimed chidingly. "When did this happen? When did my son grow so much?"

It's true that the mother I had always looked up to, I now looked at eye to eye, and I found myself as suddenly surprised by the fact as she had jokingly been. I lowered my head and walked beside her.

"This one will be a giant," one of the other women called. "I will keep my son in a basket at night to keep him from growing so large."

The women laughed, but my mother looked uncomfortable.

"My son will be a man soon," she declared to the women. Then to me, "You will have choices. Not yet, but not so far away. Will you continue in the mines? Will you be a wanderer, like your father?"

She had meant the last part to be said lightly, but had failed at it.

"My father is too good a storyteller," I assured her. "He describes the lands he sees so well that I have no need to see them myself. I will stay here."

"This village is not too small for you?" she asked.

"No. And neither is my mother, no matter how much taller I grow than her."

Her smile stretched the full width of her face, and felt like a small sun rising in my chest.

"If you are to be a man, son, you must learn the most important thing—how to serve a woman."

She passed her basket to me, and the other three women approached one by one to stack their baskets in my arms atop my mother's. Laughing, they lifted their skirts and ran down the road to the village like children.

I tried to balance the baskets, but they swayed in my shaking arms, then the top basket tipped over and spilled across the road before I managed even a single step, sending yams skittering in all directions. I put the baskets back down and began chasing after the rolling yams. On the wind, I could still hear my mother's laughter.

WHEN MY FATHER WASN'T TRAVELING, he would carve—furniture for the other villagers, or little totems he could trade, but mostly masks.

On one of our last days together, I found him sitting on a log in the backyard, tools in hand, leaning over some new work on his table.

"May I see?" I asked.

"You know you may not."

He drew a cloth across his work.

"Not even a small peek?"

My father laughed. He looked older than he was, his skin creased and weathered from his frequent travels, but when he smiled he was young again, his dark eyes lit with wonder. His skin was lighter than Mother's and mine, having come from another village to marry my mother many years ago. He was broad shouldered but thin, having been able to use his charm more than his body to provide for himself all of his life, and now to help provide for us as well.

"Every year you ask this, and every year you know the answer. You will see the mask when the festival begins, and not before then. And you shall have to guess which is me."

"I always know which is you," I said.

"And how do you know?"

I kept the answer to myself. I did not want to tell him that he always looked directly at me, through the mask, because I worried if I told him he would stop doing it.

The festival was my favorite time of year, and every man and woman in the village was preparing their costumes, their songs. The women would paint their faces white and stomp and chant while rhythmically slapping the taut skin of bongos, and the men would dance in turns, in intricately carved masks. They performed on stilts, their arms decorated with feathers and beads and their legs and stilts covered with brightly patterned cloths.

All my life I had longed for the day when I would be old enough to join them. I studied their movements—how they flicked their wrists to make the beads rattle, how they drove the stumps of the stilts into the ground, flexed their hips to explode upward, turned their ankles this way and that to allow their bodies to waver within their robes, like reeds swaying in the wind. As I watched, their movements seemed to slow, each motion its own individual moment, and I understood the purpose of every twitch and flex, committed them to memory and dream, storing the knowledge away for the day when I would be able to replicate their display.

"Come here."

I sat next to my father on the log. He placed his hand on my shoulder.

"This is your twelfth year. Soon you will go to the M'Mwera hut, with the others of your age. It is the beginning of your becoming a man. While you are there, the mwene will train you in the ways and customs of your people."

He hesitated, then reached underneath the cloth that he had covered his work with and pulled out a small adz. It was a tool he used for carving, a flat, sharp, metal plate attached to a short wooden handle. He smiled mischievously.

"But it does not mean we can't get a head start. Take this. It's yours now." He handed the adz to me.

"But we will keep this our secret. Now, fetch a piece of wood."

I ran to select a block of wood from the pile behind our hut, and my father began showing me how to carve.

A FEW DAYS LATER, MY mother made a spicy fish stew for dinner that was my father's favorite. I knew from the meal that he would be gone in the morning, off to distant places to trade wares with strange men.

I woke early, hoping to see him off. My father's cart was packed and he was standing beside my mother in the weak light of the dawn. He pressed his forehead to hers. I watched their shapes against the sunrise, connected. I chose not to interrupt.

Once my father had ridden out of sight, my mother returned to the porch. I sat beside her out front of our hut, watching the morning people come and go, and occasionally waving or calling out a quick greeting.

My mother was all the things my father was not—dark, smooth-skinned, and strong. Her arms were muscled from working in the fields and her hands were as large and powerful as those of any of the village's men, but she moved with an elegance that softened her physicality.

"I will miss you when you are at the hut," she said.

"I will not be going for a few days yet."

"And I will be here all alone."

She rubbed her eyes in a mock-crying gesture. I nudged her with my shoulder, and we laughed together. My mother leaned toward me and raised an eyebrow.

"Your father says some of his carving tools are missing. We must have thieves, no? Or maybe spirits, bored and looking for something to occupy themselves? I can't think of any other explanation."

"I . . . yes . . . I was . . . "

"Go," she interrupted. "Show me what you have been up to."

I went inside the house and returned with a mask I had been working on anytime my mother and father were occupied.

"And what is this?" she exclaimed.

"It's a rhino," I said. "Or at least I think it is. From how father described it."

She ran her finger along the wood, touched the tip of the horn, turned the mask over to inspect the inside.

"I do not know what a rhino looks like. We will ask your father his thoughts when he returns. But this is good work. You have a talent."

I beamed at my mother's praise. "When I join the festival—will you play the drums for me? While I dance?"

She handed the mask back to me and kissed me on the forehead. "I will play for you until the skins come off the drums. We will see what gives out first—my arms or your dancing feet."

THE DAY I WAS TAKEN, I emerged from the cave where the boys my age stripped rocks for ore, tired and hungry because we'd worked long past the time that food should have been brought down to us.

We had continued to work, peeling the skin of the cave, layer by layer, until the floor grew cluttered with sacks of rocks and our bellies grew empty and we clambered up the shaft of the cave with the help of the ropes we'd strung along the walls. I stepped into the harsh sun, head down and blinking, looking at nothing but my own footprints left in the flint-like dust around the cave's mouth until my vision adjusted and I could look up, my eyes registering a wrongness that I could not at first comprehend.

I stood beside the other boys and looked about the village and saw, at first, only the homes and the hearth in which we melted ore, the trees in the distance and beyond that the beginning of the slope that led down to the plains. It was only after several blinks that I could fill in the rest.

The corpses of the adults and of most of the older boys were strewn about the village. The few remaining boys and all of the younger girls were kneeling by the hearth, their hands bound behind them. I searched for my mother, but I could see already that none had been spared. I closed my eyes immediately to the dead, and when I reopened them, I looked only at the living, staring at those tied up by the hearth and not allowing my gaze or my mind to drift toward the bodies. It was only then that I noticed the strangers.

I had heard stories of white men from my father who had come across them in the cities trading for medicines and tools, but the dozen who gathered around before us were the first I'd ever seen. They had hairy faces with deep-set eyes and wore strangely shaped clothes. They had the hardened muscles of young men, but the wrinkled skin of old ones. They shouted words at us in a language we couldn't understand, the words short and sharp and violently formed in their mouths.

"Spirits!" one boy shouted. He leapt in panic, stumbled backward, and fell into the mouth of the cave. The sound of his body breaking against the rocks on the cave floor shook the rest of us into action.

We ran in all directions. Some sought cover inside their homes, some went back down into the cave, but carefully, using the ropes. One boy made it to the edge of the village and tried to shimmy up the trunk of a great tree. I ran past the strange men, toward the hearth. I saw the fear in the eyes of the boys and girls kneeling there, but I had nothing I could use to cut the ropes. I pulled at the knots with my fingers but could not get them to loosen and so I sat numbly in front of them trying to calm them.

"I won't let them have you," I repeated over and over.

It was a pledge I had no power to keep. The men collected us with little resistance. They marched us for days, barefoot across lands I'd never seen before. At the edge of the great water they thrust us forward one by one to other white men. The new men grabbed us by our testicles, shook our shoulders roughly, pushed their fingers into our mouths and rubbed them along our teeth. They loaded us into the belly of the boats, back into the darkness.

Our beds were two planks of wood side by side and bolted into the hull, barely wide enough to lie on in easy waters and impossible to grip on to in rough ones. There was a single pail in the corner but it sloshed over within an hour of leaving shore and was never replaced, so we lay shivering on the planks and fouled ourselves in our narrow bunks. We vomited as the ship heaved and swayed and could not then help but to roll in it, and into each other. At irregular intervals the door to the galley swung open and pails of a pasty gruel were poured out across the filth-caked floor for us to pick at and fight over. Boys kicked at the boards of the hull, pried at them with bloodied hands, and screamed and babbled incoherently about returning home.

Twelve times I saw new sunlight come through the slats above us before the boats came to rest. We were brought out into the open air by men who covered their mouths and noses and struck us if we came too close to them. Our legs were unsteady beneath us, no longer trusting the stillness of land. Our threadbare clothes were stripped from us and burned, and pails of water were thrown at us. The pool of effluent around our feet ran brown and gray and carried clumps of things over the side of the dock and into the sea. There were bodies on the dock as well, those who did not survive the journey and who I later learned had been hacked up and sold to farmers as feed for their pigs and dogs.

Days of little food and less rest, combined with sickness and dehydration and diarrhea, had drained us. I conserved what energy I had. I pushed everything down deep, thoughts of the past and thoughts of the future. I lived in each breath, and looked neither forward nor backward beyond it. The inspection on the dock, the rough cleaning and sorting, all happened in a blur. Every ounce of focus we could muster was placed on getting our bearings, trying to determine where we were, how much time had passed or how much we had lost. How many of us had survived and how many of us had not.

I did not know where I was but I knew I was far from home, too far for my father to ever find me. I thought of him returning from his trip. Would there be signs of violence he could see from afar, or would he ride into the village expecting all to be as it ever was? Would he smile as he approached, eager to see us as he always was after a journey? Ready to kiss his wife, only to find her dead; ready to hold his son, only to find him missing? My heart ached imagining his sorrow, his loss. I felt his pain more intensely than I felt my own.

9

I'd forgotten the shame of being sold. It had been quite some time since it happened last, and I had come to think of myself more as Valignano's servant and sometimes confidant. It was Valignano who bought me my first set of clothes that had not already been worn by another man. He was the first, since being separated from my people, to ask me my thoughts on any matter, and to listen. He taught me, but not from books, like the Jesuit priests who had educated me. He taught me from his experience, the way a father would. He'd allowed me at times to challenge him, to question him, and even, on some small matters, had sought my counsel. But in one apparently spontaneous act, he had reminded me of my place. That my fate was not my own to decide. That my estimation of myself had been too high, thinking that I had been valued more as a person than a possession. He had reminded me that I was a slave in a strange land far from home, and that I had never been otherwise, not since I was a child.

I had tried, once, to run.

From the moment I emerged from the mining cave on the day I was taken, I knew my life would be different, and I accepted it as such. It was the acceptance, I believe, that helped me to survive. We were in shock during the overland journey, but there were a few boys who started whispering about plans to escape or to overpower our captors. Even at that early stage, I recognized that the idea was a fantasy. The grizzled and gruff-bearded men with their weather-worn clothing and their watchful eyes and their wrinkled-paper skin knew their work. They had wiped out our entire village in hours, perhaps less. They'd killed the adults and the older boys precisely to prevent any possibility of revolt. They kept only those young enough to be pliable, those young enough to grow into their strength. And they kept the girls.

I had worried most about the girls, seeing how the papery men looked at them, and though I did not yet know their language, their laughs and barbs and sneers were easy enough to interpret. Yet the girls remained untouched. Only when we reached India and I saw the way in which they were inspected did I understand the white men's restraint. The girls had value only as long as they were provably intact.

Instead it was one of the boys who bore the brunt of their attentions—a boy two years younger than myself, on the smallish side, and who the slavers had pegged immediately as one who likely would not survive the journey, or would not fetch much of a price if he did. A sacrificial lamb. It had taken me many years to block out the nearby sounds of men grunting as they poured themselves into him. The empty look in his eyes when he was returned to the tent, the sackcloth he had been dressed in speckled with flecks of blood. All of us pitied him, but when the eldest of us finally took the mercy of smothering him in his sleep, we were each selfishly terrified that we would be selected as his replacement.

Nevertheless, the thought of escape was futile. We were tied to each other hand and foot throughout the days of marching, and tied even more tightly to each other before sleeping. We would have had to shuffle past our captors in unison, and in silence, slip far enough away unnoticed to have the time to work our way out from the rope, then find out where we were and where to go. We could only wait.

By the time the overland traverse was complete and we were loaded into the belly of the creaking wooden boat, the shock had worn off. Now boys talked in earnest of jumping the man who sometimes opened the portal to pour gruel upon the floor, then charging our way up the stairs and taking the ship, but already we had become too weak for such efforts. Boys shouted and cried and planned, but never acted. They clawed at the boards of the hull and whispered feverishly of swimming to safety, but they never lifted a finger against the slavers.

My new change in circumstances had been swift, just as it had always been in the past. After Valignano had offered me to Nobunaga, no one seemed to know what to do next. I should have felt anger, but instead what I felt was a profound embarrassment, as if I were some great burden that had been passed from one man to another. I bowed my head and stepped forward.

Ranmaru, Nobunaga's youthful assistant, took the cue. He touched my elbow, nodded some kind of acknowledgment toward me, and led me from the room. Brother Organtino had a pained look on his face, the soft, welcoming smile nowhere to be found. Valignano did not even bother to glance up, keeping his eyes instead on Nobunaga.

In the antechamber, Ranmaru turned his head, opened his mouth to say something, then stopped. I appreciated his silence. I seethed at what I felt was Valignano's betrayal, but I had long since learned to keep my emotions from reaching the surface.

Ranmaru walked me across the open courtyard at Honno-ji. Near the stables there were a series of small rooms, plain and square, lifted above the ground on short stilts. I entered, and he hesitated in the doorway.

"Do I need to place a guard?"

I shook my head. "I am at Lord Nobunaga's service," I said.

Ranmaru bowed, and exited. A short time later a bowl of broth and a jug of water were brought and left on the doorstep. I sat in the center of the room, cross-legged. I stared forward and did my best to think of absolutely nothing. To begin the process of erasing Father Valignano and the Jesuits from my mind, just as I had had to do with my family. It was not the first time that my life had changed in a moment. Adapting to new circumstances meant releasing any attachments to the old.

I was not visited but I was free to come and go. I ducked through the doorways at Honno-ji, ate with my fingers while the others deftly fed themselves using chopsticks, slept at night on a tatami mat that was only the length of my head to my knees—a series of reminders that the world I lived in now was one that had never been meant for me.

In the small, empty chamber that Ranmaru had led me to at Honno-ji, I resolved to do what I had always done. I would survive. I would find some way to make myself useful. I would serve this Nobunaga as faithfully as I had past masters. I would accomplish whatever task he set before me, answer whatever questions he needed answered, advise him if I were requested to, stay silent if I were not. But I would not again forget what I really was.

Making myself valuable was one element of my survival. The other was learning everything I could of my new environment.

Nobunaga's party rode out of Honno-ji temple and through the streets of Kyoto with little of the spectacle that had been on display on previous days. At the end of the first day's ride, I rose in the dark and walked out into the camp. It had always been my habit to study my surroundings by day and by night, and several times it had proven useful, possibly even saved my life.

The encampment was bracketed by cloths tied on broad wooden frames. They held the wind away from the tents, rippling violently as they did so. Each cloth bore the Oda emblem. One of the foot soldiers had told me it was modeled after the flower of a quince: a tart, spicy, pear-like fruit that grows in the mountainous regions. I stepped outside the barriers for a moment, to feel the full strength of the wind, the full weight of the darkness.

There were guards posted on both sides of the windbreaks, and a surprising number of campfires were still lit. The ashigaru, or foot soldiers, sat and talked in small groups, or milled around the encampment, their armor exchanged for thick, scratchy-looking wools.

There were a few masseuses in the traveling party, and as I walked the length of the camp, they emerged from their tents to touch my skin, slipping their hands beneath my shirt to rub my arms and back, and murmuring to each other about how it felt different or how it felt the same, depending on the masseuse. I remembered the softness of the servant girl's hands within mine before I lifted her for Nobunaga, the glint of orange in her eyes, her nervous fear. I steeled myself against the touch of the masseueses, pulled away, and continued to walk.

Others studied me as well. The soldiers had not been present during my initial audience with Nobunaga. Most would have never seen me before we started the ride from Honno-ji, and many had not seen me yet. Some jumped backward at the sight, a large black demon stalking the campsite in darkness. One drew his sword and shouted an alarm before a fellow soldier calmed him and explained to him who I was.

The commotion attracted attention from a nearby campfire. There were three men seated in a circle, and one of them waved me over.

"I saw you in the hall a few days ago. You are even bigger up close than I thought. Come, let me take a look at you."

The man was middle-aged, with jet-black hair and weathered skin, but his features were marred by a badly broken nose, the nose shifted rightward and the bridge of it nocked with a bone-white ridge. He spoke in a deep, sandpaper voice.

"It seems the Oda clan has acquired another European trinket," he said.

The two other men laughed. They wore emblems that were different than the Oda quince. It was a five-petaled flower with what could be a sun as its center.

"I am not European. I am African."

"A-fri-can."

He said the new word slowly, testing it in his mouth. He circled me in a deliberate way, then planted himself in front of me, hands clasped behind his back.

"The Africans and the Europeans work together?"

"No," I said. "Not really."

"But you came here together. You and the priest."

"Yes."

"The African and the European."

"Yes. But we are two men, we do not—"

"You come here to change us."

The two men who had remained seated stirred uncomfortably, and one of them waved their compatriot to come back to the fire.

"Hidemitsu, come, sit. Let the man be. He has done you no dishonor."

"And I do not intend any dishonor." I bowed my head toward the broken-nosed Hidemitsu. "If I have given offense, I apologize."

"You have given no offense. And I have given none in return," he said firmly. "I have merely asked why you are here, so far from your home."

"I am not here to change anyone. I have learned some of your ways, but I hope to learn more."

"The African hopes to learn the ways of the Japanese."

Hidemitsu chuckled and looked around for the others to do so in support, but they turned their attentions too eagerly to the fire. I started to speak, but Hidemitsu interrupted.

"And the European? The priest? Is he also here to learn from us? African or European makes no difference to me. You come with your trinkets and inventions, then you replace our weapons with yours, our clothes with yours, our stories with yours. Today you ask us to pray to your god, tomorrow you will ask us to bow to your king, or to eat from your hand."

I kept my head bowed. "I have no king. I have no land, and no home. I am here to serve, nothing more."

Hidemitsu spat on the ground, then grunted and waved me away.

"I wanted a closer look at you. And now I have one."

IN THE MORNING, MEN QUICKLY ate cold breakfasts, then rolled up their mats and packed their horses. There were no fires but for a small one near Lord Nobunaga's tent, where a handful of servants were preparing hot food and tea. I recognized one of the servants as the girl with the orange-flecked eyes, the frightened one who I had lifted at Honno-ji. I thought briefly of approaching her to apologize, but I recalled the dismayed expression on her face when Nobunaga had pointed at her in the hall, and I assumed she would not want the attention.

Near the fire was Ranmaru, the young samurai who seemed to be Nobunaga's right hand. He was flanked by two other men. Ranmaru spotted me, then stood from his place at the fire and the three men approached.

"Our lord requests that you ride with him today."

The two others introduced themselves as Ogura and Jingorou. They were brothers, and shared the look of it. Ogura was slightly more square of jaw, but for the most part I could only distinguish them by their hair—Ogura's tied formally into a knot, while Jingorou's hung lankly to his shoulders. Both were lithe and moved gracefully, quietly. They had the bearing of men who had seen war, while Ranmaru, smooth-skinned with charcoal dark eyes and refined features, did not, though I had learned to underestimate no one.

The three young samurai positioned themselves to ride in a protective formation around Nobunaga. Ranmaru to my side, between myself and the daimyo, and the brothers Ogura and Jingorou closely behind. They settled into place so seamlessly that it was clear they were practiced at serving as his closest guard.

Nobunaga heeled his horse and started the day's ride without a word. We had sheltered overnight in a valley and began the day on a twisting upward trail toward the crest of a grass-covered hill.

"You have been in Japan some time now, Yasuke."

I did not react immediately to the name, was slow to remember that it now belonged to me.

"Three months. Almost four," I said, recovering hastily. I was uncertain how much to say about our travels so far, but my life was in his hands now, not the Jesuits. "We arrived at Kuchinotsu. Father Valignano was received by Lord Arima, and we made our way to Kyoto from there."

"Hmm. Tell me, what do you think of our country?"

"I have not seen so much of it as to say, my lord. But the people seem kind and curious, and have treated us well."

"Except when they mob you and tear your clothes." Nobunaga smiled.

"I have yet to apologize for the disturbance I caused. I hope my lord will forgive me."

"There is no forgiveness to ask. You did nothing but be who you are. The wrong is in those who could not control their own behavior. Do not offer apologies for the actions of others."

"Yes, my lord. Thank you."

We rode silently until we reached the crest of the hill. Below us, the road led into a grove of short, leafy trees, emerald-colored in the light of the morning sun.

"Your country is quite beautiful, my lord."

"Ah, but you have not seen even the beginning of it. The cherry blossoms, the great bamboo forests, the snow-capped majesty of Mount Fuji." Nobunaga gestured to his small retinue. "But these are things we all know. Tell us of things we do not, Yasuke. Tell of us of your country."

"I was taken quite young, my lord. The country you speak of has not been my home in quite some time."

"Nonsense. Where a man is born, matters. Where he comes from, matters. Who his ancestors are, matters."

I nodded. Organtino's words to me when I was summoned to Honno-ji had been "tell him something he does not know and he will value you for it." I tried to think of what he would want to know and recalled what I could, starting haltingly.

"I came from a village that mines ore, and makes things from iron for trade. We lived in the foot of the hills, worked in the caves. On the plain below we planted beans and grew grass for our cows and goats. My homeland is large, though, and its people are very different. Some live by the sea, some deep in the forests. Some survive in the desert, while others study in great cities with large clay buildings and libraries and bustling markets. In other parts of the country, the animals are more wild than our simple livestock."

I tried to recall my father's stories without recalling my father. Without thinking of him wandering through the plains and hills and villages looking for some trace of me, without thinking of his heartbreak, his hopelessness, or possibly worse, his unwillingness to give up hope. I blocked out the story-teller and allowed only the details to come through.

I began to describe for them the stripes of the zebra, the twisting horns of the gazelle, the fierceness of the lion, the agility of the spotted leopard as it bounded from one tree branch to another. The towering grace of the giraffe and the great club-toothed maw of the fleshy hippopotamus and the intimidating charge of the armor-plated rhinoceros, who all other animals let pass unchallenged. The company listened in awe.

Ogura joked, "So it's not just the men who are giants," and everyone laughed.

I pictured the rhino mask I had carved, my mother's hands checking it for smoothness, the heat of her sitting beside me. I was shocked to realize how long it had been since I had thought about her, but I pushed down the memories and continued.

Nobunaga's interest perked even further when I told them of the elephants, their ponderous bulk, their stampeding rage and fierce tusks. How in ancient times Hannibal had dressed them for war and in more recent times, the Indians had built small castles on their backs and rode them into battle. Nobunaga absorbed it all, but seemed most interested in the topic of warfare.

"You've been a soldier?"

"Yes," I said. "I was trained when I was taken." *And forced to fight* were the words on the tip of my tongue, but I held them. "I fought."

"Tell me what you've seen."

"Anywhere I've been, men have fought for the same reason—over land or over beliefs."

Nobunaga seemed disappointed in the answer. I remembered Brother Organtino's other advice when I was first brought before Nobunaga—don't get too comfortable with him. It had been a long morning's ride, and I had settled into the conversation too easily. I thought about what other answer I could offer.

"The terrain matters," I started, looking around at the rolling hills and

74

narrow roads. "In Europe and India, the battles are fought mostly on plains. They use cannons and other large devices to assault the enemy walls. Here, among the mountains, it would be difficult to move such equipment. Your land itself renders such weapons ineffective."

Nobunaga stroked his chin, his momentary frown erased, so I carried on. I struggled to describe a trebuchet in Japanese, and was met with confused glances. I switched to talking about phalanxes, men advancing in formation behind large shields, which sparked an argument amongst Ogura and Jingorou about whether it was better to be shielded, or to have both hands free for fighting.

At midday, Nobunaga called a halt. A servant brought a stool for Nobunaga to sit on, and others hurried to prepare food. The rest of us sat in a circle on the ground, facing him. Planks of food were brought and passed around. I finished mine quickly, and Nobunaga gestured for more to be brought.

"Who is the ruler in your country?" he asked.

"No one man rules Africa. Each tribe has its own leader."

He nodded as if satisfied. "It is the same as here, then. Though it was not always so. Do you know of our history?"

"Some, my lord. Father Valignano ensured that we learned what we could before arriving."

"Tell me."

I shifted, trying to make myself comfortable. The others sat easily with their legs folded beneath them, the tops of their feet pressed flat against the ground and their weight on their heels, but they had practiced since childhood. It was painful for someone not used to that position, and they had been patient so far with my inability to hold it. I raised onto my toes, releasing the pressure on my ankles as discreetly as possible, then settled back again.

"Hundreds of years ago, the emperor's authority was absolute. But noble families competed for favor and position beneath him, and eventually undermined the emperor himself. The Minamoto clan seized power and established a shogunate, placing them under the emperor's rule, but with the shogun as head of government and of military matters. The Minamoto shogunate was itself replaced by the Ashikaga shogunate, which stood for over two centuries until my lord removed the last of the Ashikaga shogun."

Ranmaru gave me the briefest of nods, as if recognizing that I had intentionally left much out, and indicating to me that my answer had been safe. Nobunaga picked up to fill in the details he preferred.

"I removed the shogun, yes, but I did not end the shogunate. That was done by their own carelessness. They placed governors in each of the provinces and charged them with keeping the peace, collecting taxes, and retaining forces ready for war should the shogun call upon them. But with each passing generation, the shogun became weaker, more interested in the culture and arts of the capital than the difficulties in the provinces. The governors began to keep the taxes they collected for themselves, and use their forces to expand their own territories. A once unified Japan became a nation of warring states, and the shogun had little ability to stop it."

Nobunaga was no longer talking directly to me, or to anyone. He was looking out across the field. The other men in the circle had bowed their heads, and I knew I should too, but I was transfixed. Nobunaga's face burned with an intensity I had not seen before, and only then, for the first time, could I reconcile him with the picture that Brother Ambrosius had painted of a man consumed by ambition and willing to step past any bound.

"For over one hundred years, we have been at war. Not with an enemy, but with ourselves. Japanese against Japanese. We have shed each other's blood, taken each other's lands, burned each other's fields, and toppled each other's castles. Families have fought against those who had previously offered them shelter, and alongside those who had previously murdered their ancestors. Clan warring against clan, solely for the glory of their family's name. We are a house divided."

"But you will bring us together, make us one," Ranmaru said softly.

Nobunaga looked as if he'd been shaken out of a trance. He glanced around the circle, all heads still bowed but Ranmaru's and my own.

"Are we going to meet your enemies now?" I asked.

"No. Has no one told you where we are headed?"

"I had not needed to know."

The others looked up now. Two servants slipped into the circle to collect the bowls and planks and cups. No one paid them any mind.

"We are on our way to my home castle, Azuchi. We will prepare there. We will meet our enemies soon enough. Have you been given your arms?"

My spear and sword had not yet been returned to me, and I had come to assume they would not be. However, Nobunaga's simple question caused Ranmaru to bow and back out of the circle hurriedly, presumably to find a servant who could fetch my things.

"My lord, a question, if I may?"

Nobunaga nodded.

"When I was first summoned to see you, you called for a story. I'm grateful to have heard it, but I think I may have misunderstood it. Was there some message in it?"

Nobunaga stood, signaled a servant to fetch his stool and store it away.

"We should ride," he said. "If we make good progress this afternoon, we'll reach Azuchi in the morning."

The others stood and I followed. I limped toward my horse on numb feet, glad to be free of kneeling.

10

I n the morning we rode into the sun, and the brightness of it kept me from
seeing Azuchi Castle until we were almost upon it. Nobunaga had chosen
his location well—northeast of Kyoto, close enough to reach the capital in a
hard day's ride, if necessary, but also positioned to oversee long stretches of
the key route connecting the Uesugi clan in the north, the Takeda clan in the
east, and the Mori clan in the west.

The risks involved in conquering Japan from its center were clear—there
would initially be enemies on all sides, and the requirement to fight battles
on multiple fronts. Having succeeded in doing so, however, Nobunaga now
reaped the rewards of ruling from the center—the control of any communi-
cations or transport amongst his geographically separated enemies, making
it almost impossible for them to join forces, or coordinate any efforts against
him. All roads led to Oda.

As we rode out of the foothills, our first glimpse of the castle was its
golden top, glinting in the early sun like a landed star. Nobunaga turned
slightly to see my first reaction and appeared pleased.

"It's beautiful," I said.

"That is just the tip of it."

"You must be able to see for miles from atop it."

Nobunaga smiled. "I can see as far as I need to."

On either side of the road, the first green shoots of rice plants covered the valley plain. Beyond the plain were the houses of farmers and minor retainers, and then a wide bridge over an outer moat. Across the bridge there was a towering gate built into the wall that ran around the base of the mountain. To the left, a smaller road curved around the wall toward what looked like the edge of the city, but the main road continued on through the gate.

Through the entrance there were more houses, and we rode past them as we began the climb toward the top of the hill. The path from gate to castle was long and steep and narrow, which would make it difficult for attacking forces to move large numbers of soldiers quickly. It was flanked by white walls topped with dark tiles, and closer to the top of the hill the road twisted several times, creating unavoidable choke points that were well within the reach of the castle's archers.

There were several fortifications along the climb that any invading army would have to clear or destroy along the way, palisades that would offer protection for Nobunaga's foot soldiers while they peppered the road with fire from their arquebuses, and additional gates which were open now, but which could be closed to further slow an enemy advance.

A few people came out to greet Nobunaga's party with bows and waves, but for the most part, his return was quiet. At some point on the climb, I realized the column of men and women marching behind us had shrunk.

"Nobunaga ordered all men released at the lower gate," Ranmaru explained, riding beside me. "Now they ride only as far as their homes. Servants, foot soldiers, and other lower-ranking retainers have homes at the base of the hill, in the city. Higher-ranking members and key servants live higher up, closer to the castle keep."

"Where will I stay?"

"You will lodge with the guards for now, until you are assigned duties. The rooms will be small for you, but they are comfortable, and mostly quiet. I hope you will find them acceptable."

"I assure you, whatever accommodations you see fit to provide, I have seen worse."

Ranmaru looked at me appraisingly. "I don't doubt it. I hope the Portuguese were not unkind to you."

I considered, a moment, before answering.

"Father Valignano was not unkind to me. There were others before him who were much different in their treatment."

Ranmaru nodded. "And are you loyal to them? The Jesuits?"

"I served Father Valignano well, I hope. I would have given my life without hesitation, because that was my task. But I am no longer his. I now belong to Lord Oda Nobunaga. You worry I am a spy?"

"I do not wish to cast doubts on the character of yourself, or of Father Valignano, but he is a crafty thinker, and he did give you away quite easily."

I glanced at Nobunaga. He rode near enough to hear us and though he gave no indication he was listening, I had no doubt Ranmaru's questions were Nobunaga's, but ones he had deemed unworthy of himself to speak.

"I understand your suspicions, Ranmaru. I would have them myself. But while I am honored to serve our Lord Nobunaga, I was as surprised to be given away as anyone, perhaps more so."

"I think I believe you. It's not wrong for a man to have a master, but it is wrong for a man to be unable to choose his master. I hope you will find service to our lord more satisfying than any past . . . unpleasantries you have experienced. Stay in our lord's favor. There are rewards to it."

Ranmaru seemed friendly and sincere, and I had warmed to him somewhat on the march, but I sneered inside at his last comment. I wanted to tell him that one who felt free to choose his own master had never been traded from one to another against his will. That I was only here precisely because of the fact that I had no say in whom I served. My mood was turned quickly sour, and though I recognized he meant no ill will, I was in no mind to hear musings on freedom from one who did not know what it was to be without it.

Ranmaru, oblivious, pulled his horse to a halt.

"This is where the guards stay."

I nodded silently, suddenly grateful that the journey was at its end. We'd reached the plateau of the hill. The castle itself reared massively above us, seven stories tall with a foundation of packed rock and long sloping walls, a myriad of turrets and lookouts and topped with a golden keep.

Compared to the relative modesty of Arima's dirty and run-down forest castle, Nobunaga's castle keep was imposing in its size and grandeur. Each of the seven levels had wraparound balconies, but varying in size so that from the balcony of any one level there was a clear line of fire to large portions of the balcony below. The lower five levels were painted white and were fastidiously clean. No detail appeared to have been left unattended to in the castle's design, neither in terms of defense nor of aesthetics.

The guards' quarters, where Ranmaru was gesturing now, were mere yards from the courtyard gate.

"Settle yourself, rest if you like. You'll be called for later. Ah, yes. One more item."

He gestured, and a servant rode forward with a cloth bundle. Ranmaru took the bundle from the servant and handed it to me, then pulled back the cloth. Wrapped inside was my sword and spear.

"You are welcome here, in Azuchi. I am sure you will prove yourself useful."

THE GUARDS' QUARTERS WERE JUST a large empty room with nine tatami mats laid out in rows of three. I ducked my head and entered, and the six men inside started at the sight of me, my head nearly scraping the low ceiling, my skin likely black as the night with the sun at my back. They recovered quickly, though, laughing and chattering excitedly to one another. Word of me must have already spread around the compound.

"You are the African," one man stated, unable to keep the smile from his face. He waved his arm across the room. "Please, take any bed that is open."

I selected one of the beds in the corner. I made halting conversation with the men, but they were eager to rest. Food was brought—a bitter green tea and a cooked egg floating in a thin broth, a bowl of rice. I ate quietly while the others slept.

In India, I'd been taken from the docks to the market, then to a training house run by mercenaries. I'd stayed awake each night watching for any danger from the other boys in the room, and I knew from the occasional movement that they were doing the same. It was days before our collective exhaustion forced us into an unspoken truce, but once we'd each slept through a full night and woken unharmed, we abandoned our night-long vigils. Some still slept poorly—there were groans from injuries suffered during the day's training, whimpers from terrors dreamed of during the night—but I blocked them out and drifted off without trouble. It shamed me some now, that at no point had I thought of offering assistance or comfort, but each of us knew in our own way that we were alone.

I felt none of that initial fear here, but, finding myself again in a new place, amongst strangers, the same feeling of isolation settled in. These men slept soundly, undisturbed by one another's company. I curled myself up in the corner and rested as best I could.

In a few hours the men woke and exited, and a short time later six others came in to sleep. I was not called for that day or the next, but I did receive a message from Ranmaru that I was free to wander the compound. I sent word back that I would be pleased to take a rotation at guard, but received no response. With nothing else to do, I explored.

The men waved me through the upper gate and I walked the winding path down the mountainside and into town. At the top of the mountain there were sprawling estates and meticulously cared for gardens. Further down the hill were more modest homes, some with small ponds visible in the backyards. At the base of the hill, near the docks, was the town proper.

There was no organization to the town of Azuchi. There were simple homes intermingled amongst the shops and market stalls, and indeed some seemed to be selling wares from within their homes—food, fans, ceramics, teas—their doors open to the dusty streets.

Some stared at me, wide-eyed, or nudged their neighbors and pointed. Before long, I had a small gathering of people following me through the streets, though unlike Kyoto, they kept their distance. I tried to ignore the stares, but I could not escape the feeling of oddity, towering over the crowds, looking down at the tops of doorframes, occasionally having to duck under poles with flags or signs hanging from them.

I spotted a woman across the street from me, her movements familiar. I shouldered my way through the jostling mass of people, trying to catch her. The crowds seemed to part before her and close before me. She walked easily, while I fought to keep pace. I touched a hand to her shoulder. She turned, looked up at me with wide brown eyes, orange flecks dancing within them.

I froze for a moment, then bowed my head.

"I am . . . I am called Yasuke."

She hesitated, noticing the dozen or so people who had been following me, and who were watching her now.

"I am Tomiko," she said nervously.

"Yes. Tomiko. It's a beautiful name."

She started to turn from me, so I spoke quickly.

"I wanted to apologize to you. At Honno-ji, you seemed uncomfortable when I lifted you. If I offended you or upset you in any way, I apologize. I was unclear on what to do."

"No, you did nothing wrong. You did what Lord Nobunaga asked. I apologize for my reaction. As a servant, it's usually best to go unnoticed."

"I see."

She took a breath and let her shoulders relax.

"You are a visitor here. I apologize for my manners. I've heard that you are to stay with us now."

"Yes," I replied. "Though I am unclear what my role is to be. I'm staying at the guards' quarters for now, but I have no responsibilities as yet."

She laughed slightly at that, and I realized I had been waiting for her laughter, or just a smile.

"You will be put to use, I have no doubt," she said.

The smile left her face. She tilted her head and she looked at me as if she were seeing me for the first time.

"All this is new to you."

I glanced around the street. People in wide straw hats picked their way amongst the crowd. They wore squarish sandals with blocks of wood nailed into the bottoms to keep their feet out of the mud. There were fishermen with buckets hung from long poles slung across their shoulders and the stench of curdling soy from the vats of a tofu maker.

"It is all very strange," I said.

"No," she replied gently, "you are just seeing it with strange eyes."

The truth of her statement struck me dumb, and I suddenly understood how the foreign slavers and priests could look at my people as savages, not understanding our ways, evaluating our customs and practices against their standards, their experience. I resolved immediately not to make their error.

"Help me," I said too eagerly. "Help me to see it properly."

She stepped backward, her expression suddenly closed.

"It was nice to meet you," she said, the formality intentional. "I should go."

I watched her for a moment as she turned and disappeared into the crowd, then I began the long climb back up to the guards' quarters.

11

The quarters at the slave house in India slept twenty boys to a room. They were cramped, but comfortable. Chaotic, at times, but also incredibly lonely.

My legs wobbled when I was unloaded from the boat onto the dock, weak from the long voyage. After cleaning us, one of the men patted my shoulder, then my chest. He turned to the others and lifted his hand in the air in a gesture indicating my height. He pulled a rough brown cloth from his bag and held it toward me.

"Food," I said. "We are very hungry."

He looked at me blankly, not understanding my words. I was fearful of angering the man, but I felt as if I could not take a single step further. My legs were unstable beneath me and the sun, which had never bothered me before during even the hottest season, felt like a punishment. My eyes were dull, my mouth thick, and my thoughts were like air.

"Food, please," I repeated. I put my hand to my mouth in an eating gesture, but if the man understood it, he ignored it. He looked at me blankly, still holding out the cloth as if I had not spoken.

I took the cloth from his hands and dressed in it. He separated me from the others and waved his hand at the remaining white men to continue. I turned to look at the faces of the boys and girls who were all that remained of my village. The white men were separating them into groups. They shuffled on the dock, tired, confused, and frightened. They dared not look up as I was taken away. I called out to them but my throat was too dry, my voice too weak. The white man pushed me forward.

He led me through crowded streets to a strange market. We passed baskets of colorful spice and rugs woven in intricate patterns and other wares I could not identify. Toward the back of the market, the smells turned from spice to livestock. There were goats chewing on mouthfuls of hay and a few thin-looking cows flicking their tails to ward off the buzzing flies.

He haggled with a buyer in words I did not know. He gripped my shoulder and raised my arm in the air and patted my chest. The buyer considered, nodded, and gave him two bags of salt. The first man took the two bags and pushed me forward.

"I am hungry," I tried again, repeating the same eating gesture with my hands.

The buyer waved his arm at the first man and barked out a question. The two exchanged a few angry words before the first man shrugged and walked away. The buyer cursed at his back, then rummaged on the table behind him and handed me a small fist of dates. I stuffed them into my mouth and chewed them into a sweet, sticky paste, with barely enough saliva to swallow them. I ate them too quickly, my stomach twisting and cramping while I could still taste their juice, but it was still a more pleasant pain than that of hunger.

The buyer grabbed me by the wrist and led me away. He had deep brown skin and loose, flowing pants that narrowed at the ankle. I had seen Indians once, come to the village as traders, and I knew then I must be in their land. I was given a simple bed, but one that still was twice as large as what I'd had on the boat. I was given a pillow, and for the first time in weeks, a cooked meal. I was given a new name, and though the sounds of it were too difficult for me to pronounce or remember, I learned to respond to it nonetheless. I was never asked my original name.

I was one of many slaves in this new house, and over the coming months we learned an array of weapons—spear and shield and axe and mace and swords with broad, curving blades. I was even shown the working of a flintlock and a small pistol, though I was not allowed the use of either.

We trained each day in the courtyard of our owner's mansion from sunup to sundown, and sometimes longer than that, breaking only for quick meals or a hurried stitching of a wound, setting of a bone. He sometimes watched from the veranda, leaning over the railing or seated cooly beneath a canopy and picking at a tray of various fruits, his deep brown skin contrasting with the light-colored clothing he always wore. We were not permitted to share our new names with one another. Only our owner or our trainer could call us. To each other we were nameless. One boy standing in front of you was meant to be no different than another, as it would be in war.

Occasionally, new boys were brought to the compound. I scanned their faces for anyone familiar, listened carefully to their speech in hopes I would hear words I could understand. I longed to be able to talk to someone, but there was no one. My father had learned many languages, but I knew only my own, and there was no one in this place to speak it with me. Instead, my entire world became a physical one. I could intersect with it only through the gestures of my hands, my body.

With no one else to speak to, I spoke to my mother. I whispered to her at night. I tried to tell her stories the way my father had, about this new land, the food, the people, but before long I had to stop. I could not think of my mother and still do the things they asked me to do.

I SWUNG THE WEAPONS FIRST tentatively, then wildly, putting all my strength into each blow, and each failure was met with a strike across the back from the flat side of a sword. The man who trained us had the same light skin and same light eyes as those who had taken me from my village. He had a coarse brown beard and stubbled hair and a scar across his cheek that led to a gnarled stump on one side of his face where his ear once had been.

He barked orders we could not understand, grabbed our arms and legs to place them where he wanted them, and struck us any time he was displeased, but I learned. I learned to plant my foot and shift my weight so I could strike with power but maintain my balance. I learned to feint and parry, to control the weapon at all times, whatever weapon it was.

Most of all, I learned to read my opponent. To watch for the way they gripped the spear or sword, how they rolled their hands or raised their shoulders before striking. Did they flinch if I advanced, did their eyes close for a moment or look away? Did they lift their feet or turn their hips to give away their movement?

I studied them the way I had studied my father's dancing. They slowed for me the way the dancers had slowed, and I absorbed each detail of their motion. Where my father was graceful, they were clumsy. Where my father was smooth and flowing, they were jerky and erratic. Where my father's next step was always a mystery that held me enthralled, these boys trained to be soldiers were easy to read, easy to counter, easy to defeat. As the seasons changed, the man with the short sword and missing ear began to strike me less and less.

We were fed well—bowls of fruit and sticky grains, sweetened with pungent spice. If we had performed well in training we could ask for more, and I always performed well. My size and strength came back quickly and I emerged, even amongst the older boys, as someone to be feared. Only once did I hesitate.

It was during spear training. I was matched up against an older boy, tall but thin, with beaded marks on his brow and scars on his nose and lips where bones or bits of jewelry would have once pierced. I knew very few tribes, but I had seen Dinka before, and I placed him as such. He was darker even than I, but his eyes were yellow and his gums when he bared his teeth were blackening with disease.

I swept him easily off his feet with a swipe of the spear behind his knees, then put him down again by wedging the staff of the spear beneath his arm and twisting him to the ground. He was poorly skilled and posed little threat. The third time he stood, I ignored his loosely held spear altogether and simply bull-rushed him and knocked him over.

"Finish him."

I looked over my shoulder at the soldier who oversaw our training each day. The sun glinted off his simple copper breastplate. He clenched his jaw, flexing the scar that ran along his cheek from chin to missing ear.

Thinking, perhaps, that I did not understand the command, he made an unmistakable stabbing motion with both hands, gripped around an imaginary spear. I turned back to the Dinka boy. He lay on the ground, his spear in the dirt beside him. His yellowy eyes looked up at me in fear, and I knew that his journey must have been similar to mine, that he too had a family he would never see again, a home he would never return to. He, like all of us, would die somewhere so distant that perhaps even our spirits would be unable to find their way back.

But this boy would die earlier than most, for no other reason than that he had failed one time too many. My back was to the soldier, but I could feel his presence behind me. I had the spear raised in my hand, without remembering having raised it. The Dinka's expression shifted, softened. The hand he had raised to defend himself dropped. The look in his eyes changed from fear, to something that shook me far worse— permission.

I pushed the spear into his stomach, tentatively, and he twisted beneath me. My weakness proved worse than violence. Instead of a quick death from a decisive strike, his body twitched and bent and his legs kicked against the sand. Blood bubbles from his mouth and nose formed a pink froth as he heaved pulsing, whimpering breaths. His eyes held a hatred that had not been there before. I wrestled the spear free from his spasming body and stabbed once more, into the neck. This time he was still. I did not turn to face the soldier.

At dinner that night, I pocketed a few dates and a small, tightly wrapped ball of rice. I slipped from my bed in the darkest part of night and lowered myself from the window. The courtyard seemed as large and open as the ocean itself, but after a few calming breaths I sprinted across it, then climbed the gate into the street.

The streets, though mostly empty, were at that timeless hour when some street merchants were closing up their stands while others were preparing theirs for opening in the morning. Even at that young age, I was large enough to stand out, and my black skin would draw notice immediately. I stuck to the shadows and the columnal arches along the fronts of buildings as much as possible. I kept my head down, trying to shield my face. I saw two Portuguese soldiers dressed in full armor from the neck down, patrolling, but the quick bolt of panic I felt mostly fled after I saw one pass a flagon to the other, noticed both of them swaying as they walked.

I knew nothing of my location. My only plan was to get away from people, so I headed toward the end of the street that looked to have fewer lanterns. I drew only a handful of glances, none of them particularly interested in me. The town ended abruptly and I walked into moonlight. There were two paths, one leading up the hill to where a great stone building perched, with a glinting bronzed bell atop it. The other led downward, through a thicket of trees.

I thought "down" must mean the sea, and I chose that one. Beneath the trees, the darkness was absolute. Away from the city, the night was as loud as nights on the plains of my village had been, but different sounds, different insects and animals. I did not know how long my food would have to last, or what I could eat amongst the berries in the bushes, but I set my back against a tree and popped one of the sweet-tasting dates in my mouth. I chewed, and tried to forget the Dinka boy's face. His first glance meant to ensure me, his killer, that it would be okay. His final glance full of fury that I had not struck more decisively.

I kept moving a bit longer, but once I had gone deep enough into the trees I stepped off the path to find a place to rest. I curled up in a web of half-exposed roots and allowed myself to sleep. I woke sometime later to the sound of thrashing. I briefly hoped it was some nocturnal animal, but the sound was clumsy, the kind only a human would make.

I knew I should run, but I froze. I lay nestled in roots while the noise grew closer. A dog barked and pushed its snout through the underbrush, followed by three heavily armed men. I stood on wobbly legs and lashed out, flattening one of the men. The other two were upon me quickly, and my resistance was pathetically brief before one of them clubbed the back of my skull with something dull, then kicked angrily at my fallen body in the darkness.

I woke with a broken jaw, the numbly swollen tissue stretching the skin of my neck and cheek tight. I had been stripped naked and tied in the courtyard. Both hands were bound with rope, and the rope was fastened to a horizontal wooden plank. I hung suspended from my wrists and they ached with the weight, but my feet dangled just above the ground and could provide no relief.

Around me, the others were in the midst of training.

"Water," I mumbled, knowing that no one would dare bring me any.

"Halt."

The boys stopped their exercises immediately and the Portuguese soldier who trained us approached the plank from which I hung.

"You're awake," he said.

I studied the scarred, fleshy stub where his ear had been, the line along his jaw. His eyes were the light watery eyes that I had never seen before the men came to my village. His gaze was flat, without anger, but without mercy as well.

He spoke, but I could understand very few of his words. He gestured toward the second-floor veranda where our owner watched over us, dressed in immaculate white robes. He jostled his hand at his waist where a wealthy man would have kept a sack of coin and drew his hand across his neck in a symbol that I had learned the white men use when referencing death. I understood that I should be dead, if not for my master thinking me valuable.

There was no joy or malice in his tone as he spoke, no emotion or sentiment that I could read at all. He spoke in the same way he would say "lift your spear higher" or "set your feet before you strike." He lined the boys up and issued a simple command.

"Break every spear."

They took turns, beating me with their spear handles until they broke. If I passed out, the soldier cut my inner thigh with a sharp blade to wake me, then the beating continued. They let me hang for two days, twisting a wet cloth onto a stick to let me drink and feeding me a single piece of potato which I chewed slowly and painfully with my swollen jaw, then they repeated the beating. I was let down twice a day, for maybe an hour each time, just to allow the blood to flow back into my hands so that they would not need to be cut off. It should have been a relief, but the sudden swell of veins as the blood pulsed through them was agonizing, and I spent the twice daily respites writhing in the sand while my hands throbbed and swelled and felt ready to burst.

By the time each boy had broken his second spear handle across me, I could not tell one part of my body from another. I ached everywhere, and with every breath. Blood dripped from the cuts on my inner thigh, down my leg and off my toes. The only single pain I could distinguish from the others was the constant pull on my wrists from the hanging. I was certain one wrist had dislocated, but I refused to take inventory of my injuries.

They left me again, hung naked in the brutal afternoon heat, the bug-infested evenings, the frigid, dewy mornings. My lips caked, my eyelids sealed shut with mucus, snot and saliva pooled on my chin before falling to the ground. The skin on my wrists peeled and flaked away.

Hanging there in the courtyard, swarmed by insects, consumed by pain, I had a choice to make. I could go mad, or I could push it all away. I had run, but with no destination. If I were given a map, I would not be able to point out where my village was, and would have no idea how to get there. Even if I had, there would be nothing to return to. Another tribe moved in, likely, mining our caves, maybe even living in our homes.

I had no home anymore. I had no people. I had nowhere to go. I excised all memories of my village, my youth. I let the faces of my family slip away from me. I buried my pain. I let go of my dead.

When they cut me down, the Portuguese soldier threw a spear on the ground beside me. With slow, deliberate movements he unbuckled his copper chest plate and removed it. He threw it in the dirt, then drew the short sword from his scabbard and threw it down as well.

"Kill me," he said.

I looked at the spear. My body ached, everywhere. The backs of my hands were a purplish-blue, the skin swollen and stretched tight. The palms were bloodless and pale. The skin around my wrists was almost completely peeled away and what was beneath it was gray and soft, like rotting fish. Even grasping the spear would be an exercise in agony, but I knew what I had to do. I chose the nameless boy beside me, for no other reason than that he was closest. I picked up the spear and I didn't look at his face and I didn't hesitate. Not then, and not one time since. I ran the boy through, then collapsed to one knee on the ground.

"Water," I said.

The soldier nodded at me and grinned. In the veranda above the courtyard, my owner sipped from his coffee, then turned and went back into the house.

From that point forward I learned how to accept violence, to keep the two things separate in my mind—who I was, and what I had to do. If killing one of the other boys meant an extra bowl of grain, then I would kill and sleep soundly after. Over the course of months, I trained and fought and killed and ate. My arms rounded and hardened, my legs thickened, my hands grew strong. I was still a boy, but there was little to tell me from a man. And I never again hesitated to follow an order.

I was a slave. I no longer needed my chain.

12

Azuchi was a city preparing for war. I could feel the familiar tension and anticipation that always hung over an encampment about to march. Tokugawa Ieyasu, Toyotomi Hideyoshi, and Akechi Mitsuhide, the three generals who had sat just below Nobunaga on the dais, had ridden ahead of us from Honno-ji and had been in Azuchi for days, drilling formations in the courtyard.

Each general had their own standard—Tokugawa, three leaves of wild ginger, turned inward; Toyotomi, a stylized leaf from a Paulownia tree, known for their rapid growth; and Akechi, the five-petaled bellflower. I recognized Akechi's bellflower as the same emblem that had been worn by Hidemitsu, the broken-nosed soldier who had confronted me by the campfire on the march to Azuchi.

I saw Hidemitsu several times, leading his own unit through their movements, his crooked nose and bone-white notch concealed beneath his helmet, but his gravelly voice unmistakable. He conferred frequently with Akechi, but seldom with the other two.

I settled into a routine of watching the troops each morning, for hours. Most days there was a small contingent of women who trained as well. They practiced with weapons, mostly the long-poled naginata, or bow and arrow, but they didn't join the men in the formation drills, and I made a note to ask Ranmaru or one of the guards about it.

I was also struck by the uniformity of the armies. The army I had been a part of after being sold had Europeans, Africans, Indians. The ship I had sailed to Japan on had sailors from all parts of the known world. Even in my small village, there were occasional traders from India, or sometimes even further. Here, there were just Japanese, and realizing this I felt foreign in a way that I never had before. From somewhere unseen a sudden loneliness settled into my lungs, caused my breath to hitch. It is not the absence of people that makes you feel alone, it is the presence of people, and the awareness that you don't belong amongst them.

I tried to see myself through the eyes of these men and women who had never seen another race, and I could not fathom how impossibly strange I must be to them. Even worldly Nobunaga, scrubbing my skin, expecting it to be some trick. Seeing them work together made me feel further apart, but I watched anyway.

They were guided by a complex series of flags and drumbeats, moving swiftly and efficiently in coordination with the signals. They were disciplined and quick to correct any errors. A few of the younger amongst their men were either eager or nervous or both, but most of the men carried themselves as seasoned fighters and knew full well what was ahead of them.

War stories are stories of glory or tragedy, but the experienced men among them would have learned, as I had, that most of war is boredom. Most likely they would leave the gates for a long march, then a short battle on the open plain, followed by weeks of a castle siege. The early days of a siege are a reprieve from the days of marching and the intense rush of battle, and bring the hope of a quick surrender from the opponent.

Once a castle holds out through the initial days, the inevitability of a long siege sets in, and all the horrors that accompany it. Screams and cries from inside the walls at any hour of the day or night, sometimes cut short, other times allowed to continue far too long. Emaciated bodies launching themselves over the side of the walls. The soldiers taking bets in the morning on whether or not it will "rain" that day. Coins changing hands, then changing hands again the next day, and again the day after that. Sometimes

a cheer when a body crashes, if the bet was large enough. Mothers holding dead babies and screaming obscenities at the soldiers below, or worse,
bashing the head of a living baby off the bulwark to give it a quick death as
opposed to letting it slowly starve. Those inside the walls turning on each
other, if left long enough, eating first the dead, then the weak, while outside
soldiers would shoot arrows into any approaching supply wagon long after it
was necessary, just for the target practice, or to relieve their boredom. Even
though most in the wagon are farmers, innocents. In war, no side fights hon-
orably.

In the afternoons I trained on my own, working through movements
with spear and sword until I was covered in sweat despite the cooling weather.
I tried to move like the Japanese. To strike swiftly, with minimal motion of
the body, and draw the weapon back to be ready to strike again, but it went
against my instincts. The Indians and Europeans taught me to strike with fe-
rocity. To swing with all my force whether sword or axe or mace, and launch
my body into each blow. I had only my crab sword and my long spear, but I
tried to imagine the grip of the Japanese weapons in my hand. I had studied
them carefully. I learned the women preferred the naginata spear because
its long shaft gave them leverage which allowed them to match a larger opponent's strength; that the foot soldiers used the shorter yari spear to defend
against horsemen or dislodge them from their mounts.

Watching the samurai and the ashigaru drilling in the courtyard, I
realized that, regardless of weaponry, I had always fought with the force
of my arms and my legs. The weapon was just the sharp or blunt object at
the end of my force. The Japanese struck precisely, and with only as much
force as is required, wasting no movement. They trusted the blade over
the body.

I mostly trained behind the guards' quarters where, other than the
times that one shift of guards rotated with another, it was quiet. But one
day I noticed a young boy peeking around the corner of the quarters' back
wall, watching me. He pulled back quickly behind the wall when I noticed
him, then slowly edged one eye out into the open again. I ignored him and

continued, but the next day there were three kids, the day after that, seven. They went from peeking around the corner to standing openly at the side of the guardhouse, pointing, giggling, and mimicking my movements.

I'd been a sailor, a soldier, a seminary student, and a slave. It had been years since I had seen a child laugh. I tried not to react while they pointed and giggled, but I could not help the slightest of smiles.

At nights I drew what gossip I could from the guards coming off duty. They scoffed when I asked if Nobunaga was preparing for war.

"Our lord is not preparing for war, he is at war already. What you see here are his main forces, but he has many other armies at his command, led by many other daimyo."

"And they are fighting now? Where?"

"Iga. Other places as well, but Iga is our lord's obsession."

The guard who said it looked down, as if saying the name itself was a curse. I'd heard some of Iga, first from Brother Ambrosius aboard the boat at Nagasaki, and later from the pirate Murakami, who had provided us passage to Sakai. Iga was not subject to rule by any daimyo or lord. The only authority was an Ikko, a band of individuals tasked with ensuring the province's defense. The assassins of Iga were legendary, and viewed in almost mystical terms. Some believed them capable of invisibility or even of instantly transporting themselves from one spot to another, over any distance. Some thought them not men at all, but spirits or demons. They answered to no one, killed for money, and rarely failed. There were stories of them waiting for hours or days, holding a single position if necessary, waiting for their target, or for the right moment.

Another guard slapped the first hard on the back.

"The men of Iga are men. They will fall just like all other men. Have they not tried three times to assassinate our lord, and failed?"

"They've sent assassins? Here?" I asked.

The guard shook his head.

"No, no. Not here. The first assassin waited in Koga, where he knew Lord Nobunaga would be passing through. The assassin held his position for days, waiting for his target to show. He hit our lord twice with shots from a musket, but they hit his collared plate. He was thrown from his horse, but unharmed. The assassin was hunted down and tortured for days."

The room had gone otherwise silent while the guard continued.

"The second assassin entered a palace where our lord was staying, but he was quickly discovered by the guards. He killed himself to avoid suffering the same fate as the first, but Lord Nobunaga still displayed his body on the palace gate for everyone to see. The third came closest. He had entered yet another of Lord Nobunaga's palaces, made it onto his rooftop while he slept. He lowered a thread dripping with poison down into our lord's bedchamber. Lord Nobunaga awoke before the poison fell into his mouth, but the assassin managed to escape."

"Yes, but Nobunaga has not stopped searching for him. With the price that Nobunaga has offered for him, every Oda man in Iga will be searching for him."

After years of serving as Father Valignano's protector, the stories put me on edge. Three assassination attempts. One in which they had known the exact route he would ride, two others in which they had entered the palace where Nobunaga was sleeping. I resolved to have a more critical eye while walking around Azuchi, to be more cognizant of its potential weaknesses.

The guards had continued on with their discussion of Iga. ". . . they fight well, yes. I would not want to fight them myself, I will not deny. There are five passes through the mountains into Iga, and our lord has ordered an army sent through each. Lord Nobunaga has sent forty thousand men in all. Iga will fall. The real battle is west, with the Mori."

"Who will go?" I asked.

"The men already have their orders. Hideyoshi's men will march west along the southern route, Akechi's men will march along the northern road."

A guard in the corner with his back to the wall, playing a hand-carved pipe amongst his fingers, offered a prediction.

"Hideyoshi will reach first. No one is better at seizing castles. The little mouse never fails."

"Hmm. He succeeds, yes, but not quickly. Hideyoshi squeezes men from their positions. He is the better tactician, but the old man Akechi is the better negotiator. He will whistle and everyone will walk out the front gate."

"Whistle," another sneered. "More like beg."

There was a short burst of laughter, then the men stopped suddenly, turned toward me. I offered what I hoped was a reassuring gesture, and they relaxed, but not fully.

"There is a man under Lord Akechi. Hidemitsu."

"Ahh, Hidemitsu." The guard smiled and pulled his nose to the right side of his face, drawing laughter from the others. "He is Akechi's son-in-law, and most trusted lieutenant. You don't like him?"

"I have no cause to dislike him," I said cautiously.

The guard shrugged. "Sometimes men dislike men without any cause. It does you no good to pretend otherwise."

"I fear I may have made an enemy of him," I probed, hoping for more information.

"You would not be the first. Hidemitsu makes enemies more readily than he makes friends. Just stay away from him. He'll do no harm."

Not wanting to push further, I changed the subject.

"So Toyotomi and Akechi will both head west. And Tokugawa? What of his men?"

I had seen the three generals in the fields and courtyards preparing their men, but I reached back to the first night at Honno-ji, when I had seen them up close. Toyotomi Hideyoshi, short, wiry, with a wrinkled face and sparse beard, his jaw working back and forth as if he were constantly chewing; Akechi Mitsuhide, the oldest-looking of the three, with a bald pate and partially gray hair pulled back from the sides into a short knot, the one who Brother Organtino had described to Father Valignano and I as more of a philosopher than the other two; and Tokugawa Ieyasu, heavyset, his jowls sinking into his neck and his bulk hidden under a flowing formal robe.

"Tokugawa's men have been ordered to hold," said the guard in the corner. "If the western campaign starts poorly, he will support whichever army needs it. If the western campaign starts well, my guess is he will go east, to tear down what remains of the Takeda clan. Their power has been broken, but Takeda Katsuyori remains in charge of the lands, and they still hold the territory around Mount Fuji."

"And what of you? The guards?"

That brought another round of laughter.

"We stay here. We guard the castle. The one place no one dares attack or can even reach. We have the most boring job in all of Japan."

The guard kicked his feet out in front of him and crossed his arms, threw his head back, pretending to snore. The others laughed, but before long they had all settled back onto their mats, and the fake snores were replaced by the real thing.

13

The crowd of children watching me train behind the guards' quarters had swelled to almost two dozen. It had also grown to include a handful of interested soldiers, merchants, and tradesmen who, unlike the children, pretended to be occupied with some other business while they watched. Their naked curiosity made me keenly aware of my strangeness. I was the only African in all of Azuchi, and likely in all of central Japan.

I warmed up slowly, stepping through my motions—thrust, breathe; circle, slice, breathe—then began moving faster, combining sequences. Before long I was sweating, swinging, spinning, all to the background of the whispers and laughter of children.

"Do you actually fight with that thing?"

I turned to see Ranmaru, leaning against the corner of the quarters, smirking. He pushed himself off the wall and walked toward me, putting his hand on the Portuguese crab sword and briefly studying it.

"I heard children laughing," he said. "Now I see why."

"This weapon has served me well," I said somewhat defensively.

He took the sword from my hand and dropped his hand to the ground in overexaggerated fashion, much to the delight of the now giggling crowd.

"Heavy," he said, lifting the sword again for further inspection, then swishing it slowly through the air. "Slow. It's a wonder you're not dead. Speed and precision, this is how you win a fight. Not with strength."

He puffed his arms and chest out and waddled around the semicircle, making himself as big as possible and drawing uncontrolled laughter from the children. He grasped the tip of the blade and held the handle of the sword out to me.

There was no meanness in Ranmaru, but I still felt my blood rise at being mocked.

"I am open to learning," I said carefully. "How would you defeat someone stronger than you, an experienced fighter?"

The casual smirk returned to Ranmaru's face. He looked around, his eyes settling on a merchant's cart.

He walked over to the cart and selected a tough-looking gourd from the top. He bounced it back and forth in his hands, checking the thickness of the skin. In a flash, he turned and launched it at me, but I was equally as quick in my response. I set my feet and sliced upward. The strike was accurate but the angle was wrong, and the gourd caught on the blade, my sword lodged over halfway through it.

Ranmaru clapped, and the children joined him in applause.

"So your weapon can catch things. That is impressive."

I looked down at my sword, a thin dribble of juice dripping down the black metal.

"That blow will kill a man," I said.

There was a blur of motion and Ranmaru's sword was drawn. I raised my blade to counter. The instincts of thousands of days of training told me my reaction was quick enough, but the gourd was still lodged on the blade, slowing me. Ranmaru's katana was at my neck a mere moment before I could block it. Just enough to make the difference between life and death.

"It will kill a man, yes. But what about the next man?"

He sheathed his sword, smiled, and took a step back.

"You strike more powerfully than you need to. If you did only what was necessary, your sword would be free. It affects your footwork, your balance. You step further, shift your weight, use your strength, even when the smaller movement will accomplish the same."

He patted me on the shoulder.

"You'll train with the rest of us from now on. And once you get your sword unstuck, come with me. Lord Nobunaga says you're to have new clothes. He's arranged for entertainment, and you're to join us."

NOBUNAGA HAD CALLED FOR A sumo tournament to mark the beginning of his western campaign. Ranmaru brought me to be measured so that I could attend in more traditional Japanese garb. Since being gifted to Nobunaga, I owned nothing but my sword and spear, and three sets of trousers and one blouse, which I had been rotating through.

The tailors chattered excitedly about the measurements. They were likely unaware that I could understand them, but I said nothing. I watched them as they worked feverishly to stitch together materials.

It would be my first time inside the castle. Seven stories tall, it towered over the series of administrative buildings and courtyards that covered the flattened mountaintop, the private properties and military stations dotted along the route up the mountain, and the small but burgeoning city at the mountain's base. Above the sloping rock foundation, the first five floors of the castle were painted mostly white, with some minor details visible in black and gold. The sixth floor was a vibrant red, and the seventh, the golden castle keep that had shone like a star in the sunlight on our approach.

By evening, my clothing was ready. Ranmaru summoned me to the castle and presented me with the new outfits. In addition to four kimonos there were two pairs of pants he called hakama, billowing down to mid-calf with a pleated front, and tied around the waist with a thick belt; and three loose-fitting shirts of light wool, in blue and orange and white, open down the front like a robe. He selected the blue and showed me how to wrap the shirt across my chest and tuck it into the sash of the hakama to hold it closed.

After I had changed, Ranmaru had the Portuguese clothing, the clothing that Valignano had purchased for me, taken away. He gestured to a glass mirror and I turned toward it. The hakama were tied high on my midsection, the robe-like shirt pulled across my body in an angle, making my torso look short but broad. They were clean and comfortable, and despite myself, I waved my arms to feel the shirt move against me. I made a slashing sword motion that brought laughter from Ranmaru, and I laughed with him.

"Come on." He waved for me to follow.

Inside the castle, the outer hallways were ringed with private rooms for meetings, for more intimate social events, and for quartering esteemed guests, but the inner part of the castle was completely open. Visitors from all seven floors could view the central main floor opening. Great columns ran from first level to seventh, painted with dragons and peacocks, herons and outsized fish and other, stranger creatures, but people as well—philosophers and warriors and other historical figures.

The inner balconies of the first five floors were painted in black, and the sixth in red. The seventh floor was coated entirely with gold flakes and marked with the symbol of the emperor. I knew from Valignano's training that the emperor never left the capital, and recognized the audaciously powerful statement Nobunaga had made simply by building with his visit in mind. Visiting daimyo or their emissaries would see the golden viewing area on the castle's highest floor and understand Nobunaga's message loud and clear: "The seat of power is here, not Kyoto. In time, even the emperor will come to me."

"I do not know much of sumo," I whispered to Ranmaru as he led me up the stairs.

"It is like most things Japanese," he responded. "It is very simple, until you begin to study it. Then it becomes complex."

We stopped on the fifth level. There were a dozen others already lined against the railing, all dressed more finely than I. I recognized Ogura and Jingorou amongst them. The two brothers greeted Ranmaru respectfully when we entered, and then did the same to me, somewhat more uncertainly. Food was brought, rice flour dumplings dyed green and pink and yellow, and tea and sake, much better fare than I had been enjoying in the guards' quarters.

A hush fell over the crowd as Oda Nobunaga appeared on the level above and across from us. The emperor's box was empty and unlit, and so Nobunaga, in the sixth level's red box, looked out over the gathering. I could see larger and larger groups gathered together as the levels went down, from small pockets of minor dignitaries down to the crowd of soldiers packed into the lower level. All rose to acknowledge Nobunaga, who merely nodded, allowing the proceedings to begin.

A raised platform had been brought into the main floor earlier in the day and dusted with sand. It was circled with bales of rice-straw and marked in the center with two short, painted white lines.

There was a single gong from a drum, then an older man in a dark shimmering kimono entered the main area, carrying a long sheaf of lit brush. He circled inside the ring, waving the smoking brush around the ring's edges. Ranmaru touched my elbow.

"The dohyo is sacred. This man is the yobidashi. He will administer the competition but first must purify the dohyo."

When he finished, he handed the still-burning incense to assistants outside the ring, and the yobidashi sat cross-legged alongside one white hash mark. Twelve competitors entered the area, heavyset men with serious faces and tightly tied topknots, naked but for a loincloth and a twisted rope belt. There were no cheers as they entered, just respectful murmurs. On the lower levels, I could see whispered discussions, bets being discreetly placed. Beside me, Jingorou placed two coins on a table and looked at his brother Ogura, who smiled and nodded.

The first two competitors stepped into the dohyo. The yobidashi stood and proceeded to the two white hash marks. He held out an emerald-colored war fan. The competitors lined up opposite each other, one on each hash. They slammed their closed fists down to the line and charged. The crowd, respectfully silent to that point, erupted, all the way up the castle tower from level one to six.

As quickly as the fight had started, it had ended. The younger of the two competitors had been rooted from his feet and pushed outside the ring of rice-straw bales. The loser bowed to the winner and exited the dohyo. The yobidashi showed his fan to the winner, then shouted, "Oshidashi."

"What is 'oshidashi'?" I asked Ranmaru.

"It is the technique used to win the bout."

"How many ways are there to win?"

"As many ways as there are to lose."

I turned to Ranmaru and saw a playful smile on his face, and suspected that my question had been a dumb one. I watched money change hands at the levels below me. The dohyo was swept quickly with a long brush and the next two men entered. Ogura had collected his brother's coins from the table.

The bouts proceeded quickly, and I focused on the wrestlers. The floor seemed to shake when they collided into each other, and though that was most likely due to the boisterous stomping of the crowd, it was easy to imagine that it was the force of the contact between the two men instead. Yet, despite the violence and power on display, there was an elegance as well. The competitors were nimble. They stayed balanced on the balls of their feet, feinted and countered, stepped and side-stepped, defending their positions and setting up their attacks with an incongruous grace. The cheers rose louder as the tournament ran on, no doubt spurred by the generous pouring of sake. It was after either the seventh or eighth bout that I first heard someone call for the giant.

"Kyojin" started as a single shout, but was quickly picked up, becoming a chant among the lower level, then rising to the second level, then the third. The crowd had turned their eyes upward again, but this time they were not looking to Nobunaga, they were looking to me. I stepped back from the balcony's edge, but short of leaving altogether, there was nowhere to go to completely escape sight.

The dozen or so men in the balcony alongside me laughed, and first one, then another, picked up the chant.

"Kyojin. Kyojin."

From below there came a shout of "Let us see Yasuke fight."

"Well, at least one of them knows your name," commented Ranmaru wryly.

The others in the viewing box turned toward me, sizing me up. Ogura and Jingorou whispered to each other about my prospects, and whether they were worth betting on.

I looked up to Nobunaga's balcony. He was seated at the edge of the crimson viewing box, accompanied by Toyotomi, Tokugawa, and Akechi. He had a bemused smile on his face, but otherwise gave no indication of his wishes. The decision was mine to make.

I wondered if there was danger here. Were there consequences if I were to perform poorly, or to make some mistake of custom? Were there enemies to be made if I won? When there were so many things I still needed to learn, even the simplest of choices had to be made carefully. I could only rely on my own instinct. My instinct was that the greatest risk lay in avoiding the challenge, and having made the decision, I realized one thing more—I wanted a fight.

I nodded at Nobunaga and he nodded back, giving his permission.

I raised my hand and the chants turned to raucous yelling. It beat against my ears like waves while Ranmaru led me back into the hallway and down to the lower level. By the time I reached the bottom, someone had already tied a loincloth for me. The crowd had picked up my name, and as I changed into the loincloth, the chant of "Yasuke" echoed through the chamber.

Ranmaru offered quick instructions.

"You must crouch and touch your hands to the white line, then the bout begins. After that, it is simple—stay inside the bales, and do not let any part of your body other than your feet touch the ground."

I nodded and walked out into the main chamber. I should have been nervous, but instead I was excited. I had been cooped up in the guards' quarters for days, the only release being my daily training sessions. During months spent on the Portuguese ship, I had been tempted to enter the fights belowdecks that the sailors sometimes organized, but I was unwilling to forsake my duty of remaining ever on alert in Valignano's defense. I felt the shame, still, of being so easily given away by someone I had trusted, so crudely reminded of my place, my value. I was relieved to finally be able to test myself against someone, at anything. Relieved to finally have some release.

My competitor was already in the dohyo. He was short and stocky, with powerful-looking calves and arms. His face was toward me, but he seemed to be looking past me rather than at me, as if I were not worth his full attention. He shook his shoulders, rolled his neck, bounced lightly on his thick legs.

People in the crowd were shouting animatedly to get last-second bets in, the night's earlier discretion long gone. I entered the dohyo, bowed to the yobidashi, then bowed to my opponent. He smirked.

We stepped to the white hashes, pounded our fists to the ground, and when he charged I wrapped my arms around his chest. In a single motion I lifted him from his feet, rolled him over my hip, and slammed him down on his back in the center of the dohyo.

The wave of shouting became a tsunami. The yobidashi was so shocked he initially forgot his tasks and simply stared at me. When he recovered, he rushed to me, held up the war fan and shouted, "Tsukaminage!"

I turned to leave the dohyo, but the next man had already entered. He looked me up and down, then gritted his teeth and clenched his fists. I smiled at him. Behind me, the crowd roared.

14

Sometimes men paid to watch us fight. They wore clean robes and leather sandals in the same style as our master, had the same brown faces and thick dark beards. They stood in the dirt of the courtyard, cheering us to violence and sometimes passing a coin to our Portuguese overseer if a fight was entertaining enough.

We walked out into the training yard one morning, and our overseer was flanked by four men who were dressed similarly to him, but with heavier armor. It was the first time other white men had come to the compound.

We lined up as we always had, picked up the weapons before us. It had taken weeks for me to heal from my wounds after being let down from the hanging board, but once healed I resumed training, quietly and ruthlessly doing whatever was necessary. I brushed aside a too-eager spear thrust from an older boy and struck his head with the flat of a sword hard enough to bring blood trickling from his ear when he fell. I ducked beneath a mace swing from a light-skinned opponent with deep-looking scars and slashed the back of his knee, sending him to the ground.

The white men did not cheer, nor did they wager, and I wondered why they were there. They watched impassively, sometimes whispering amongst themselves, then to our overseer. After a few more fights, the overseer called for us to halt. He pointed at a dozen of us. A few bags of coins were passed, then the four new men led us down to the docks, to board another ship.

In the hold of the ship there were twenty to thirty slaves already waiting. They were silent when we entered, but after our captors went above deck, whatever talking we had interrupted slowly resumed. I recognized a few words, not in my own language, but a close enough dialect that I could understand.

"You are Lomwe?" I called out.

My voice sounded strangled in my throat, and I realized how long it had been since I had used it. It was dark in the hold and difficult to see, but an older man made his way toward me, picking carefully amongst the legs and feet. In the thin light I could see half of his face, deeply lined, and his hair, long and gray and braided.

"How old are you?" he asked.

"Thirteen."

"Hmm," he muttered to himself, shaking his head. "Younger every year."

"Where are you from?"

"I am from here," he said. "This boat. And so are you."

He sank back into the darkness. I did not speak again the rest of the voyage.

WE SLEPT IN A STONE fort with its back set to the water, and high walls on the front side which were subjected to shelling at any time of day or night. I had never seen cannons before, and the first time I felt the shake of them thundering against the walls, I fell to the floor. No one noticed. Men ran to and fro, dirty, bleeding, and tired, sometimes shouting orders, other times their expressions still. The white men were still faceless to me—I had not yet learned to tell one from another except those who had scars.

I found the old Lomwe man again on the third day. I recognized him by the ropy gray braids that splayed across his shoulders and his sweat-soaked back. We'd been set to all manner of work since our arrival—building braces for the walls and gate, sharpening and cleaning weapons, clearing debris where stones had cracked and partially crumbled in—but we had not yet been called to fight.

"We will," the old man said, passing a bucket of mortar to me.

I dipped a cloth-wrapped stick into the bucket and applied it to the space between stones, as I'd been shown.

"Who are they?" I asked, pointing with my chin to the army camped outside the walls.

"These men call them Ottomans. They curse their names, and one they call Suleiman they curse most of all."

"What has this Suleiman done?"

"It has the feel of an old curse. I don't think this Suleiman exists, or at least not anymore. This is an old war. Different men fight it now from those who began it."

"And what do they want?"

The old man shrugged and reached for another bucket, passed to him by the next man in line.

"The Ottomans, the Portuguese"—he gestured vaguely in the direction of the inner fort—"they want the same thing. They both believe this land belongs to them."

"Does it?" I asked. "Is this where they come from? The Portuguese?"

The old man seemed confused by my question, then laughed. He took the empty bucket from my feet, replacing it with another.

"Here? No, boy, you are still in India."

"And how far is that from home?"

Though I knew it was impossible, I could not suppress the thought of my father, searching for me and finding me here. The old man stopped his work, grown suddenly very serious. He glared at me sternly.

"Forget home. You will never see it again, do you understand me? Forget home." Then, as he turned away from me, "Forget everything you know about it."

A shell struck the wall, sending dust drifting down on top of us. The old man shook himself off.

"I think they both believe *all* land belongs to them," he said.

I LEARNED TO SLEEP, EVEN when the cannons were fired. The slaves worked from the rising of the sun to deep into the night, and the few hours we had for rest could not be wasted. Whenever possible, I tried to get chores atop the wall, so I could look out at the enemy army. The clothes the Portuguese wore beneath their armor were mostly gray, or a dull red, but the Ottomans wore vibrant blues and greens and yellows. They stood out against the gray landscape as if they wanted us to see them and to know where they were at all times.

I studied how they joined themselves together and how they divided, how they moved, and when. I had learned during my training how to read men's actions to predict what they would do, and I tried to apply that now to formations of men.

Sickness set in amongst some of the men. They could be heard at night, groaning and uttering words into the darkness that must have been prayer. In the morning they would be lying in the dirt, the dew wet on their clothes, having tried to crawl back to their tents from the latrine and failing.

If they were still alive, they would be taken to a room beneath the fortress and kept apart from others. If they had passed during the night the bodies were burned, and it was our job to carry the stiff and stinking corpses away, to pile them up and light the flames.

We dug deep trenches around the fire pits and filled them with water to keep the flames from spreading too far. We left only a small strip of land undug, just wide enough to drag a body into the moat-encircled fire pit. The white men turned away from us in disgust, not willing to see their fellow soldiers treated in such a way. Afterward they would splash buckets of water on us and order us to scrub ourselves, but they would still not come near us. From atop the wall, I could see fires in the enemy camps, and I could tell from the color of the smoke and the smell upon the wind that they were struck with the same illness as well.

"Who will win?" I asked the old man one day. We'd burned six more bodies and were shoveling dirt over the embers, and the remains.

"Why do you care?" he responded, then returned to his work. After a moment he stopped to lean on his shovel and looked at me.

"I don't mean to speak to you gruffly, but you are still a child, and you can't afford to be. Not here. You belong to these men. As do I. We mean less to them than the dirt we are shoveling. If you want to survive, you don't ask questions. You do what is asked, and you hope you are not noticed."

He returned to his shoveling and so did I.

The war had settled into day after day of drudgery, hour after hour of mind-numbing sameness, and it was because of this that the attack surprised us.

I had just awoken and dressed myself. The sun was not yet visible on the horizon, though its earliest rays had turned the sky from black to a palish purple. From nearby I heard a shout cut short. Some men ran toward the shout and some men ran away from it. I joined the former group and saw a dozen or so men in brightly colored robes and thick-looking chain mail.

The cannons had cracked the wall overnight, and Ottomans were spilling through the base of the breach. A horse cloaked in chain mail leapt over the rubble, followed by another. Their riders pushed them into the small crowd of Black slaves and Portuguese soldiers, creating chaos, and giving cover for more men to enter the fray.

The old man had gotten there ahead of me, and I saw him trying to drag one of the wounded slaves away from the fight. I took a step toward him, then stopped and crouched upon hearing the crack of a rifle. A Portuguese soldier fell dead, less than two arm's lengths away from me.

There were a few more shots fired, then the Ottomans slung their guns behind them. I knew from the little training I had had with such firearms that they would not have time to reload them before Portuguese soldiers were upon them. One of the Ottomans drew his sword and moved toward the old man. I rolled the dead Portuguese soldier over and took his spear and sword. Without thinking, I heaved the spear. It struck the Ottoman in the shoulder. It clanked harmlessly off his armor, but it drew his attention. The Ottoman spun and ran toward me, followed by two others. The old man's eyes met mine, but only briefly. He continued to haul the fallen slave to safety.

The fortress had turned into an ant colony of activity. The white men rushed into battle with the screams of beasts, while others behind them lined up with their rifles. The air was soon thick with smoke and the smell of gunpowder.

For a moment, everything seemed to freeze. I could see the faces of the men on both sides, curled into expressions of anger and hatred. All reason had left them, and they flailed at each other with a bloodlust I had never known existed before. Stunned and frightened, I thought to run, but before I could turn to do so, the first Ottoman was upon me.

The Ottoman who I had thrown the spear at was close enough that I could hear him exhale. His long, curved sword caught the first glint of the morning sun as it swung down at me. I dropped to a knee and heard the blade whistle in the air above my head. I still held the Portuguese sword, and I struck the man's knee with the handle of it. He buckled, but the two others who had followed him stepped into his place as he fell backward.

The second man swung his sword, and I raised my own sword to block it, but he was too strong, and I only managed to deflect the blow. I felt cold metal against my upper arm, followed by a steady trickle of blood. There was no pain yet, but I screamed regardless.

I scrambled to my feet, blocked a thrust from the third Ottoman and another swing from the second, but then felt a slash across my right thigh, just above the knee.

I looked at the blood running down my left arm and down the front of my right leg, and I panicked. I was strong, but strong for a boy. These were men, armed and experienced, and trained or not, I knew if I tried to fight them I would die.

I turned and ran, all three men in pursuit. I leapt over rubble and fallen braces and gained a little space, my bleeding thigh throbbing with the effort. The heavy chain mail made the men slow, but I knew they would catch up with me eventually. There was only so far I could run.

Calm yourself.

The words came from somewhere within me, and I listened. I pictured my father, dancing, and everything slowed. I controlled my breath as best I could. I ran still, but I watched the courtyard while I ran, looking for opportunities. I pictured my pursuers in my mind, their size and weight, their armor, their weapons, trying to find some advantage.

There were three of them and one of me. I needed to keep them moving and separate them, or to find a closed-in space where their numbers would work against them.

The fire pits.

The moats we had dug around them were too wide for a man to leap across, and the thin strip of dirt we left undug so that we could drag the bodies to the pile was only wide enough for a single man.

I reached the pits quickly and made my stand atop the remnants of the sick and the dead. The Ottomans had no choice but to line up and come at me one by one. The first charged at me like the rhinoceros of my father's stories, and I knew he was hoping to push me backward to make space for his friends to cross. I lowered my shoulder to the ground and rolled my body at his legs, knocking him into the ditch of water. I stood and swept my sword across his throat, then reestablished my position at the end of the short land bridge, just as the second man crossed.

The sounds of violence in the courtyard had reached cacophonous levels and I could barely hear the man's battle cry, though he stood right before me. He slashed and I dodged, but he followed his attack with a punch to my face. I felt the metal of his glove crunch into me, felt my nose break and bleed, and I fell backward.

I blinked and stared up at the sky but there was no time to recover. I stood. The third Ottoman was already crossing the strip of dirt and if I allowed that I would have to fight them both at once, in the pit's center. My survival depended on holding them on the other side, where they would have to come at me one at a time along the narrow path. I threw my full weight at them, desperately, and pushed the second man into the third, forcing both to recover their balance, and for the third man to retreat to the other side of the moat to avoid falling into the water.

I swung the sword and struck the second man on the side of the head. His helmet rattled and the sound of it seemed to throw him off guard. I picked out an uncovered spot in his armor and thrust the sword into his armpit, as deeply as I could manage. He stumbled, tottered, and fell, but as he did so, the sword slipped from my grasp.

The final Ottoman soldier, the one whom I had struck with the spear, took his time. He stepped over his fallen comrade and studied me as he approached. His chain mail hung down below his knees and clinked against the plated armor on his shins with every step.

I looked around for anything I could use. I picked up a shovel and held it out in front of me with both hands. The Ottoman circled, watching my feet, the way I had learned to watch other men's feet, their hands, their eyes.

The cut on my thigh began to ache. Blood from my broken nose flowed down my face and onto my chest. I breathed through my mouth and tasted the tint of it on each inhale. We watched each other, evaluating one another, standing in a pit of mud and ash and charred bones.

He said something to me in a language I couldn't understand. He came forward with a short thrust, but only to test me. He probed again, this time swinging his sword more aggressively. I deflected it with the blade of the shovel and watched sparks flash orange and blue from the scrape of contact.

We circled once more, and I picked my point of attack. I swung the shovel at his midsection in a controlled feint. He raised up to block the blow and I rolled my hands over the handle of the shovel, driving it instead into the joint of his armor between foot and ankle. His lower leg caved inward despite the armor, and there was a loud snapping sound. He screamed and I let my momentum carry me forward, throwing my shoulder into his chest. He fell backward, his helmet toppling away. I did not hesitate. I drove the blade of the shovel into his face, once, twice, then a third time.

I slumped down, leaning on the shovel, and examined my wounds. Some time later a Portuguese soldier approached, shouting angrily at me. He stopped when he got close, looked at the bodies of the three fallen Ottomans, then stared at me, speechless.

THERE WERE MORE BATTLES. SOMETIMES the Ottomans surged inward, other times we went out to meet them on the plain. When we killed more men than we lost, the white men cheered and drank deeply from clay mugs and shouted at the stars. When we lost more men than we killed, they would sit quietly by the fire and grunt at each other like animals.

I killed men I didn't know and fought for reasons I did not understand, but with our walls breached and our backs against the sea, it was only a matter of time. The men pulled down their red and green flag and replaced it with a white one.

"What does that mean?" I asked the old Lomwe slave.

"It means we are done here. It's the flag they wave when they no longer wish to fight."

I had still learned very little of the Portuguese language, but I didn't need their words to recognize their fear. It showed in the set of their faces, the tightness in their shoulders. They gathered atop their wall and watched anxiously as one of their own rode out on horseback to the open-sided tent where the opposing army sat shaded, watering their horses and sizzling skewered meat over open flames. I sat on the wall with the old Lomwe and a few other slaves. We watched from the corner, well away from the white soldiers.

The white man was brought before a chair at the center of the tent. The man in the chair was dressed in fine silk and wore a tall blue hat with a tassel of yellow at the top. The two talked for a short time, then the man in the tasseled hat stood and walked over to the fire. Two soldiers held the white man's arms and forced him to his knees. Across the distance we could hear him scream.

One of the men on the wall stood to leave. He spoke to the others. I recognized the words "boat" and "morning," and understood that they were preparing to leave. Some others followed the man down the ladder, but most stayed, as did I.

In the tent on the plain, the man in the tasseled hat took a pair of tongs and lifted a fist-sized stone from the fire. He walked slowly and deliberately over to the white man and forced the stone into his mouth. The soldiers held him while he twisted and kicked and heaved, and released him when he was still.

The white men who remained on the wall said nothing. They turned and climbed down the rickety ladder.

Our tasks turned from preparing for war to preparing for voyage. There were supplies to be checked and packed, sail rigging to be inspected, weapons to be cleaned and stored. No one slept, but the victorious Ottomans seemed content with allowing the Portuguese to leave.

"Where will we go?"

The old man paused for a moment. "Come with me."

He brought me to where the captains of the white men were circled over a table. He cleared his throat and clasped his hands in front of him and bowed his head. He spoke a few words of Portuguese, and gestured toward me. They glanced at me, but with little apparent interest. They turned back to their lists and inventories.

One of the white men cocked his head, continued to look at me. He stepped out from behind the table. He curled the fingers of his hand to beckon me forward. I recognized him as the soldier who had found me at the fire pits, the day of the first breach. He spoke to the others, and something was agreed upon. The men turned back to their table.

The old man took my arm and led me away.

"You will go with them," he said.

"What about you?"

"Most likely I will stay here. They will only take a few."

We walked in silence for a few steps.

"Is it better to stay or to go?"

"For me, to stay," he said. "But I am old. You are young and strong. For you? I don't know. But I hope it will be better for you to go. You have value. Maybe you will be treated well."

The old man waited for a response, but I said nothing.

"What?" he questioned sharply. "Why do you hesitate? What keeps you here?"

"My father . . ." I cleared my throat. "My father may be looking for me."

"He will not find you here."

I put my head down, knowing it was true but still unwilling to accept it. "He won't give up."

The old man sighed. He grasped the sides of my head, forced me to look at him.

"No, he will not give up. You are his son. He'll put his hand on the shoulder of every boy he sees your size and age, and hope that when the boy turns toward him, the face will be yours. But it never will be. Your father will never give up hope, but *you* must."

He released me and slipped away before I could say anything further. As I watched him walk away, I knew I would never see the old Lomwe again. But I could not yet give up the hope of ever seeing my father.

15

The armies of Toyotomi and Akechi marched out the next day, westward, toward Mori-controlled lands.

The guards shook me from sleep. I usually rose before the sun, but as the two men standing above me attempted to rouse me, the sun was already high and bright in the doorway behind them. The tournament had not gone late—in all, I'd fought ten men before retiring to thunderous applause from all six levels of the castle, including from Nobunaga himself—but afterward, a small group of soldiers gathered around the guard hut with sake and a few bottles of foreign wines. I had never been given to drink but something in the men's faces told me they needed the distraction. Some of them would be heading off to war the next day, and they were not quite ready for their last day of peace to come to an end.

I grunted and reached for my pants and shirt, then remembered that they had all been discarded. I now had a bundle of four carefully fitted kimonos to choose from, plus two pairs of short, loose pants, and three thin cloth shirts. I washed my face in the basin and dressed quickly.

Once again I descended the long mountain path in a small crowd. Outside the top gates and slightly below the flat mountaintop there were a series of small residences belonging to Nobunaga's concubines and a few high-ranking pages—anyone who he might wish to summon immediately. After a few more downward twists and turns, the next level was divided into much larger swaths of land on which Tokugawa, Toyotomi, and Akechi had built their own residences. Continuing down the mountain there were the homes of the samurai, spread mostly without regard to rank, and of other key servants, then finally the farmers and other citizens in the town at the mountain's base.

In the valley beyond the city walls, the armies of Toyotomi and Akechi stood in formation beneath their fluttering standards. Columns of cavalry on sleek horses, and countless foot soldiers. Their armors were every color, but mostly blue, red, yellow, and black. They carried all manner of weapons—swords and bows; the Portuguese arquebuses, as well as the yari—wooden poles with savagely sharp blades on the end; and naginatas, which were similar, but with a longer, curved blade. They also carried a bamboo canteen each, a rations bag, a sleeping mat, and hung from their waist, a reel of string in case a bow needed to be restrung.

The samurai were on horseback at the front of the cavalry, wearing the distinctive long and short sword and a horo, a cloak bearing their clan emblem, attached to the back of their armor, which would billow out behind them as they rode. If they defeated an enemy noble or samurai, or other combatant of sufficient importance, they would use the horo to wrap the fallen opponent's head, to secure it until it could be sent back to the camp.

Brother Organtino had explained the head viewing ceremony to me. The heads would be cleaned and dressed, and presented in a traditional manner, sometimes with a wooden plaque indicating who they were and who had killed them. The victorious lord or general would dress himself formally, examine each head, address the more important ones with some final message, or even a drink, often covering their own face with a war fan so that the spirits of the dead could not identify them and avenge themselves. The samurai who had claimed the heads would be given gifts and rewards based on the value of who he had killed. It was something the Jesuits would have condemned as godless and barbaric on the parts of the African tribes, but conducted by the Japanese, Valignano simply referred to it as "their ancestral way," albeit somewhat distastefully.

The assembled samurai wore metal helmets with leather flaps on the side and back marked with metal studs, tied beneath their chin with thin red ropes. The helmets were intricately marked and decorated—rabbit or fox ears, peacock feathers, lobster shells, antlers and crescent moons and family crests.

Flags were attached to the back of horses, or held by standard-bearers. The black-and-gold quince of the Oda clan. The Paulownia leaf of the Toyotomi forces. Akechi's men, marching under the five-petaled Japanese bellflower on sky-blue cloth. Toyotomi at the head of his forces, long golden spikes arrayed at the front of his helmet to represent the rising sun, and Akechi at the head of his, his helmet brown and plain.

There was little ceremony. The generals barked their commands and the armies marched out to the road, west. The farmers and soldiers and guards and servants watched them until they grew small in the distance and then returned to their day.

AT NIGHT I WALKED THE compound. The stories of the three assassination attempts had focused me, and I returned to my habits. The courtyards were lit with lanterns hanging from the edges of rooftop tiles, but I counted my steps, oriented myself so I could move in darkness, if necessary. From the guards' quarters to the gate. The gate to the castle steps. The castle steps to the temple, and from the temple to the foundation of the new Jesuit church, recently begun. The building of which had undoubtedly been agreed to after my gifting to Oda Nobunaga.

I'd heard few updates on Valignano's movements, but I knew his plans. He'd be moving throughout Japan, shoring up Jesuit settlements where they existed, establishing them where they did not, spending just enough time in each place to recognize shortcomings, assess opportunities, and leave behind a set of orders.

Returning to the guards' quarters, I passed near the stairs of the castle.

I saw Tomiko exiting the castle and walking toward the front gate. If there was a shift change in servants, there would be several walking together. I was surprised to see her alone. She walked quickly, checking over her shoulder.

I started to call out for her, but sensed a presence nearby. A shadow stepped out from beside the guards' quarters. A noticeable girth, but the movements graceful, controlled. The movements of Tokugawa Ieyasu, the watchful and battle-hardened general who Nobunaga trusted most.

I let Tomiko go. I watched her pass through the gate and begin what would be a dark descent along the road into town.

I approached Tokugawa and bowed. "To what do I owe this honor?"

He had come into the light now, and I could see his face. His eyes were red-rimmed and heavy-lidded, wet and rheumy like an old dog's.

"I came to commend you on your bout last night. Or should I say bouts? Walk with me."

Tokugawa turned to leave without waiting for an answer, and I fell in step slightly behind him. He waved me forward.

"There is no need for that. Tell me, where were you coming from?"

"Nowhere. I was merely walking the grounds, trying to learn my way."

Tokugawa nodded approvingly.

"I was a bodyguard to Father Valignano," I continued cautiously. "I would like to have some role here, however minor. I am grateful for our lord's generosity, but I am not accustomed to idleness."

"There is no need to apologize for ambition. Ambition is rewarded here, provided your ambitions align with Lord Nobunaga's. Tell me, what do you know of me?"

I hesitated, recalling Brother Organtino's brief description, and wondering how much would be safe to relay.

"I have heard you described as loyal and patient," I began hesitantly, "and I know of your defense of Hamamatsu Castle with only five men."

"Hmmph. I had only five men because Takeda Shingen crushed our armies at Mikatagahara. The Takeda outnumbered us three to one, but they did not come to fight me. They were on their way to Oda lands to fight against Nobunaga. The Takeda cavalry was one of the most feared forces in the country at the time. Every one of my generals urged me to simply let them pass through my lands."

"And why did you not?"

"I could not stand by and let them march on Oda territory."

"You were loyal to him even then."

"I am loyal to him always," Tokugawa stated emphatically. He stopped and turned to face me. I ducked my head in deference, but I could feel him staring at me. After a moment, he turned and continued walking.

"As a boy, I was given to the Imagawa clan as a hostage. My father needed their help to defend Mikawa Province against invasion, and it is custom to seal such deals by sending a family member to live in the other clan's home. Any treachery or betrayal on my father's part, anything other than loyalty to the Imagawa clan, would have resulted in my death."

"You were a slave," I stated wonderingly.

"I was a noble, still. I was raised with all the same privileges and opportunities that the noble children of Imagawa were. But no matter how well you are treated, you never forget that you are not a person. You are just a thing that has some value, no different than a vase or a prized animal. This, I think, you know already."

I did. It was the lesson I had learned many times over and should have never forgotten. That no matter how many years I had served Father Valignano and the church, no matter how faithfully and how well, and regardless of the good treatment and fine clothes and training and occasional freedoms, in the end I was still a thing to be traded. I was still property.

"Is that what I am here?" I asked.

Tokugawa tucked his hands behind his back and continued walking, silently. He stopped as we approached the beginnings of a building. Little more than a trench dug in outline, with large rocks piled into it.

"This is the site of the new Christian church to be built here. It was the promise your priest extracted in exchange for you."

"I know," I said quietly.

I knelt by the trench, placed my hands on one of the stones which would serve as the foundation of Father Valignano's new church. I knew Valignano's mind, his singular devotion. One life would mean nothing to him in balance against the souls he would save here. He built churches in glory of God, preached sermons in glory of God, baptized the converted in glory of God, and while I had known him long enough and well enough to know his faith was sincere, I also knew he was not ignorant of the glory these accomplishments brought to him personally.

Tokugawa placed a hand on my shoulder.

"You are not here because of a deal with the Jesuits. You are here because Lord Nobunaga wanted you to be here. This is simply the price."

"I don't understand."

"Do you know how Nobunaga came to greatness?"

I shook my head. I removed my hand from the rock of the church and stood.

"The Imagawa clan sought to march on Kyoto. The Imagawa could prove lineage to the Minamoto and Ashikaga clans, which meant Imagawa Yoshimoto, if he was successful in his campaign against Kyoto, could claim the title of shogun."

"And Nobunaga could not. It is why he could only overthrow the shogun, not claim the title for himself." I almost added *and that's why he needs the emperor*, but going that far seemed unwise.

Tokugawa nodded and continued. "Nobunaga's home province of Owari was on the path to Kyoto. The Imagawa had no quarrel with the Oda clan, they were simply in the way. Owari is a small province, and the Oda were seen as a minor clan. I doubt Imagawa even considered any significant opposition there as part of his campaign, and indeed, he swept through the southern part of Owari with little difficulty. So much so, that he camped overnight in the valley of Okehazama. He celebrated his early success with a head-viewing ceremony.

"Nobunaga was at Gifu Castle, in the north. He had two thousand men, while Imagawa had twenty-four thousand. His generals urged him to fortify the castle, send for help, and try to withhold a siege long enough for assistance to come. It would have been the wiser choice, really. But our lord has never been one to mistrust his own instincts. He rode out, outnumbered twelve to one. They approached the very lip of the valley undetected, under the cover of a great storm. They rode down onto the unprepared Imagawa forces and slaughtered them. Those who survived scattered and returned home. The Imagawa campaign came to an end. Yoshimoto was killed, and all of Japan took notice of Owari, and of Oda Nobunaga. And I was freed."

"This is why you are loyal to him."

"Yes. And no. Nobunaga allowed me to return to Mikawara Province, where I eventually ruled in my father's stead. I was a hostage and he made me a daimyo. Toyotomi's ascent is even more unlikely—he was born a peasant, without even a family name. He came into Nobunaga's service as a sandal bearer, but with each new task and new responsibility, he proved himself able. Now he is one of Oda clan's top generals. The point, Yasuke, is that Nobunaga respects tradition but is not bound by it. In Nobunaga's service, a man is not limited by his birth, or by his name. In Nobunaga's service, a man can be whatever he proves himself capable of. This is why I am loyal. Perhaps someday you, too, will find a reason in it as well."

Tokugawa bowed his head slightly to me and walked away, while I remained standing at the church's foundation.

16

In the morning, a prisoner arrived from Iga. I was awakened by the pounding of hooves, the shouting of men. Behind the horsemen and the prisoner was a small parade of other soldiers and curious citizens, and all of the whispers that inevitably come with a crowd.

It was the third assassin of Iga, the one who had tried to poison Nobunaga. He was dragged inside the gate by a small band of soldiers, his hands tied, his face bloody. He wore loose black pants but no shirt, no shoes, and tattered strips of flesh on his feet suggested he had been that way for some time.

A soldier entered the castle and returned quickly, bounding down the steps and shouting orders.

The soldiers dragged the man to the training courtyard on the castle's east side, and two workers started digging. In less than an hour they had dug a hole almost deep enough to hold a man. By that time, a crowd of hundreds had gathered, but all gave respectful distance, forming a circle around the soldiers and the prisoner. The prisoner remained expressionless while they forced him into the hole and buried him up to his neck.

The workers and the soldiers then backed away. The crowd parted and Nobunaga entered, accompanied by Ranmaru at his side, Ogura and Jingorou close behind. Nobunaga wore a simple black kimono, and the others had selected solid colors to match, none of the intricate patterns or pageantry of more formal occasions.

Nobunaga approached from the prisoner's front, so that the prisoner could see him coming. I made note of the fact that, much like Father Valignano, it appeared no detail of Nobunaga's went unplanned. He looked down at the prisoner, but only briefly, before addressing the crowd.

"They said that the men of Iga are wizards. That they appear and disappear like ghosts, that they transform into animals, can stop their own breathing for days at a time, that they can control men's minds. They say that the assassins of Iga never fail, but three times they have sent their assassins against me, and here I stand. They said that the province of Iga would never fall, but our messengers bring news that Iga *has* fallen. The Takeda will follow, and the Mori. Soon, all of Japan will be united under the Oda emblem, and all of our enemies will bleed into Oda soil."

The crowd cheered and thrust their hands into the air. Nobunaga turned his attention back to the prisoner, and Ranmaru held both hands outward, presenting a long, thinly sliced bamboo reed. The prisoner was still mostly calm, but was now breathing heavily. The weight of the dirt compressed against his chest, forcing him to gulp for air.

Nobunaga took the bamboo slice from Ranmaru. Without a sound, he pushed it into the top of the prisoner's forehead. Blood gushed down the man's face and into the dirt. Nobunga continued to push the reed through the man's hair and scalp, until it passed all the way through to the other side. The man screamed and struggled to move. Nobunaga removed the thin layer of scalp and placed it in front of the prisoner where he could see it.

I had lived a life among soldiers. I had seen men subjected to worse tortures for lesser crimes, and the punishment Nobunaga chose to mete out was one I deemed fair by the standards of war.

I scanned the crowd for reaction. Some smiled, some wore shocked expressions. Some had turned away. Most of the crowd, however, appeared unmoved or indifferent. I remembered Valignano's lessons. There had been war here for over a hundred years. No man or woman standing here had ever lived a day in a country at peace. They were a people accustomed to horrors.

Nobunaga dropped the bamboo reed to the ground, blood dripping from his hands, and the crowd parted again. The small entourage returned to the castle. Once they had ascended the stairs the crowd dispersed, leaving the screaming assassin alone in the courtyard.

LATER IN THE DAY, I was summoned to the castle for tea. Ranmaru led me to the tea room, a seven-mat room on the fourth floor. He quickly but patiently walked me through the customs, but I was already familiar with them from Father Valignano's lessons on the long voyage over.

The tea room was one of the few rooms in the castle without artwork. It was instead painted entirely in gold flake and the sun striking the walls gave the room a glittering appearance. Nobunaga waited inside. He wore a simple robe with a sleeveless jacket atop it, its shoulders wide and starched stiff. The Oda crest was displayed discreetly on the breast of the jacket, then displayed larger across the back of it.

I knelt across from him on an intricately woven tatami mat, and the same hands which had a few hours before removed the top of a man's head now wiped the instruments of tea with a silk cloth, ceremoniously purifying them. He snapped the cloth open after each wipe, then refolded it carefully and wiped again. He then set the cloth aside and collected a ladle of water from a pot sitting atop still-glowing rocks. He poured the hot water into a bowl, then dipped a whisk into the water twice, swirled the bowl gently, and dumped the water into a second pot to his left.

He spooned a small quantity of ground tea leaves into the cleaned bowl, ladled hot water over the powder, and whisked the tea in rapid circular motions. As per custom, neither of us spoke. There was the sound of birds, and the occasional snippet of conversation from the courtyard below, but the inside of the castle was silent. I admired the movement of Nobunaga's hands, the grace, the discipline. Even the simplest of motions was executed in a precisely prescribed manner, but despite their grace, the hands were marked with cuts from training and calluses from long hours of gripping a sword or a spear, from countless draws on the string of a bow. His hands were a study in the contrast of shocking violence and inspiring artistry that I had glimpsed in all cultures, but none so much as here.

He whisked until the tea frothed, then broke the froth with a shake of the whisk. He set the tea aside and passed me a plate with a single confection. It was in the shape of a flower, pink with a yellow stamen. I cut a third and placed it in my mouth. It was overpoweringly sweet, but intended so, to balance the bitterness of the tea. I cut the remainder of confection in half, and ate the final two pieces as well, then set the plate aside.

Nobunaga picked up the tea with his right hand, placed it in the palm of his left, and turned the bowl twice. We bowed to each other as I accepted, then I returned the respect by turning the bowl twice. I drank the bitter tea in three sips and wiped the rim of the bowl, bringing the formal ceremony to a close.

"I apologize for the briefness of the ceremony. I am still learning its ways. The emperor's tea master, Sen Rikyu, sometimes holds tea for hours, without a word, and all of his guests leave feeling enlightened."

"Your apology is unnecessary, my lord. You honor me with this service."

"As you honor me with yours."

"Forgive me, lord, but I have performed no service."

"You've entertained. Every man and woman present was thrilled watching you wrestle, and I understand the children are equally amazed watching you train."

Nobunaga chuckled, and I looked down at my hands, unsure how to respond.

"Hmm." He sighed. "Yes, I have spoken with Tokugawa. He has told me that you do not feel useful here. Why are you so eager to serve?"

The mention of Tokugawa's name made me aware that there was no conversation at Azuchi that would be safe from Nobunaga's ears, and that encountering Tokugawa last night was likely no accident. I hesitated. I did not possess Valignano's skill of always knowing the correct thing to say, so in place of that, I offered the truth.

"For as long as I can remember, my survival has depended on proving my value."

"Every man has value."

"Not every man has a master he must prove his value to."

Nobunaga considered this. He leaned back as servants entered the room, clearing the instruments from between us and carefully packing up the hot kettle and coals. They backed out of the room, holding the trays of instruments out in front of them and bowing.

"Some of my vassals whisper that I prefer the ways of the Europeans to the ways of my own people, but it is not true. I value our histories and traditions as much as any man, but I will also accept any new thing that is useful, regardless of where it comes from."

"I have not heard any such whispers, my lord."

Nobunaga threw his head back and laughed. "I said they whisper. I did not say they do so carelessly."

He stroked his short, triangled beard. "You take well to our ways."

"Father Valignano thought it important that we understand the Japanese. All the members of our mission were trained aboard the ship, and before."

"You have learned well. Still, I will tell you a story you may not know. Do you know of the battle between Takemikazuchi and Takeminakata?"

I did not. Nobunaga straightened himself further and folded his hands across his lap. I had been practicing my sitting, but my ankles were already starting to burn from being pressed flat beneath me.

"There was once a conflict between the heavenly gods and the earthly gods. The earthly gods had multiplied and grown unruly and disrespectful of the heavenly gods. The heavenly gods turned a blind eye to this, and showed little concern about what happened on earth. Until, one day, Okuninushi, the leader of the earthly gods, proclaimed all of the land to be his own. This angered the heavenly god Amaterasu, because all of the land, by tradition, belonged to her.

"Amaterasu summoned one of her sons to go to earth and restore order, but the son looked down on earth and was too afraid to go against the earthly gods on his own. Amaterasu summoned a second son, and sent him to earth, but this son sought out Okuninushi and switched sides. She summoned yet a third heavenly god, named Ame no Wakahiko, and she armed him with a magical bow and sent him to earth to restore her rule. But years passed, and no word came from Ame no Wakahiko. Amaterasu sent a pheasant down to earth to get word from him, but the pheasant was struck through with an arrow. The arrow passed all the way to heaven and landed at Amaterasu's feet.

"Another god picked up the arrow and recognized it as Ame no Wakahiko's, and said, 'If he is a traitor, let this arrow strike him dead.' Ame no Wakahiko had met a woman on earth, and fallen in love with her and married her, but the arrow from heaven, his own magic arrow, found him and struck him down.

"Amaterasu was now furious. For years now, Okuninushi had ruled over *her* land, and turned her sons against her. She summoned a final god, a fierce warrior god named Takemikazuchi. Takemikazuchi traveled to earth and sought out Okuninushi, and demanded that he return the land. Takemikazuchi then planted his sword upright in the ground, handle down, and sat cross-legged atop the sword's tip. Okuninushi trembled at the sight of this fierce god, but asked permission to consult his son.

"Now it was Okuninushi's turn to find a champion. His first son took one look at Takemikazuchi, and was so overcome by fear that he cast a spell and turned himself invisible. Takemikazuchi again demanded the return of the land, but Okuninushi asked permission to consult another son. The second son, Takeminakata, was more fearless than the first. He looked at Takemikazuchi sitting atop his sword, and he picked up an enormous stone, balancing it on the tip of his finger. He demanded the warrior god leave earth and for Amaterasu to send no more of her sons, but Takemikazuchi refused.

"The earthly Takeminakata tried to wrestle the heavenly Takemikazuchi to the ground by grabbing his wrist, but Takemikazuchi turned his arm to a block of ice, forcing Takeminakata to let go. Takeminakata grabbed his other wrist, but Takemikazuchi turned this arm into a sword, forcing Takeminakata to let go again. Then Takemikazuchi grabbed Takeminakata's wrist, and easily broke the wrist of the earthly god. The earthly god Takeminakata fled, but the heavenly god Takemikazuchi followed him to Lake Suwa. Takeminakata surrendered and promised to never leave the lake if he was spared.

"Afterward, Okuninushi surrendered control of the land back to Amaterasu. She sent one of her grandsons, Ninigi, to earth to rule over it. She gave him three gifts to aid him in his rule—a fabulous jewel called the Yasakani; a mirror called the Yata; and Kusanagi, a great sword her brother Susanoo had pulled from a monster's tail. The emperor can trace his lineage all the way back to Ninigi, and thus Amaterasu, and is still in possession of these three items today. They are the proof of his divine ancestry."

My ankles throbbed painfully beneath me, but I remained focused on the story, knowing that Nobunaga would not have told it had it not had meaning.

"This is the origin of Japan?"

"Of the empire of Japan, yes. But also the origin of sumo. The wrestling match between Takemikazuchi and Takeminakata, to determine whether people would be ruled by the earth or by the heavens, is the beginning of the sumo tradition. Each sumo bout is a battle for the soul. Your performance the other night must have made many think of Takemikazuchi himself, come down to us once more."

Nobunaga smiled broadly, and I bowed my head to the floor.

"I am no god, my lord. I am your servant."

I picked my head up and Nobunaga looked at me thoughtfully, his smile gone.

"Does it make you uncomfortable, my speaking of the Shinto gods? Do you believe in the faith that your Father Valignano teaches?"

"I believe what I am told to, my lord."

A dark look crossed Nobunaga's face. He appeared angered by the answer.

"I have a hundred thousand men I could call into this room and they would kneel and tell me exactly that. I brought you here because I sense that you are not one of them. Speak freely. And sit comfortably."

I gasped in relief and leaned forward, resting on one knee and releasing my aching ankles. Nobunaga laughed, but not condescendingly.

"It will come in time," he said. "Tell me—you were in the courtyard today. Do you think it cruel to torture a man?"

I rubbed my ankles and considered the question. Nobunaga's demand to speak freely appeared genuine, I could see no trap in it. I found myself liking him and cautioned myself to remember that I was nothing more than another of his foreign gifts, which he prized so highly. Nevertheless, I was here to serve. If he wished me to speak freely, I would do so.

"When I was first taken from my land, I was sold to a mercenary. He trained us to fight. I killed other boys for a little bit of food, saw things done which were worse. I never considered the morality of it, because I was trying to survive."

I held back the memory of the young Dinka writhing beneath my spear, blood frothing at his mouth. Held back the memory of the boy beside me when I'd come down off my hanging, killed only because of where he stood. To say I had never considered the morality of it was not quite true. I'd merely placed necessity above it.

"And now?" Nobunaga asked.

I stretched my legs and looked briefly at Nobunaga, then down at his feet.

"When I grew to be a man, and after I had proven myself in war, I began to dream of revenge. I would lie awake at night trying to recall the faces of the men who had come to my village, killed my family, but their faces had been so foreign to me at the time that I could not identify them. I realized they could be anyone, and anywhere. They could be faces at the market, or in the stalls. They could even be men I fought alongside, and I would not know for sure. I began to see them everywhere, convinced that every white man I saw was one of those slavers who had come to us.

"It drove me to constant anger. You ask me what I think of the Jesuit teachings—I think there are many good lessons in them, but the forgiveness they preach is something that has never felt right. Some things can be forgiven, some cannot and never should be. If I ever were able to find those men, if I could do to them what you did to your would-be assassin today . . . I would do so and more. And I would not think myself cruel because of it."

Nobunaga stroked his chin and studied me thoughtfully. "So you believe cruelty is justified, if it is dealt in revenge?"

"The Jesuit teachings have given me a different perspective on many things, but survival is still paramount in my mind. I think if a man means to rule, he needs to have the capacity for both cruelty and mercy. Judgments on these things are for those who won't bear the responsibility of their necessity."

"How should such a man know when to be cruel and when to be merciful?"

"Your question assumes cruelty is an action. I believe it is not. An action is neither cruel nor uncruel. The cruelty is in the enjoyment of it."

"Did Father Valignano teach you this philosophy?"

"He did not have to, my lord."

Nobunaga paused, tilted his head. His hands, previously still, opened in front of him and then steepled together. "I suspect you've seen many such actions."

"My people . . ." I started and stopped.

"Please . . ." Nobunaga gestured encouragement, but waited patiently.

I reached back to old memories, buried deep, and exhumed the facts of them. I was surprised to find there was no pain in the recalling of them. I cleared my throat.

"When a man is accused of something, the matter is brought forward to our mwene. He is not our leader, but something of a settler of disputes, or source of advice. If the mwene could not get to the bottom of the matter, he would force all concerned to take oaths, what we call mwaavi. A date would be set for the mwaavi to be taken, and all the village would gather. On the given day, those being judged arrive before sunrise. A pot of water is boiled, and the elder appointed as the administrator of the mwaavi chants over the water. Then the accused is ordered to stick his hand in the pot. If he is burned, he is guilty. If he is unharmed, then the accusation against him was false."

"But does not every man burn their hand in the pot?"

"Yes," I said. "Because every man is guilty. The Jesuits believe in right and wrong. I am not so convinced of their rightness, or the rightness of any man."

Nobunaga stood and walked over to the window, turning his back to me while he looked out over the courtyard.

"Do you know, I have been only a week's ride on horseback in any direction? You have sailed the ocean, seen Europe and India and Africa. I will soon be the ruler of all of Japan. And yet, I have seen only a fraction of what you've seen."

He turned back to me and I bowed my head, still leaning upright on one knee.

"Every man under my command has lived as I have lived. We have studied the same histories, learned the same lessons. I take counsel from men and women who think as I think because what they know, I know. If you were to advise me, Yasuke, would you speak bluntly?"

"No, my lord. Not at the risk of losing my skin to a bamboo reed."

I smiled and hoped that the Nobunaga I spoke to now was the same one from the reception at Honno-ji, who enjoyed stories and entertainment and the company of his men. His laughter, when it came, free and authentic, was my reward for the gamble.

"You will do well here, I think."

Nobunaga's laughter subsided, but the spark in his eyes remained, and I could understand the loyalty Tokugawa felt for him.

"The men I fought for—the ones who bought me, trained me—they should have lost," I said. "I knew little of why they were fighting at the time, but I have learned much since. They were on foreign soil. They were greatly outnumbered. They held on as long as they did by keeping their enemy divided. The rulers of the different regions each wanted the Portuguese gone, but each fought them individually, and sometimes fought each other."

I dared to look Nobunaga directly in the eyes.

"Today you have foreign traders and missionaries," I said, "but a day will come when you will have foreign soldiers. You are right to unite Japan. Under one banner. Under one man."

Nobunaga crossed the room and placed his hand on my shoulder.

"You wanted duties. You will serve in my personal guard. You kept Father Valignano and the Jesuits safe, you will do the same for me. I can teach you to sit without looking like you've been stabbed in both legs," he said, smiling broadly. "In exchange, you can teach me what you have seen of the world."

17

In the school of the Jesuits, I learned I was a savage.

The great ship I boarded after the Portuguese defeat hugged the coast for the first few days of sailing before it was set to go out to sea, but at a stop in port we were given new orders, and redirected to break up a siege at Hormuz.

The first strong winds and rains signaled the beginning of the monsoon season, and we sailed toward another battle as the ship's captain carefully watched the skies. I carried cannonballs to supply the men who lit and fired the deck cannons. The ship rolled and yawed in the rough waters, and though we were close enough that we could see the faces of the men on the enemy carracks, any strikes landed against them were more a matter of chance than of aim.

Through the barricade we dropped anchor and rowed the skiffs into the shallower waters, our arms aching from straining against the storm.

Ashore, the town had suffered heavy damages. The slaves were deployed to tear houses down to clear lines of sight or deprive the enemy of advantageous positions. We dug trenches, erected earthen walls and other fortifications, repaired the walls of the garrison, which had been punched repeatedly with heavy artillery fire, and we were beaten or kicked or whipped if we stopped to rest.

The combined forces of the Indians and Ottomans were separated from us by just the edge of eyesight distance. They shoveled dirt into the shallow-est part of the river by shifts, building a land bridge, and we raced to prepare the defenses for their eventual charge. Every day we watched their progress, and they watched ours.

The storm was in full force when they launched against us, and we fought in wind and rain that turned the normal chaos of battle into something unknowable. Relaying orders was impossible. Enemy sol-diers appeared from the lashing gray sheets without warning. The flash of matchlock pistols popped in the darkness like fireflies, and the sound of a musket ball passing by your ear was drowned out by the gale, detectable only by a muzzled whine and a momentary sensation of heat, if it passed close enough.

I was struck once, in the forearm, and I could barely hear the crack of bone, but I had no choice but to fight on, swinging a halberd with one good arm. We slipped in the mud and fell against our enemies and dragged each other to the ground and killed there, rose again. When the night brought a reprieve from fighting, an officer pulled my arm to set the bones and tied the arm against a short wooden stick to keep it straight, then sent me back out to continue the digging, the repairs, the preparation for the next day's battle. I was bone-tired and was still yet a boy, but I was forced to my tasks under threat of a whipping, or torture, or execution.

In the early days of the siege, the officers were fed first, then the sol-diers, then the slaves, but as supplies dwindled, the slaves were not fed at all. We scrounged what we could by picking amongst the clothing of the dead soldiers for rations and scavenging what few items remained in the stores of the town outside the garrison, competing for scraps with the rats and the wild dogs.

After months of fighting, the garrison was secured and the weather lifted and we pushed inland. The season of the rains came and went three more times while we fought, until our leaders and theirs finally settled a peace. During that time my first hairs came to my face, but slaves were not allowed blades except under the supervision of officers, so I scraped them clumsily from my face in a large tent and dripped blood into a bowl while men watched and laughed.

When it came time to return to the ship, it was loaded with rugs and spices and lumber, any plunder that had survived undamaged, and we set sail once again.

I had learned enough Portuguese by then for simple conversations, and I fell in with a group of three soldiers.

"You fought well. When we get back to Europe, we'll see you're taken care of."

"You stick with us," another said. "I'll keep a lookout for you personally."

They were gaunt from their time at war, the bones beneath their skin too visible around their neck and shoulders. Their faces were smudged and bruised beneath patches of coarse beard and their fingernails were bitten ragged. They passed around a skin of foul-tasting liquor and patted their chests, constantly checking for the purses of buttons and buckles they had each managed to acquire. I did not trust them but I was too tired to be wary, and had no other choices. I figured myself safer with men I did not trust than with men I did not know.

I wanted to let my arm heal, my body rest, but there was little time. When the wind was still I was set to an oar. I scrubbed the deck, repaired tears in the sails, washed the sick, and wrapped and carried their corpses to the deck if they didn't recover.

When we finally docked, the men rejoiced in a way that made me know this must be their home. The three soldiers I had stuck with led me through cobblestone streets and offered me to a farmer in exchange for a sickly look-ing hog, and I did not resist. The farmer, in turn, offered me to the church, apparently in payment of a debt.

"I can work," I said in Portuguese. "I'll be useful."

"Have you been baptized?"

I didn't recognize the last word, so I did not respond. The priest turned the corner of his lips up in displeasure, but gave the farmer an accepting nod.

I was taken to the courtyard and given a bucket and a bar of soap. It was better treatment than I had received from the white slavers on the deck who had thrown buckets of cold water at us from a distance, and the simple act of scrubbing myself clean in the open air felt like a luxury.

I slept for two days, rising only to relieve myself, or to drink from the basin that had been provided to me. When I awoke fully, the priest dressed me in a white robe and dipped my head in water. He chanted a few words in a language I had not yet heard. From the inflection in his voice I could tell he had asked me a question. His face expectant. I nodded, not knowing what I had agreed to. He dipped me again into the water. When he lifted my head he welcomed me and told me I was saved.

"You said you can work?" he asked as I shook myself dry.

I nodded.

"Good. We do not allow for idle hands here. You've seen the garden, you can start there. It should be watered daily, and weeded every other day. There will be clothing to mend, meals to cook, and of course we need to keep everything clean."

"Thank you, Father. I will do all that you ask."

The priest frowned. "You'll attend lessons as well, but do not be concerned if they are too difficult for you. We'll start with that accent. You talk like an animal."

My days were chores and lessons, exactly how the priest had laid them out for me. I had learned their words from the soldiers and sailors, but I spoke them the way an African would. They punished me until I could make their words sound the same way they made them sound.

I was instructed in history, Latin, and religion, and when I could find time between lessons and chores, I trained. I used the snapped wooden handle of an old broom. I gripped it as I would a spear. I set my feet and I swung, and turned and thrust, working through the motions I had practiced time and time again, my body sweating but my heart, my breathing, controlled.

My hands and feet and hips and shoulders moved, but my thoughts were stilled, my memories pushed down deep.

The chores and lessons I was given by the priests were not difficult, but the price of imperfection was steep. There were lashes across the back of my hands for spots missed while cleaning, for clothes not pressed flat enough after washing. When calluses formed on my hands and I could no longer feel the strike of the leather, they removed my shoes and struck the bottoms of my feet. Each night I lay in my bunk and let the rhythmic ache and the pulsing of blood through my damaged hands and feet lull me to sleep.

My lessons also included geography, but when they spoke of Africa, it was not the Africa I knew. They spoke of tribal savages of low mind and low morals, bathing in rivers and praying to trees, half-naked and quick to violence, conductors of incomprehensible rituals.

"We do not pray to trees," I said without thinking. "We bring gifts to lay at the Msoro tree and pray there to God for safe work in the mines, and good harvests, and health for our families."

The priest snatched me by my hair, his face smoldering with anger, and dragged me from the benches.

"Apparently lashes across the hand are not enough for you."

He brought me into the courtyard and cut a fresh switch from a vine and struck me across the back with it. It was sharp enough to split skin through my thin shirt, and the pain of it buckled my knees, brought me to the ground. One of the other brothers brought him a plaited flail and he let the switch fall and lashed me with the flail instead.

I couldn't breathe. On my hands and knees in the courtyard, saliva dripping in long strands from my chin, I waited for the beating to end. When it did, a large wooden yoke was placed on my neck, heavy enough that it took three of the brothers to place it.

"Stand."

I pushed myself up to one knee, but could not lift my head from the ground. The flail snapped angrily across my back again.

"Stand."

I struggled to get my feet beneath me as best I could, then planted my hands to either side of the yoke and pushed myself upward, groaning and staggering, legs shaking. I gained my feet and felt the full, crushing weight of the yoke on my neck and shoulders. The priest stepped forward, and with me hunched beneath the yoke, his eyes were finally level with mine.

"Do not speak to me of your heathen traditions. And do not contradict me again. You will stand here, for the remainder of the day and through the night. If myself or anyone else sees you sitting, your punishment will begin again."

He turned to leave and the other brothers followed.

I stood. As the dusk fell and the sky grew darker and the temperature cooler, my legs grew weak, my shoulders grew numb, and my back pulsed with pain, both from the whipping and the weight. The Lomwe's message sunk into my bones. There was danger, for a slave, in making your thoughts known.

When they lifted the yoke from me in the morning, I collapsed to the stone floor of the courtyard, and for the first and only time in my life, I wept for mercy.

From that moment on, I listened. I walked on swollen feet, completed my chores with cracked and numbing hands, then I sat on their wooden benches and repeated their lessons back to them better than any of their novitiates could.

I kept even more to myself than before. I worked, I learned, I stayed silent. Even when the subject was Africa I would sit quietly, shamefully, and listen to my own history, taught to me wrong. It was how I would survive.

I did not try to tell them of Ichiyao, where all members of the community would join together to help a family with a task, or of the M'Mwera hut, where I would have gone at the time of my cutting had I not been taken by the white men so young, where I would have stayed for a moon, learning our people's customs before returning to the village as a man.

Day by day and month by month their words set in and I allowed them to. I let their words replace mine, their beliefs replace mine, their history replace mine. The memories of my village faded, the memories of my father's stories faded, the memories of my family faded, until I started first to question whether the priests were wrong or I was, and then, in time, stopped questioning that at all.

18

Each morning in the courtyard, the reed was produced and another small slice was taken from the assassin's skull. By the third day he was crazed, snapping at bugs that crawled across his face, trying to catch them in his teeth for food. He lapped his tongue at the water that an attendant would periodically dribble into his mouth, and sometimes also at the blood that dripped and caked on his cheeks and chin. He was conscious but not present, and looking into his eyes one could easily come to believe in the promised Jesuit hell.

I could not help but think of my own torture, hung from a board in the center of the training house courtyard, desperately angling my mouth to catch water dripped from a cloth. I understood how easily a man can break.

I was called to the castle daily now. Sometimes I caught glimpses of Tomiko, the quiet servant with the orange-flecked eyes, but I never had the opportunity to speak to her. I had spotted her once again, on one of my nighttime strolls, leaving the castle quietly alone. If I thought I had frightened her at Honno-ji, I certainly had done so by abruptly asking her to teach me about her culture and people when I had approached her in town. I was curious about where she was slipping away to, but she was through the gates and down the road into town before I could stop her to talk.

The duties I was given were simple. Nobunaga hosted a variety of diplomats and supplicants and high-ranking servants in various audience rooms throughout the castle, depending on his visitor's station. I stood guard at Nobunaga's side, still sporting the painted black crab sword and long spear that had accompanied me across a sea. Each of the visitors bowed to Nobunaga, but then risked a sidelong glance toward me before beginning to discuss matters of business. I knew I was there for novelty and intimidation as much as I was for security, but I accepted the role and responded to most looks with a hard-faced scowl, laughing inside anytime someone started at the sight of it.

Yet I knew that Nobunaga had enemies. The would-be assassin being slowly scalped in the courtyard was evidence enough of that. I remained vigilant, learned what I could. I watched the men and women who came before Nobunaga in the way that I watched soldiers, looking for signals of their intentions, indications of anything they held back, or offered nervously. I noted that those high ranking enough to be allowed swords in Nobunaga's presence always removed the scabbard from the sash on the left of their waist and placed it on the ground to their right when they knelt before him. After seeing this repeated enough times, I recognized that a sword placed on the left side was ready to draw for a right-handed fighter, but the sword placed to the right was a peace offering, a signal that no aggression or threat was intended.

There were matters of war brought forward, certainly, but also a broad range of administrative issues—land surveys, tax disputes, the quality of rice harvests, the output of silver mines, land delegation, wages, apprenticeships and appointments, marriages, castle repairs and additional fortifications, the cost of arming men, feeding them, favors to be shown and favors to be withheld, requests for funds for upkeep of the Imperial Palace and grounds in Kyoto, and religious disputes as well, temples insisting on payment for having prayed for Nobunaga's success, or subtly requesting that the activities of the Jesuits be more tightly restricted, or outright banned.

These Nobunaga mostly brushed off, and progress on the Jesuit church proceeded apace. As activity increased, so too did the presence of priests sent to oversee the construction. I recognized a few of them, but mostly avoided them regardless. A revulsion flared up in me any time I saw the familiar frocks or noticed the walls of the church rising higher, knowing this building was the measure of my value.

Nobunaga was far from predictable, but he was consistent. In each new territory coming under his control he standardized the currency, formalized the tax structure, demanded accurate census and survey missions, ordered roads to be kept in a proper state of repair, abolished customs barriers, and promoted trade and industry. Nobunaga was at times impatient with those who were hesitant to make their request, at times harsh with those who he felt had managed their tasks poorly, but he gave true consideration to all information presented to him, and judged soundly and fairly. You could ask for little more from a man of his stature.

On the military front, the first heads from the western campaign began to arrive, evidence of General Hideyoshi's and General Mitsuhide's early victories. The heads were given to specialized attendants, to be prepared for presentation. They would be cleaned and perfumed and dressed for display, the expressions pulled serene, the hair oiled and tied tightly into a knot, the teeth blackened with charcoal. They'd be displayed on wooden boards with tiny carved plaques.

The bodies were fastened to posts in the courtyard for far less ceremonious purposes. They'd be used to test new blades, struck and hacked at until the weapons were deemed worthy and the bodies fell to pieces small enough for the birds to carry away. The smell of stale blood and turning flesh hung in the air, and I suspected that this, too, was intentional. A means to harden and prepare the less-experienced fighters against what was ahead.

I WAS INVITED TO JOIN Nobunaga on hunting trips with Ranmaru, Ogura, and Jingorou. The castle town of Azuchi backed onto Lake Biwa, creating a formidable barrier and giving clear line of sight for miles. The lake had three major islands and it was a short row to the closest of them, Okishima, to seek game in the marshes and woods.

Nobunaga was an accomplished falconer, and appeared most content when one of his birds returned to him with a rabbit or some other small creature. All of them were more proficient than I with bows, both on foot and on horseback, but I still managed to impress them by spearing a wild pig at thirty paces.

As we rode up on the felled animal, Ranmaru halted and shouted, "All hail Yasuke, slayer of pigs!"

He turned to me, and seeing no change in my expression, he patted me on the shoulder to let me know he was joking.

"Come now, Yasuke. You're a warrior, are you not? You must practice your boasting. Ogura excels at it."

On cue, Ogura pulled a small rabbit from his saddlebag, dangling it by his legs. He set his face to a mockery of sternness. "I am Ogura, and no creature is fast enough to escape my eye, or my bow. I have fired a thousand arrows and taken a thousand pelts. Never have I placed a weapon in the dirt or in a tree, only in flesh."

"Yes, yes," interrupted Jingorou, his expression much less serious. "My brother is the scourge of small animals and rodents, but for every pelt he has taken, I, Jingorou, have taken three. My brother hunts what runs from him, I hunt what runs toward me."

"You hunt what you hit by mistake," jabbed Ogura.

The two brothers smiled. Ranmaru pointed his chin toward me. "What will you boast of, Yasuke? Your hump-backed desert horses? Your giant tusked beasts?"

I laughed, then quickly swallowed it, used to hiding my reactions. Ranmaru had a glint in his eye, and I could see these mild jests were his attempt to make me feel comfortable. It was a simple gesture, but I was moved by it.

"I wish he would have boasted of his wrestling," said Jingorou. "It might have saved me a few coins at the tournament."

Ranmaru gave an almost undetectable nod of encouragement. I turned to Jingorou. I gave him an intimidating glare, then stuck my chest out in the most exaggerated way I could manage and pounded my fist to my breast.

"My modesty is matched only by my strength, Jingorou. I'm sorry that both cost you so dearly . . ."

I meant to continue, but Nobunaga gave his horse a sudden quarter-turn, nocked and fired an arrow, then another, then a third.

The grass ahead of us had hardly yet stirred when he fired the first, but three quail burst up from the long grass and fell back to the ground just as quickly, each with an arrow in its breast. All of us sat back in our saddles for a moment, stunned into silence.

Nobunaga slung his bow back into place and turned the corner of his mouth up into a slight smirk. "I am Oda Nobunaga, and Japan's most boastful warriors collect my kills."

Ogura and Jingorou bowed and laughed, and rode ahead to pick up the fallen birds.

There was nothing in the way of pressing business to return to, so we set a small fire by the shore. It was not yet dark, but the cicadas had begun their evening song. Ogura and Jingorou cleaned the birds. One skinned rabbit hung drying from a makeshift rack, and I worked at skinning another while Ranmaru built up the flames. Three other birds were already in a pot hung above the fire, boiling to loosen the skin and feathers.

"You shot well today," Ogura said to his brother.

"Thank you. I've been avoiding pears."

Ogura stopped carving the skin of the small quail in his hands and looked across the fire to where Jingorou was sitting.

"You've been avoiding pears," he repeated, a question in his voice. Beside me, Ranmaru's shoulders bobbed up and down two quick times, as if he was stifling laughter.

"Yes," Jingorou said, plucking feathers from a bird that had boiled and cooled. "Pears make you see poorly. They affect your aim. I've been avoiding them."

Ogura thrust his hands wide in exasperation. "Who told you this? I will strike down the man who has made my brother sound like a such a fool."

"Too many pears makes you see poorly. Everyone knows this."

151

By now Ranmaru had stopped trying to contain his laughter. "Jingorou, your wife must have eaten every pear in the region on your wedding night."

Jingorou feigned anger at the jab, but soon collapsed into laughter, joined by Ogura and Ranmaru. I smiled but held my laughter inside. If Nobunaga heard the conversation, he gave no indication. He sat with his back to the fire, watching water bugs as they skipped across the lake's placid surface. He turned and our eyes locked for a moment before I lowered my head.

He cleared his throat, just subtly, and the laughter ceased.

"I'll see to it that the archers are given no more pears," he said wryly, turning now fully to the fire. "In the future, please see that all such sage military advice is presented to me immediately."

There was a quiet charm and wit to Nobunaga. His curiosity, his sharpness, and his attention to detail reminded me of Valignano, but where both men showed ruthless focus, I could not recall ever having seen Valignano joke with his men. Still, I had allowed myself to be charmed by Valignano as well, only to find that I was nothing but property to him. I resolved to remain more vigilant with my loyalties, though I could not deny that I liked these men.

Ranmaru dropped the two branches he had been using to manipulate the fire, apparently satisfied with its heat. He lifted his chin in my direction.

"Yasuke, who are the most fearsome archers you have seen?"

"The most fearsome?" I glanced at the faces around the fire, all now turned toward me. "The most fearsome archers I've seen are the ones shooting at me."

There was general laughter.

"Do you prefer the bow or the arquebus?" asked Ogura.

I considered the question for a moment, pulling another long strip of rabbit pelt beneath my knife.

"The bow is still more accurate, in the right hands. But it requires skill and practice that the arquebus does not. The arquebus can miss and still cause damage, or at the very least spook a horse, or even a soldier."

"They are effective," Nobunaga inserted. "Not all would agree with you, though. There are traditionalists who believe I am wrong to use the Portuguese guns. Akechi prefers his men to use the bow. He says that wars are won by warriors, not by weapons."

This last was said with a sneer. Nobunaga picked up a whetstone, began sharpening his knife, the sparks adding to the fire Ranmaru had built.

"We have always been slow to change," he said quietly.

The others nodded, and a silence settled in.

"In India there were cannons . . ." I paused for moment, lost in the memories of my first experiences with them, the terrifying noise and destruction, the shaking of the walls when the shells struck, the feeling that everything would collapse and we would all be buried in the rubble. I thought of the old Lomwe slave and wondered where he was now, or if he was no longer. I shook my head, regathered.

"The cannons are weapons of great power. Meant to intimidate and destroy, and able to be used to deadly effect with only a little training."

"Where did you see them?" asked Ranmaru.

"Several battles. Malacca. The Strait of Hormuz. I knew little about the fighting at the time, but I was caught in a war with two great empires, the Portuguese and the Ottomans."

Nobunaga had leaned closer to the fire at the talk of empire, but his face remained passive. Ogura and Jingorou had set aside their skinning.

"One of them invaded the other?" Jingorou prompted.

"No. Both fought over land that neither had claim to, other than the claim they had staked themselves. There were riches to be had in trade, and so they fought for supremacy over the ports. Every great empire has depended on controlling access to the sea."

I trailed off, lost in my own thoughts. Remembering the rolling decks of the Portuguese ships in the storm outside Hormuz, men lashing themselves to the rail while the slaves scrambled on the spray-slicked boards to secure the cannon shot, risking being washed into the sea to drown so that our masters could fight for riches which did not belong to them. The enemy ships bobbing in and out of sight with the rising and crashing of the waves, the wind sending the icy cold rain slicing through us like knives.

The others had continued talking. I missed most of what they said, but a mention of Nagasaki brought my attention back to the conversation. Ranmaru had been listing off ports and the lords who controlled them. ". . . smaller ones throughout the islands, but for large trade ships, Nagasaki is the best-situated port. Lord Sumitada controls the region there."

I hesitated, waiting for someone to correct Ranmaru, or for him to correct himself, but he did not. He carried on, listing off Sumitada's enemies and allies.

"I'm sorry," I interrupted. I turned to Nobunaga, bowed my head. "I apologize if this is something my lord already knows. Perhaps word has not yet reached Azuchi."

I paused, nervous, but Nobunaga gestured at me to continue.

"When I first came ashore here, we were to land in Nagasaki, but made the decision to anchor in Kuchinotsu Bay instead. Lord Sumitada controls the region, but no longer controls the port."

"Then who does?" asked Ranmaru.

"Lord Sumitada has ceded control of Nagasaki to Father Valignano."

Across the fire, Nobunaga's expression seemed to darken for just a moment. There was silence, waiting for his response. He gathered his jacket about him and stood.

"Let us return," he said calmly. "We've had enough idleness for one day."

19

Nobunaga received most of his visitors in a small antechamber on the castle's second floor. More important visitors would be presented to him on the main floor, in the central dais where the sumo tournament had been held, but Nobunaga preferred a less august setting for more informal business.

The second-floor chamber could hold about ten men comfortably. It forced visitors to ascend one flight of stairs, seeing just enough of the ornately decorated central pillars to arrive in front of Nobunaga suitably awed. He sat cross-legged on a wooden platform against the back wall, elevated just enough to place him above any who came before him, but not ostentatiously so.

I stood to the right of the dais, while he listened to reports of the war from one of his riders.

"The western campaign is progressing, but slowly. Both Akechi and Toyotomi have won early engagements, but against lesser Mori retainers. Toyotomi is moving more aggressively along the southern route. Akechi's forces have . . . bogged down with a siege at Yakami Castle." The rider cleared his throat, hoping the news would not be received poorly. "However, both armies are in good position, my lord."

"Any movement from the Mori?" Nobunaga asked.

"The Mori clan have not yet committed their full forces, my lord. They cannot allow this assault on their vassals for long, though. We know they will engage soon."

Until the Mori were drawn out, there would be no decisive confrontation, but they seemed on the cusp of doing so. Meanwhile, Tokugawa's forces were on the move as well. With Iga secured and Tokugawa's forces no longer needed as a reserve, he was sent east to complete the conquest of the Takeda lands. The Takeda clan had been severely weakened by a series of devastating losses, most notably at Nobunaga's own hand at Nagashino. But Takeda Katsuyori had yet to yield. Tokugawa had taken his army out quietly in the night, none of the pageantry with which Akechi and Toyotomi had deployed.

All that stood between the Oda clan and the reunification of Japan was a crippled Takeda clan to the east, and a still dangerous but outnumbered Mori clan in the west. Nobunaga stood, his mood seemingly brightened by the reports.

"The people need entertainment."

To CELEBRATE THE VICTORY AT Iga, Nobunaga ordered there be a play. Noh actors rode in from Kyoto to perform at Nobunaga's request. We gathered around the stage in the same ranks as we lived—those closest to the top of the mountain were closest to the stage, those who lived lower on the mountain were seated further away. The stage itself was a permanent fixture in the courtyard, a wooden stage that had pots half-buried beneath it to amplify the sounds, a shrine-like roof built over the top of it, and a pine tree painted on the back wall. To the left of the stage there was a slanted ramp for the actors to make their entrance, with three short pine trees planted in front of it. The stage was surrounded by polished white pebbles that reflected the light from the lanterns and gave the stage a glowing appearance.

A small chorus chanted and sang at the right of the stage, and four musicians kneeled at the back of the stage, three with small canvas drums and one with a flute. There were five short plays. Each one featured a single actor wearing a wooden mask, while the other actors were bare-faced. The costumes were elaborate—broad-shouldered golden robes and seashell-patterned silks and fans with embroidered dragons and scorpions. The movements were sometimes subtle, sometimes dramatic.

I could follow little of what was actually happening, but I felt deeply unsettled as I watched the men stomp and dance and chant. The masks the lead actor wore were ever-changing—a sad-faced woman, a fierce demon, a crazed elderly man, a serene monk.

In the longest play of the set, a traveling monk came across a woman crying in front of a shrine. When the monk inquired about the shrine, she urged him to pray for the man entombed there, then revealed herself to be a ghost and disappeared. In the play's second act she returned, in full battle armor, lamenting that she had not been able to join her lord in death.

At one point during the performance, Ranmaru placed his hand on my arm and looked at me with concern. I looked at him, then quickly away. I was shaken by the performances, but was not sure I could put into words why. The plays were brief and slow-paced, but to me they were a blur.

By the time the performances were complete I was sweating. As the crowd migrated toward the castle gate, I went in the other direction to get some air. I walked out to the stone wall at the back of the courtyard, looking out over Lake Biwa, and I sat there on the ground at the wall's base.

The play brought back memories of home, memories that I had spent years fighting off and holding at bay. Festivals held during my childhood, the women painting their faces white with a paste made from minerals and dancing and playing drums while the men performed on stilts, wearing masks of spirits and animals.

One day I had found my father's festival stilts hidden beneath his carving bench. I snuck away to the edge of the village to dance on them—falling, rising, dancing, and falling again. I scraped the skin from my knees and elbows, bloodied my chin, but continued to practice until I could at least perform a short routine, lifting my feet high, twirling my arms, throwing my head back, and offering my throat to the sky. When I returned, I could not hide what I had done, but my mother and father had not punished me, nor could they disguise that they were more amused than they were angry.

I didn't know if my father was still alive. I didn't know if he was still searching, still hoping, despite all the years. I did not know where my mother was buried. My father would have looked for her, amongst the bodies, ensured the traditions were completed. Perhaps he would have done it for all of them. None of them had been spared.

I was twelve when I was taken. My dreams were of going to the M'Mwera hut with the other boys my age, learning the customs of adulthood, and returning to my family to be recognized as a man. Instead I'd been sold in far-off places, killed boys, killed men, buried bodies, burned bodies, or wrapped them and thrown them into the sea. I'd seen sickness and death, cruelty and violence. I'd seen what men were, and seeing it all made me want to be a boy again. To sit with my mother while she slapped her hands against the skin of the drums, and to watch my father while he danced.

I had not allowed myself to weep for them in the hold of the ship, or in the training grounds of the mercenaries, or in the classes of the Jesuits, but I wept for them now, in the darkness at the base of a fortress wall in a land so far away I had never known it existed.

After I had composed myself, I headed back toward the guards' quarters, passing by the theater stage as I did so. The crowd had dispersed, seeking either rest or further entertainments. The performers were still there, brushing the stage clean and storing their instruments. A man in a gray robe was carefully folding the costumes and placing them in a chest, and I could tell by the grace and control of his movements that he had been the actor under the masks.

"I want to thank you for your performance. It was moving."

He turned toward me, looked up at me with a wide-eyed gaze, then recalled his manners, tucking his chin in a quick nod.

"I am glad you enjoyed it. It is an honor to perform for Lord Nobunaga." He risked a glance upward. "Forgive my curiosity. I was in Kyoto when you arrived. I heard the commotion, but was unable to catch a glimpse of you myself."

"Curiosity should never require an apology. I am curious myself . . . the masks. They are wonderful."

"Ah!" he said excitedly, diving back into the chest to produce one. "Yes. The mask-making is an art."

He held up the carved mask of a man with a neutral expression—lips curved, but not quite enough to be called a smile; eyebrows high and arching, but not emphatic enough to evoke surprise. The actor tilted the mask, showing how with the movement of his head he could use shadow to create many emotions from a single expression.

"It is remarkable," I told him. "Where I come from, we also carve masks. The men wear them in festivals for singing and dancing. Seeing you perform tonight reminded me of home."

He bowed deeply. "You honor me."

I reached for the mask, and he allowed me to take it. I ran my fingers across the face, the wood smooth beneath my touch.

"My father taught me how to carve, but only a little. I would have learned more . . ." I trailed off, thinking of all the things I had been dragged away from. I handed the mask back to him and he accepted it slowly, placing it back in the chest.

"Could you make one for me?"

"Sadly, I cannot. It is tradition that we carve our own masks."

"I understand. Thank you. And thank you for your performance. I will not forget it."

I bowed and turned toward my quarters.

"I could teach you, though."

I stopped, looked over my shoulder at the actor.

"It would be my honor to assist one of Lord Nobunaga's servants, and a foreign guest. I cannot teach you as your father would have. But we can take what you have learned and what I have learned, and we can create something new."

* * *

THE PERFORMERS RETURNED TO KYOTO, but the actor stayed behind. He gave me a block of cypress and showed me how to draw the face upon it. We sawed the edges to get the rough shape, then he showed me how to use a chisel and wooden mallet to peel back the wood in layers. The chisel had the same feel in my hand as the adz that my father had given me so long ago, but the metal head of it was lighter than that of the adz, and the cypress was softer than the acacia I carved as a child.

At first I stabbed too deeply and marred the wood, and he would patiently correct it if he could. If he could not, he would provide me with a fresh block of cypress and encourage me to try again. Soon I learned the correct angles, the correct weight on the hammer, and was rewarded by seeing the wood curl away in thin strips.

"Do you have family?" I asked him.

"They'll not miss me if I am gone a few days more than expected."

"Do your performances take you far?"

"Further now. Ah, ah, careful!" I pulled back the chisel to shave more lightly, and the actor relaxed.

"Further now? Why?"

He shrugged. "The more land that is under one rule, the safer it is to travel. Less need to worry about the politics of performing for one lord one week, and then his enemy the next."

He reached out to steady my hand.

"Lord Nobunaga asked me once if I thought him cruel."

The actor looked at me sharply. "Does he treat you poorly?"

"No," I said hastily. "He treats me well, just as well as he treats the others in his company, men of his own country who have been with him much longer."

The actor shrugged again, testing the wood with his finger. "A man like Nobunaga must at times be cruel. But he does not need to be kind. His kindnesses are by choice."

I studied the man for a moment, but he was staring intently at the mask. "I think it is ready for painting," he said.

"I had another master who also gave me a high place. I trusted him. And I think I was wrong to."

The actor crossed the room and dug into his chest, looking for the painting materials. He spoke with his back to me while he rummaged.

"When trust is broken, the fault can only lie with the man to whom trust was given, never by the one who gives it. Will you judge all men by this now?"

He found the paints he wanted, and the brushes, and started pulling them from the chest.

"Trust is a strange thing. A man cannot prove himself worthy or unworthy of it in advance. Trust can only be earned once it has already been given."

Still he did not turn. He opened the paints and readied them on a thin board. I watched him work. He had stayed and helped me when he had no reason to. This kindness was his choice, one with no gain offered, and perhaps Nobunaga's kindnesses were as well.

The actor handled the mask deftly, respectfully. I thought of my father in his mask, dancing above me, eyes never leaving mine, as he moved effortlessly on his stilts. About how much I had longed to dance beside him, just once.

"Do you have a little more wood?" I asked. "There is one more thing I would like to make."

I HAD LITTLE TRAINING IN the ways of my own people. I had watched, and those memories and observations were all I had to guide me. The actor had returned to Kyoto, leaving a small chisel from his tool kit with me as a gift. He wished me luck, as I did him as well. We'd finished waxing and painting, and while the mask I had crafted was no match for the quality of his own, it was more than passable.

One morning, after Nobunaga had completed his breakfast, I asked him to come out into the courtyard with me.

"I have something I wish to show you."

Nobunaga, always curious, seemed pleased, and came without question. Ranmaru, Ogura, and Jingorou accompanied him.

Once down the steps of the castle, I excused myself to go the guards' quarters. A few moments later, I emerged from the quarters as something else altogether.

I had constructed two wooden stilts, each two feet long, with pegs for me to stand on. It had been harder to describe them to the old actor than it had been to build them. He looked at me in confusion as I explained what I wanted to do, and in the end he just shrugged and handed me his sturdiest pieces of wood, then peered over my shoulder as best he could as I cut them to size and pieced them together.

In place of a more traditional outfit, I tied a long silk sheet around my waist, long enough to hang almost but not quite down to the bottom of the stilt. Above the sheet I wore no shirt, just a simple necklace and bracelets made of rice hay, a few feathers of pheasant tucked into each bracelet. And on my face, the mask of a rhino, the face painted gray, the expression angry, the short curved horn attached with dry clay.

I snorted and flexed the muscles in my arms and chest and shoulders and walked out into the courtyard. There were gasps from the small number of people milling about the base of the castle. One of Nobunaga's guards reached for his spear in fright, but did not level it. I was more nervous than I had been since I was a boy. My heart beat heavily and the mask seemed to pulse on my face with each breath. A small crowd gathered. They all looked up at me, some in wonder, some in shock, some in fear.

There were whispers first, then points, then a few began to laugh. I could feel the heat of my own breath beneath the mask. I worried that I had made a mistake, that they would judge me for a mindless savage and a barbarian, just as the Jesuits had judged my people. Nobunaga silenced those gathered with a sharp glance. He called for a stool. He stepped forward and sat in front of me, alone, while the others gathered in a circle around us.

I stomped twice into the ground, sharply. I reared back my head, throwing the short gray horn toward the sky. I moved tentatively at first, remembering the motions rather than feeling them. I had taken metal tabs from the armory and tied them around my fingers and thumbs to clack out a rhythm.

In my village there would have been drums, a row of them, slapped with palms hardened to callus in the mines or in the fields. There would have been carved reeds, blown by the elders to make high whistling notes. The other dancers would have wrapped cords of dried macadamia nuts around their ankles, which would rattle inside their shells while the men stomped and leapt. I moved awkwardly on the stilts, but grew more comfortable with each step.

My mother would have been amongst that row of drums, hers the only smiling face amongst earnest ones, because she could not contain the joy she felt at playing, nor I my joy at watching her. There were features of her face I still could not recall, but I knew every detail of her hands, how she pulled her fingers tautly back to stretch her palms, rolling her shoulders back and forth as she slapped the flat of her hands against the skin of the drum, how the vibration of the strike seemed to make her whole body shimmer. The memories washed over me, then settled somewhere deep inside me, and I felt ready.

I remembered one of our last conversations together, when I had asked her if she would play for me when it was my turn to dance at the festival. I remember the smile that had come to her face, vibrant and wide. The spark of joy in her eyes. The feel of her kiss on my forehead. Beneath my mask, tears came to my eyes at the memory.

"I will play for you until the skins come off the drums," she had said. "We will see what gives out first—my arms or your dancing feet."

Nobunaga gave me his full attention, and I focused on him, performed for only him in the same way my father had performed solely for me. The movements felt foreign. I'd now lived in other lands longer than I had lived in my own. I remembered the sweet smell of mango and orange on the breeze, the sound of my people singing, the pride I felt each time when my father turned toward me, hidden beneath his mask. I remembered his face, then my mother's, my grandmother's, all more clearly than I had ever been able to picture them before.

The movements started to come more naturally. I dug the stilts into the ground and scraped my right foot beneath like a rhino about to charge. I kicked the stilts up high behind me and spread my arms wide and spun and leapt, and with each movement I released some of the shame the Jesuits had taught me. Within me I could hear the sounds of the drums, the singing, I could, for the first time, feel a connection to my ancestors, and my village, and the life that I would have led. A lightness. An awareness. A connection to something inside me that had not been taken away, but which I hadn't known how to find. I danced until I was sweaty, until my muscles ached from clenching and my feet were sore from the pegs of the stilts and I heard the drums within me stop beating.

I collapsed to the ground, exhausted. The crowd was silent, looking to Nobunaga for his reaction. He stood from his stool, approached the spot where I lay pooled in the dirt, and he bowed before me, touching his forehead to the ground.

A murmur worked through the crowd, then a rustling of clothes as they bowed themselves before me as well. But while they were simply following Nobunaga's lead, Nobunaga's bow was one of true respect. I was humbled almost to tears. I had stood by him for weeks now while visiting lords brought extravagant gifts and lavish displays of gratitude, but I had nothing to offer other than my service.

I removed the mask and handed it to him. Ranmaru stepped forward to accept it, but Nobunaga waved him off. He took the mask from my hands himself and we sat together in the dirt, for a moment, as equals.

20

While Nobunaga's mood improved, the mood at Azuchi overall grew more somber.

The soldiers, focused and disciplined in their training before, were even more so now. The remainder of Nobunaga's forces knew they would be called to the field soon; it was only a matter of determining whether it would be west to support Akechi and Toyotomi against the Mori clan, or east to support Tokugawa against the Takeda.

I sometimes trained with them, sometimes on my own. With them, I practiced keeping my body aligned, snapping the wrists to slice with the sword rather than swing and chop, using the precise amount of force. Without them, I would leave the sword and practice with just my feet, sliding them forward and back, side to side, keeping them squarely beneath me at all times, learning to move the way I needed to. The small crowds that had previously been drawn to watch grew bored and drifted away.

Some nights I slept, and dreamt of the people in my village, not tied to the iron hearth but buried up to their necks instead, the Portuguese slavers peeling away pieces of my people's scalps with razor-sharp reeds of bamboo, holding the strips of flesh and hair aloft and dancing wildly, shouting to their god in the sky.

Other nights I walked. I avoided the church during the day, did not want to see the priests, or the growing number of Japanese who were drawn to them. At night I allowed myself to stand before it, though. Progress had been swift. They had wisely built it to be smaller than the neighboring Shinto shrine, which was one of Nobunaga's prized constructions, but the Christian church was no less impressive in its own way.

The walls were tightly fitted stones of varying shades, subtle but beautiful. The door was thick oak, imported at great expense, and there was an oblong aperture beside it, angled at the top and flat at the bottom, currently blocked in wood but soon to be replaced with a stained glass window that Father Valignano had commissioned. It would be the first such window in all of Japan.

My feelings on the Jesuits were complex. There were good men amongst them, and others who could not be trusted. The Portuguese priests whom I'd first been given to had treated me like an animal, but Valignano, despite his betrayal at Honno-ji, had not. I had learned hard lessons from them, but valuable things too—languages, culture, history. Their message of mercy and forgiveness was a worthy one, though some who preached it were unworthy of the words, and I wasn't sure how to separate the message from the men, the words from the actions.

I caught a glimpse of movement out of the corner of my eye. A shadow, slipping down the steps of Azuchi Castle, one that I knew must be Tomiko. I hurried to follow, and caught her at the gate.

"Tomiko."

She turned sharply, her expression the same shocked look as she had worn when Nobunaga had called on me to lift her at Honno-ji.

"I'm sorry I startled you. And I'm sorry for earlier, if I asked too much."

There was a long pause. She seemed almost on the brink of tears, but her voice was steady when she answered.

"I saw you dance. It was . . . beautiful."

I choked down a sudden lump in my throat and looked away.

"Thank you," I said quietly.

She reached out and touched my forearm.

"You want to understand us. It's not too much to ask. Come."

She led me through the gate. Guards were in place to check anyone who entered the castle grounds, but they had little concern for who left. We walked down the mountain road in darkness, and in silence.

"Is this where you come every night?" I asked when we reached the valley plain of the surrounding town.

She continued to walk. There were a handful of lanterns still glowing outside of shops and homes and a few small groups of threes and fours walking the streets, but it was mostly quiet. We passed through the town to a collection of a half dozen shacks near the water's edge, so dark I had not even seen them from the street.

A woman waited in one of the doorways. She saw me, looked to Tomiko sharply.

"It's alright," Tomiko told the woman, waving me forward.

The smell struck me first, the smell of spilt blood and flesh soon to turn rotten. It wafted into the street, assaulting my nostrils. It was a smell I was all too familiar with, but it was unexpected. I gagged, pressed the sleeve of my shirt against my nose.

The shack inside was tiny, just a single room with a tatami mat set in the corner, two candles burnt half to their base, and a pile of a dozen heads lying on the floor. Some had their eyes and mouth open, gaping at the low ceiling in perpetual horror. There were scrips of paper folded into their ears and nostrils indicating who they were and who had killed them.

"These heads are from the west," I said dumbly.

The woman was one of the head-cleaners. These were their shacks, pushed to the very edge of town to execute their gruesome art, working their canvases of muscle and bone, well away from those who would reject them.

"Yes," Tomiko said, kneeling in front of the pile of heads, seemingly unaffected by the smell. The woman stood against the wall, still frightened of me. Both Tomiko and I ignored her.

"I was born Mori," Tomiko continued. "I was married into the Saitō clan, and came into the service of the Oda when the Saitō were defeated."

"I don't understand."

Tomiko studied the heads, gently picking them up one by one, inspecting them.

"My brother and father are samurai, sworn retainers to the Mori clan. I come here to look for them."

The woman stared mutely at me and pressed herself more tightly into the wall. Tomiko turned a head carefully in her hands while the words dug into me. I had more questions than I knew how to ask. Was she relieved to not find her family's heads amongst the dead? Was she angry with Oda for its war against her ancestral family? Would she turn? Tomiko seemed to read my thoughts.

"War is this country's nature. We have grown up with it, lived with it daily. It's not a thing to be feared or hated or raged against. It just is. You can't understand us without understanding this. If my father's head or my brother's head shows up here, I will know that fighting against them was considered an honor."

She placed the last head back on the pile, wiped her hands against her robe as she stood, then nodded in gratitude to her host. Tomiko passed the woman a single coin, and she glanced at me fearfully before accepting it and pressing herself back against the wall.

"And what will you do?" I asked. "If . . . if they do show?"

Tomiko looked me in the eye, chin held high, none of her previous fear present.

"I will honor them. I will wash their heads with my own hands, and let them know that they were loved."

21

I walked Tomiko back to the castle, the guards recognizing me and allowing me to bring her through. I was shaken from the experience, whereas she seemed to have been calmed by it. Nobunaga was not her enemy. Oda against Mori was something bigger than any individual man. It was an inevitable conflict, and for Tomiko to rage against it was as useless as it would be to rage against the rising of the sun. In a strange way, I understood. I thought about the Portuguese mercenaries, the Jesuit priests. I knew what it was like to accept your captor, and to serve.

A few days later, I met Ranmaru at the front gate. I had not been called to duty since my performance. When word finally came to the guards' quarters for me to see Ranmaru, I was both relieved and concerned. He waved for the front gate to be opened and indicated we walk down the mountain a ways.

"Any word of the war?" I asked.

"Toyotomi makes progress. Akechi remains bogged down outside Yakami Castle. Tokugawa sends little word, but when Tokugawa is silent that is generally good news."

"You think we'll deploy west, then?"

"No. Tokugawa will reach Takeda Katsuyori before either Akechi or Toyotomi are engaged by the Mori. Nobunaga will show both clans respect. He will ride east first to remove Katsuyori from the head of the Takeda clan personally. He will ride west only when the Mori take the field."

I pushed back thoughts of Tomiko, waiting for the heads of her brother and father to come from the west. I was relieved at Ranmaru's belief that we would go east to face the Takeda instead.

We descended past the generals' homes as we spoke, minor castles in their own right, set slightly below Nobunaga's and just outside his own gates. The three compounds laid out below Azuchi Castle reminded me of the way the three men sat below him on the dais at Honno-ji, the night I first saw them—wiry, chipmunk-eared Toyotomi who had risen from peasantry; the overweight and ever watchful Tokugawa, released from a genteel bondage and returned to the head of his clan and province; and the balding, gray-bearded Akechi, the poet and philosopher whose winding road had brought him from the Saitō clan to the shogun, and now to Nobunaga.

"Will I ride with him?" I asked.

"Are you so eager for war?"

"I am eager to be of service. War is what I am trained for."

"I thought you were trained for dancing?" Ranmaru looked at me coolly for a moment, then broke into a wide grin.

"You know I could crush you with one hand?" I joked.

"Hmm. Do not be fooled by how pretty I am," he retorted. "I don't fear you like the other men do."

"Fear me or not, the outcome will be the same."

Ranmaru merely raised an eyebrow in response. I suspected that he had indeed been underestimated many times, based on his looks. He had the delicate appearance of a pampered noble, but none of the arrogance that usually came with it. His words were often boastful, but his actions showed the humility of a servant, and both words and actions were always peppered with small kindnesses. The way he had led me quickly and skillfully from the room after Father Valignano had offered me, back at Honno-ji, or his words of encouragement and advice on the night of the sumo tournament, or the playful barbs on hunting trips intended to make me feel relaxed, feel welcomed.

"I should thank you . . ." I started, but he was already speaking.

"You seemed upset the other night. During the play."

I nodded and cleared my throat, then turned to look ahead.

"It brought back . . . memories."

"Of your home?"

"Yes."

"You don't speak much of it."

"It is a place I will never see again. For a long time, forgetting it seemed to be the best choice."

"And you feel that way still?"

I thought of the old Lomwe man, back in my earliest days of slavery. He had talked to the Portuguese on my behalf, convinced them to take me with them. If not for his assistance, I would likely still be toiling under them. When I had hesitated about leaving, the old man had put his hands on either side of my head and tilted me toward him.

"Your people come from a village near Mount Namuli, yes?"

"I have no people. Not anymore," I said bitterly, but the old man ignored me.

"Your mother, I am sure, taught you how the first woman walked out of the cave at Mount Namuli, and all life followed her?"

I nodded. I heard my mother's laughter on the wind as she ran down the road with her friends, saw her silhouette touch the shadow of my father in the morning sun as they said goodbye to each other for the last time.

"Some of us never leave that cave. We are content to stay safe in the dark. But you are young and strong and brave. You, I think, are meant to step outside of the cave. To leave a footprint on the world."

It was he who told me I should forget my mother and father, forget my home. He was surely either in chains or dead, and no more happy for having accepted his fate. I changed the subject.

"What was the play about? The longer one, with the girl crying by the shrine?"

"Tomoe Gozen?" Ranmaru visibly brightened at the opportunity to tell a story. "It is one of Lord Nobunaga's favorites. He recited portions of it at

Atsuta shrine, when he stopped to pray before riding into battle against the Imagawa. She is one of our most celebrated warriors."

"I have seen women training. Do they fight?" I asked.

"Do the women not fight where you are from?"

"Our village had no trouble with our neighbors."

"You grew up in peace." Ranmaru chuckled. "Some would call it a blessing, some would call it a weakness."

I thought of the slavers coming to our village and how unprepared we were for such an attack, what little resistance we had offered. My anger flared for a moment, but I knew Ranmaru meant nothing by his comment, and I suppressed it.

"Our people's villages were run by the women. They farmed, mostly, but also determined who would get which plots of land, how food and other resources would be distributed, and who we would trade with and how much. When there were marriages, it was the man who would leave his home to move in with the woman, and minor disputes would be settled by them, though more significant matters were taken to the mwene. Their word was final in all matters. It is very different from here, or from most places I've seen."

"Perhaps that is *why* you had peace," Ranmaru said, and I was unsure if he meant it jokingly or not. He continued the walk, and picked up his story as if it had never been interrupted.

"The women you see in the courtyard are Onna-Bugeisha. They do not join us in battle, but they train to defend the castle and the town in the event Azuchi is attacked while our armies are away. Tomoe Gozen was onna-musha, a female samurai, decorated in battle. It is written that she was worth a thousand soldiers, with either sword or bow, and that she was ready to confront a demon or a god, whether mounted or on foot. She served Yoshinaka of the Minamoto clan in the Genpei War, and was always the first captain he sent into battle.

"In the play, the ghost of Tomoe Gozen prays at the shrine where her beloved Lord Yoshinaka was interred. She tells the traveling monk of his final battle, and final command. Yoshinaka had led the defeat of the Taira

172

clan and positioned the Minamoto to rule, but he was betrayed by his cousin Yoritomo. When Yoshinaka was gravely wounded at Awazu, Tomoe encouraged him to take his own life, and vowed that she would take hers as well, but Yoshinaka ordered her to live, and to take his amulet and his kimono back to his home province.

"She went out to meet the band of approaching Yoritomo soldiers. They did not recognize her, so she feigned fear to embolden them and draw them close, then cut them all down. In doing so, she gave her Lord Yoshinaka time to end his own life with dignity. She returned to his body for the amulet and the kimono. In the play, she laments not having been able to join her lord in death, but she did her duty."

"You would do this?" I asked, already knowing the answer. "You would commit sepukku if Lord Nobunaga were to fall?"

"Without hesitation," he said proudly.

"And what if he ordered you to live?"

Ranmaru paused, as if he had never considered the question before. Then his expression changed, and instead of answering, he pointed.

"Ah, we are here."

We had stopped approximately halfway down the mountainside, just below the homes of Nobunaga's wife, and that of his concubines, right around the level where his high-ranking servants and pages lived. Ranmaru was gesturing toward the courtyard of a modest pine house. Flowering plum and magnolia trees lined the short path to the doorway and from the rear of the house, I could hear the soft splashing of either frogs or fish in a small pond.

Ranmaru opened the door, and I followed him inside. I did not have to duck to get through the doorway. Inside, the ceilings were unusually high. There was a small reception area, then another doorway into a larger room. A sprawling tatami mat covered most of the floor. A window looked out over the rear pond and sunlight fell in through the branches of the blossoming backyard tree. Two young men in simple yellow kimonos stood at the far end of the tatami mat, and bowed as we entered.

"These are your servants. I'm sure you will treat them well, as they will you."

"I don't understand," I muttered, truly confused.

"What's to understand?" Ranmaru laughed and looked up at the ceiling. "Clearly this is a home made for a giant. Did you think you would live in the guards' quarters forever?"

I looked around the room again, with new eyes. The timber panels had a wet sheen and were almost still green in places, freshly cut.

"This is mine?" I stammered.

I had spent most of my life sleeping in tents or under the stars. When I had slept beneath a roof, it was always one which belonged to another man. I was overwhelmed and unsure how to respond.

I bowed to the two servants and thought to give them some small task in respect of their service, but I had never given men orders before in any matter other than battle and could think of nothing to ask of them. Ranmaru placed his hand on my shoulder.

"There is one other thing."

WE RETURNED TO THE TOP of the mountain, inside the gate, and Ranmaru walked me past the nearly completed Jesuit church to where its Shinto counterpart stood. Nobunaga waited on the steps, dressed formally in a rich purple kimono with golden inlays patterned throughout.

Ranmaru bowed. "I will return."

Nobunaga nodded at Ranmaru and he departed. I started to thank Nobunaga for the gift, but he waved the words away.

"You were a boy when you were taken, yes? Do you remember much of your home?"

"Pieces, my lord. I do not think of it often, and when I do, I feel more emptiness than anything else. I remember some of my people's ways, but not as many as I have forgotten, or as many as I never learned. I remember details of people and places, but I rarely recall any *feeling*. My memories, when I have them, are like someone else's."

"Hmm. My home province of Owari is only a short distance from here, but my memories of it are the same. Clear, yes, but somehow empty of any connection. As if they were things that had happened to someone else. There is one event, however, that has stuck with me always."

Nobunaga descended a few stairs to stand on the one just above me.

"I was reckless in my youth. Disrespectful, even. I thought my father, and his retainers, weak. I was angered at how lowly we were regarded by the other clans, and I blamed them. I did not understand at the time that my own actions also brought shame to us. I dressed slovenly, I paid little attention to affairs of the province, or to its people. My father favored my older brother to be his heir, though he was born illegitimate. I fought with them often, even in front of servants and commoners, even when their counsel was wise. The people whispered at my arrogance. My worst act was at my father's funeral. I should have been honoring him; instead I threw a bowl of incense and cursed at his body."

Nobunaga seemed to cringe at the memory.

"They called me the Fool of Owari. Throughout all of Japan, that was how they saw me. They scoffed at me, at our clan, at our province. And they were right."

"But now they all bow to you."

He waved his hand dismissively at the comment.

Nobunaga turned his back to me and regarded the shrine. Valignano would not be happy to see a Shinto shrine sitting beside his new church at Azuchi, but if Nobunaga were able to unite Japan under his rule, Valignano and the Jesuits would have little choice of who to work with, or what they would accept.

"I supervised the building of this shrine myself. For weeks stones were brought in by oxen and levered into place by teams of men. I had a women's orchestra play all through the day on the hill so that the music would encourage them."

Nobunaga turned back to me, some fire lit just behind his eyes.

"I named this temple Masahide-ji. When my father died, his retainers were so concerned about my behavior that they plotted to install my brother as the head of the clan. They did not want the Oda to be guided by the so-called Fool of Owari. But one of my father's retainers, a samurai named Masahide, refused to give up on me.

"He gathered the other samurai in the shrine at Owari. He read a letter he had written expressing his disappointment in my conduct, but also his hope that I would accept my responsibilities and lead the Oda clan with honor. Then he committed seppuku. He knelt on the mat in the center of the shrine and used a small tanto blade to first stab himself, then draw the blade up and across his midsection. Then his young page, acting as his second, used Masahide's own katana to behead him, slicing expertly to leave a small flap of skin at the front of the throat to prevent his master's head from touching the floor.

"This is a long-standing custom amongst the samurai, but never before had I seen it performed. And it was because of me. Because I *was* a fool. I live every day with the shame that Masahide had to give his life to put me on the right path, and I come here, every day when I am home in Azuchi, to remind myself of it. That day, Masahide taught me responsibility, honor, sacrifice. That day, Masahide taught me what it means to be a samurai. And I built this shrine to honor his memory. But I also built it to remind myself of how foolish I once was."

I felt the need to say something, but could not find the right words. Nobunaga appeared to be in the grip of genuine emotion.

"I asked you before, what you believe in. Let me tell you what I believe in. I believe in Japan. I believe in our ways, our customs, our history. But I believe also that we must accept change. We must honor our customs, but not be held back by them. And I believe that we have fought against each other too long, that we must again become one. You are a free man now, Yasuke. A slave believes what he is told. What do you believe?"

I bowed my head to the ground. His words were like a blow to the stomach. I had considered the nature of freedom many times, but seldom given any thought to it as a practical matter. What I considered freedom were the small objections Valignano had sometimes tolerated, or the times when I was consulted on questions of strategy. What did true freedom mean, here in this place?

I did not know, but I knew this: if my choices were now my own to make, I would choose to stay. I would have given my life for Nobunaga's on my first day in his service, because that was what I was meant to do. Now I would do so regardless of service. I was given to him as a gift, but he had treated me as a man. He had humbled himself in the dirt beside me. If I were truly free, I would use that freedom to stand in his company, protect him from his enemies. I knew what I would choose to fight for, and in this moment, that was freedom enough.

"I believe in honor," I said. "I believe in loyalty, and service, and sacrifice. All my life I have fought for other men's causes, but if you will have me, I will fight now for your cause as my own."

Nobunaga nodded. "Come inside."

At the top of the stairs, two of Nobunaga's servants waited. They opened the shrine doors. Just inside were two wooden racks, one holding a pair of swords and the other holding an oversized set of armor. Wordlessly, the two servants began pulling the pieces from the armored rack and helping me dress.

I was already wearing short pants and a shirt with a belt and slippers. They handed me leggings, which I pulled overtop of my trousers. I tied the shin guards, then I stood as they attached the skirtlike greaves around my waist. Next came the gloves and armored sleeves, then the shoulder and chest plate. The armor was black with a single golden quince, the Oda emblem, painted on the chest plate. The laces were bloodred and tied together in the back to be out of the way. Finally, a cream-colored sash was wrapped twice around my waist, pulled tightly. Once those were all in place, the two servants stepped back, giving distance.

Like the home, I knew the armor had been custom built for me. This was not some whim from Nobunaga, but something he had planned for some time. His face betrayed nothing, and as overwhelmed as I felt inside the armor, I took his cue to respect the solemnity of the moment.

The scabbards of the two swords were black, the grips red and gold in a crisscrossed diamond pattern. I lifted each carefully from the rack and tucked the scabbards through the sash. When I turned to face Nobunaga, Ranmaru had returned. He passed Nobunaga my helmet. It was all black but for a short, upward-curving rhino horn jutting from the center, the same rhino horn that I had carved and stained gray and attached to the mask that I had danced in, that I had given to Nobunaga. There was no face plate. I kneeled before Nobunaga and he placed the helmet on my head.

"Let them see your face," he said, "and let them run from it."

22

T he rank of samurai had never before been given to a non-Japanese person. The citizens, the guards, and the ashigaru now had to bow in my presence. I was relieved from guard duty, so that all of my free time could be used to train and to maintain the simple home and garden and pond that had been provided for me, though much of that work was handled by the pair of servants I had been given.

To ease my mind I trained. I now had a garden of my own, no longer did I practice in the patch of open space behind the guards' quarters, studied by a crowd. I moved from sun to shade to sun beneath the plum and cypress, watched only by frogs and birds. I stepped off the stone walkway into the soft soil of the garden, carefully avoiding the shoots of carrot and potato so I could practice in unsure footing. A challenge was as likely to come in mud or snow as on stone, and I would be ready regardless.

I slid my feet forward and back, stepped to the side, turned, and repeated, all with my sword still tucked in my sash. I envisioned an opponent, created him in whole in front of me. I watched his hands, his feet, his eyes, and only when the time was right did I draw and strike, a single downward slice to the crown of his head.

I reset, sheathed the katana, began again. Forward, back, forward, left, forward, then flashing the katana one handed across his line of sight to draw his block and plunging the shorter wazikashi left-handed into his chest. I sheathed both, and reset.

Most nights, I was invited to the castle to dine with Nobunaga, sometimes with Ranmaru and the other samurai, sometimes privately. I was given additional clothing and a small stipend. It was the first time in my life I had ever been paid.

I was worried about the reaction of the other samurai, and the commoners. I was an outsider who had been elevated to an honored position, but that could be met with respect or resentment. I was relieved, but still somewhat uneasy with how well I was accepted. I had sealed my popularity at the sumo tournament. Everywhere I went people bowed and smiled and sometimes even cheered when they saw the two swords tucked through my sash and recognized what it meant.

I returned their bows, even more conscious now of observing the proper customs. I did not want to bring shame to either Nobunaga or myself. I had been given an honor but felt there was still more I needed to do to prove myself worthy of it. At night, in my new home, I practiced kneeling, eating, speaking.

The servants looked to me for orders, but I had none to give them, so they cleaned and prepared food and tended and watered the garden, cared for my armor. My hands were something they had never been before—idle.

I looked at them, gnarled and calloused and thick with muscle and scar. They had been put to the cave walls in the mines of my village, put to the tar at the walls of the Portuguese fortresses, to the oar on their ships, to the scrubbing of the seminary floors, and to the perfection of sword and spear and bow in the training courtyard in India.

They were also hands which had never held another in love, never brushed the soft skin of a cheek, or stroked a plait of hair. They were hands that had killed, but never caressed. Hands that had gripped whatever was necessary to survive, but that in the end had remained empty, and would perhaps always remain so.

* * *

"Isaac."

I had taken my spear to the blacksmith for sharpening and was waiting outside in the courtyard. The name failed to register at first, bounced around the air before landing, before I realized it had once been my own. I looked up to see the familiar robes of the Jesuits approaching. The smiling face of Brother Organtino and the stern expression of Father Valignano.

Some of the new revulsion I had developed rose in me, then settled, mixing with my old feelings of loyalty. I bowed my head to them, instinctively. Old habits die hard.

"Greetings."

"Look at you, dressed like a proper Japanese." As always with Valignano, I could not detect whether his words were meant as approval or as disrespect. His glance fell to the red and gold hilts of the two swords at my waist, and while I had worn them with pride since they'd been given to me, his single glance turned that pride sour and I dropped one arm to my waist to cover them.

"You look well," Organtino interjected. "It pleases us to see you so."

"Thank you, Brother. I am well. What brings you?"

For weeks I had been speaking Japanese exclusively, and the transition back to Portuguese was jarring. I remembered the priests at the small seminary administering punishments whenever I pronounced words wrong, but I also could not help but remember Valignano, later, teaching me Japanese and patiently correcting any mistakes. The Portuguese words now felt foreign in my mouth. I had to think while I spoke, and the discomfort of it made me feel I was on the defensive.

"We have been invited to oversee the completion of the church."

"Are you excited," Valignano said flatly, "to have a place to worship again?"

I looked into the face of the man who had given me away. "It will be a beautiful church, no doubt. I'm sure it will be well worth the price that it was purchased with."

Organtino looked down, but Valignano's expression didn't change. "Any price would be a small one. Any loyal servant of the church would agree."

His tone was questioning, feeling me out to see what level of loyalty he could still count on from me. I tried to give him nothing to read, but knowing Valignano's tactics did not necessarily protect me against them, and I looked away.

The blacksmith's shop was open to the street and I watched as he sharpened my spear, sparks leaping from its tip while he struck the flint against it. Beside him, an armorer was weaving together metal tabs half the size of a palm, running a thread through a hole in the corner to make a row, then threading the rows together to make a light, flexible chest plate. Another was smoothing a wooden stock that would be bored out and used for an arquebus, one that would be equal or better in quality to the weapons the Jesuits relied on so heavily for trade. If Valignano was surprised to see its construction, or had even taken notice of it, he showed no sign.

"The quality of the wood in Japan is excellent, and their eye for good stone is, I must say, unmatched. It did take some time to teach their craftsmen about the stained glass window, but they have taken to its design quite well. I do think it will be magnificent."

"A church that will look like a church, then," I said.

Valignano frowned in disapproval at my tone.

"A step forward. Churches built as shrines or temples were always meant as a beginning. A way to give comfort to those who are hesitant about receiving the Word. There is a difference between receiving the Word and accepting it, however. Accepting it requires shedding attachments to the old ways. I think many here are ready for that, don't you agree?"

"You have been successful in your travels, then?"

We stared at each other for a moment, Valignano half turned toward me, half away. He stroked his chin, considering, then turned fully toward the church before answering.

"Quite successful, yes. Many are eager to hear our message. As I've told you before, though, spreading that message requires resources. I have heard that Nobunaga has . . . concerns about our control of the port at Nagasaki."

"It seems your spies are well placed, as always."

Valignano shook his head, disgusted.

"I do not use *spies*. Nevertheless, you understand the importance of remaining well informed. Just as you understand the value of Nagasaki in advancing our mission here. Not just as a foothold, but as a source of funding for our activities. Surely someone who would control the whole country would not begrudge us this small thing?"

"Nothing you demand is ever a 'small thing.' You know quite well that I have seen armies fight over less."

"And is that what Nobunaga intends?"

"I do not speak for my lord."

"I do, speak for mine. And His Word cannot be ignored."

The blacksmith appeared behind me. "Your spear is ready."

He offered a short, crisp bow before reentering his shop, and Valignano smiled.

"It's good, that you are respected here. You have always been a good servant, and I trust that I have always treated you as such. I hope that you will continue to be helpful to us."

Valignano turned before I could respond, and after a brief, apologetic glance in my direction, Brother Organtino did the same. I felt locked as I watched them walk away, then released when they slipped from view.

23

I had never met a man of God before I'd been sold, first to mercenaries, then to the church. My people were farmers, traders, and craftsmen, but most of all miners. The men in our village visited the Msoro tree daily to leave gifts, and pray to God for the health of their families, for safe work in the mines and for good harvests, but otherwise religion was secondary in our lives.

The Portuguese priests who traded for me and named me enforced their beliefs on me in the way they thought best—namely long days of labor and martial punishments for any sign of transgression.

When word came that the seminary would be receiving an important visitor from Italy, the local priests went into a panic. For weeks leading up to Father Valignano's visit, the priests inspected every corner of the church grounds, handed out painful stripes for even the most minor of infractions. They bent their knees and lowered their heads before the shadow of this tall Italian visitor who everyone feared had even crossed the doorway.

After a meal of the finest meats and wines they had been able to secure, they sent the sons of nobles before Valignano for recitations, but he waved them off and gestured toward me.

"Who is this?"

The priests stiffened, exchanged glances. One stepped forward. "We named him Isaac. He's a—"

"A student, I assume," Valignano interrupted. "He wears the robes of one."

He gestured and I stepped forward to present myself.

"Do you know the catechisms?"

I gave them in Latin I knew to be flawless, and while Valignano did not react, I could feel the Portuguese priest rustling behind me, could feel the stare of the other students on my back. Valignano looked down at the roast chicken and potatoes and pie that remained laid out in front of him, but he seemed suddenly disinterested in them. A Portuguese priest cleared his throat, and I returned to my seat in the corner of the dining hall.

Later in that evening, I was called back to the hall. Valignano and three of the local priests were seated at a small table. I kneeled down before them.

"Have you given confession?"

"We had not thought it necessary . . ." one of the priests began.

"Does he not have a soul?" Father Valignano asked sharply. "Why do we send our missionaries out to the farthest reaches of the world if we don't believe the people we find there to be God's children?"

The priest offered no answer, other than the reddening of his face and the souring fear of his expression. I admired this man who commanded such respect, who could wound others with nothing but his disapproval.

"Leave us."

The priests scrambled out of the room, heads bowed and robes tucked up around them. The small gesture sparked a memory of my mother, tucking up her skirt and racing down the road to our village, the smile on her face incandescent. I pushed the memory away as quickly as it came.

"You have scars. Were they given to you here?"

I shook my head. "Before here. I was a soldier."

"You are not old enough to be a soldier," Valignano scoffed. When I didn't answer, he leaned forward, tilted my chin up with his hand, turned his head as if he were evaluating some new object he had discovered.

"Where?"

"In India. With the men who brought me here."

"You survived," he said, letting go of my chin. "You must have inflicted some scars as well. Did you kill men?"

I hesitated, nodded.

"You do know that is a mortal sin?"

I nodded again, braced myself for him to call for lashes, or worse. He leaned back in his chair.

"Let us call that your confession. It's not the proper way, but it will do for now."

A few days after my confession to Valignano at the Portuguese church, I had been told to pack my things. That I would be leaving with him.

"Does this mean my sins have been forgiven?"

"There is no need to forgive. You did what you had to do. How can something that is necessary be evil?"

I had nothing to pack, so I walked out of the Portuguese seminary in Valignano's wake, my hands empty and my back clothed in nothing but the scratchy wool robe of the novitiates. We'd stopped first at a tailor, and while he measured and cut, Valignano taught.

He told me that he had not come to Portugal looking for men, but for ships. The waters we were to sail to were known best to the navigators of the Portuguese, and of the Protestant Dutch. He told me that the seminary I'd been given to was the dumping ground for lesser sons of nobles. That first sons would be raised as heirs and second sons would be raised as protection against mishaps of the first, but that third and fourth and fifth sons were sent to seminaries and colleges, where they could bring merit to the family name without being burdensome on the family fortune.

He talked of his plans. How he believed those before him had failed by trying to force Christianity onto others without compromise. His vision was of a church that integrated the word of the Lord into the local customs and languages and mythologies, rather than demanding that they be abandoned. He would couch his religion inside of theirs. He would make enemies in this, he said. He would need protection.

I understood little of what he said at the time, and knew even less of how much of it to trust. I said nothing, only nodded when he seemed to need some bit of encouragement to continue. I liked him immediately.

When the tailor was done, Valignano inspected the new clothing.

"Make two more sets," he said. "One a size larger, and the other a size larger again from that. We have a long voyage ahead. He will grow."

THE JOURNEY FROM PORTUGAL TO Japan had been almost five years, with time spent in Goa and Macau along the way, both Portuguese-controlled ports in India and China respectively.

On the decks or in the galleys, Father Valignano taught me the history of Japan, the customs, the language. I had already learned Portuguese and a fair bit of Latin, but Japanese was much different than either. I struggled, and Valignano was patient.

His lessons extended to include European warfare, trade, and of course, the church, the latter two of which he considered to be intertwined.

"It is unfortunate to have to rely on such material concerns, but missions are expensive—new seminaries, schools, printing presses—the spreading of our word is not possible without them."

In Macau, Valignano was appalled to find that none of the priests had learned to speak Chinese, and wrote for the church's best linguists to be sent at once. In the streets there were bandits, some of whom had marked the priest as a target. They would attempt to shepherd us into a quiet area, or sometimes confront us in full view of crowds of people, knowing that they would not intervene. On such occasions I would step to Valignano's front, stand to my full height, and lock eyes with whichever bandit I thought was bravest. Sometimes there was violence. Other times they slunk away to try again with an easier mark.

In Goa, we walked through bazaars that reminded me of the one in which I had been first sold. There were stalls with pearls, coral, porcelain, velvet, peppers, and medicine, but most of all, spice. Great sands of it, in all colors and smells.

In the streets outside the bazaar, Africans and Indians were auctioned. They were pushed up onto a raised platform one by one to be displayed, some frightened, some confused, and I could not look at them without seeing myself there, in their place.

I watched the slaves paraded to and from the dock in Goa while Valignano stood beside me. I recognized the frailty and weariness of that long walk, the confusion of it, the submission after the hardships of a long journey, but also the terrifying spark of hope at that journey's end, the unquenchable hope that would only serve to deepen their misery. I could do nothing but lower my head to avoid meeting their eyes. After a few days of this, Father Valignano, without a word being said, began altering our routes, walking up to an hour out of our way to avoid the markets.

I thought him a friend.

24

At dinner that night, Nobunaga had an announcement.

"In the morning we ride east."

The words turned the usually relaxed dinner suddenly somber. Nobunaga continued.

"Tokugawa has flushed out the remains of the Takeda leadership and has them on the run. He believes they are heading for Tenmokuzan. We should be able to catch up with them quickly."

The brothers, Ogura and Jingorou, nodded in agreement. As usual, Ogura had his hair tied formally at the back of his head in a knot, while Jingorou allowed his hair to fall about his shoulders. Fresh planks were brought forward, with small plates of chestnuts, kelp, and abalone, and cups of sake. I remained silent.

"And news of the west?" Ogura asked. "How do our other generals fare in their campaigns?"

"Toyotomi makes good progress along the southern road, but the Mori have not yet been shaken out of their tree. On the northern road, Akechi is . . . stalled."

Jingorou sneered. "No surprise there. The wily mouse succeeds while the old man gets bogged down."

Ranmaru ignored him and continued.

"Akechi has been unsuccessful in his siege on Yakami Castle, but he has negotiated a surrender."

"He's still in Tanba Province?" Jingorou joked. "I bet if we look out the window we can still see his horse's tail."

"And what was the price of this surrender?" Ogura asked quietly.

"An exchange of hostages. Akechi has promised the safety of the Hatano to secure the surrender of Yakami Castle. Hatano Hideharu will come here to Azuchi, to serve our Lord Nobunaga. Akechi's mother will go to serve in the house of the Hatano clan."

The news was roundly greeted by scoffing. I could imagine the reaction of the guards when they heard the news, remembered them laughing that Toyotomi would fight his way west, and Akechi would progress west with begging.

"The man offers his mother as a hostage, when the Hatano have no chance of victory."

"By the time he catches up to Toyotomi, the man will have no family left."

"Maybe he was simply that eager to get rid of his mother, that he gave her up so quickly."

The brothers both laughed, but Ranmaru quickly silenced them.

"Let me remind you that Akechi is out in the field leading thousands of men, while you sit at our lord's table, comfortable, warm, and well fed. Save your laughter. You'll soon consider trading your own mother for a comfortable bed as well."

The men nodded, duly chastised. Nobunaga had not looked up from his bowl and did not seem to share Ranmaru's compassionate view of events. "I have recalled Akechi. The southern route is proving more promising, Toyotomi will draw the Mori out on his own. Diplomacy has its place, but Akechi pays too high a price for too small a prize. We will not meet the Mori with weakness. Akechi has new orders to bring his men east and meet up with ours. I've asked him to deliver the Hatano family here to Azuchi personally, then ride to meet us."

"Akechi will not be happy at being pulled from the western campaign."

"Akechi is loyal. I'm not concerned with his feelings on the matter, he has his orders."

The men mumbled in consent. Ranmaru turned toward me.

"And what is your trouble? You've been eager to see battle for weeks, and now that it is upon us, you look as sour as a lemon-taster. Has our giant gone frightened?"

He said it teasingly, and drew a little laughter from the men, though none of it harsh. When I did not reply, Nobunaga looked up from his bowl.

"All men speak freely here."

I swallowed my last mouthful and put down the plate and bowl.

"Are the Jesuits to remain here?"

"Does this bother you?"

I clenched my hands into fists, released them again. I did not know the answer. There was no reason for me to be angry, and no reason for me to be against their presence, but seeing them in the courtyard was another reminder that I had seen as allies those who saw me as property.

"I should have warned you they were coming," Nobunaga stated. It was the closest he would come to an apology in front of the men. "Nevertheless, the answer is yes. They will remain here. They are my guests, and will be treated as such by all."

"Of course," Ranmaru agreed. "I am curious myself, though, my lord—why do you entertain the priests when your own armorers have learned to make arquebuses of almost the same quality that the Portuguese offer?"

"The Jesuits have their uses besides their guns. Their ideas have spread, and it has managed to keep the Buddhist and Shinto priests . . . unsettled. They'll give us no more trouble if they have their full attention upon the Jesuits."

"Yet they hold our most critical trading port," Ranmaru ventured.

"All Japanese land will come under our banner, whether it is currently held by foreigners or our own. For now we have other enemies to deal with."

"Are they enemies, then?" Ogura asked quietly.

All eyes turned to me, and I thought on it a moment. I tried to separate out my personal feelings to give the truest answer.

"Valignano does not consider any man his enemy. But he does have objectives, and he always believes himself in the right of things. He can be . . . determined."

The others nodded, contemplating.

"It might not be a good thing to allow their ideas to spread too far," Ranmaru pushed.

Nobunaga bristled, answered sharply.

"They will not. I will see to that."

After a few moments of tense silence, Nobunaga turned to speak to me directly.

"You asked, once, about the story of the Mongol invasion and the Divine Wind. Why I chose that story on the night you were brought before me. I will tell you. Tokugawa told you the story of the battle of Okehazama, did he not?"

I nodded.

"The forces of the Imagawa clan outnumbered ours twelve to one. There was no reason whatsoever for me to ride out against him, but one—*I believed*. I believed we would win, regardless of the odds. The Imagawa clan, fat off their early victories, were camped in a ravine that I had played in as a boy. A ravine that I knew like the back of my hand. I took that as a sign.

"Along the way, I stopped at Atsuta Shrine. While Imagawa Yoshimoto drank sake and viewed the heads of our fallen clan members, I prayed. And after I prayed, I rode, hard. By the time we reached the mouth of the ravine, Imagawa's men were tired or drunk or both, but still, there were too many of them. Still, we needed a miracle. And we received one.

"The skies opened up and sheets of rain came down so hard that you could not see more than a few feet in front of your face. We used that storm to ride right up to the edge of their camp. The first they knew of us being there was when they felt our arrows in their bellies, our spears in their necks. They scrambled, broke, and scattered, and we rode over their remnants. The storm came just when we needed it, and broke as soon as we needed it no longer. You heard the story of the Mongol invasion and took it as one of Japan's forces being overwhelmed by foreign invaders. I hear it as one where Japan fights in its own defense. As it fought for our clan, sending a storm raging upon the Imagawa on the night we faced our most dire threat.

"When I choose to believe something, that belief is unshakable. I believe in every man here, and I believe in you. You are one of my samurai now, Yasuke. Father Valignano may view you as something to be traded, but I do not."

The men all nodded and lifted their cups toward me. I lifted mine as well.

"To our Lord Nobunaga."

We drank.

"Tenka fubu," Ogura said softly as he placed his cup back onto the tray. The words were repeated in turn by each man present.

"Tenka fubu," I offered, going last.

The realm under one sword.

"Finish your meals," Nobunaga said. "Visit your families, see to your households. Tomorrow we ride for war."

III

Tenka Fubu

Tokugawa:

Little Bird, if you do not sing, I will wait for you

Toyotomi:

Little Bird, if you do not sing, I will make you sing

Oda:

Little Bird, if you do not sing, I will kill you

—Japanese proverb of the Three Great Unifiers

25

I dreamt of laying beneath the stars, after the long march from my village to the coast. The lumbering sea turtles had buried their eggs and returned to the sea, leaving almost no trace of themselves behind.

We would walk out onto that beach soon with our baskets, digging up the places we'd marked, collecting what eggs we needed and leaving the rest, but for now we were content to sit or lie amongst the thin reeds at the beach's edge.

I was full-grown, but my mother beside me was the age I remembered her being. I started to tell her stories of where I'd been, what I'd seen. The fragrant markets of India, the spiraling churches of Portugal, the vibrantly packed streets of China. The quiet dignity of Nobunaga's reception hall at Honno-ji, the glittering gold leaf keep atop Azuchi Castle.

She said nothing. She was staring upward, her fingers connecting the stars to trace pictures in the sky. I was content to lay back and watch her.

The stars were countless, shining brightly against bands of green and purple in the night sky. The sand beneath my back vibrated and I slowly sank down into it, amongst the just laid eggs. I could feel the warmth of my parents as they lay beside me. But I could also feel the pull of the sea.

IT WAS GOOD TO BE away. In the weeks leading up to our march east, the ranks at Azuchi had swelled. Soldiers and samurai from smaller cities and rural areas had been called to arms, and with the increase in men came additional enterprising merchants, courtesans, masseuses. It had become a dangerous mix. The rural men had the same code of honor, but not the same manners, nor the same respect for the customs of the court.

Men restless for war have a tendency to find their own battles. Fights broke out over women, over gambling debts, over insults both real and perceived. The citizens of Azuchi learned to stay off the streets in the evening. By law, a samurai could strike down a commoner over any slight or show of disrespect, without any consequence. These rough village men, called to war, their blood up, did not hesitate to do so and took offense far too eagerly. The only thing keeping the town from exploding entirely, the only universal law of Azuchi, was fear of Oda Nobunaga.

Once, a short, bearded, and seemingly quite drunk samurai shouted something at me in the street that I did not recognize. He moved toward me and sneered and shouted again, and though I did not know the words, his intention was clear. His hand was already on his blade when two of his companions grabbed him, whispered to him, then bowed and apologized profusely while escorting him away.

Even in the faraway towns, word had reached ears of the giant Black samurai who had wrestled ten of Oda's strongest men, and now rode daily with Nobunaga and had been taken into his inner circle. No man in Oda's service would dare challenge me.

I told the story of the drunken samurai to Ranmaru, Ogura, and Jingorou as we readied our horses and waited on our orders to ride. Jingorou laughed.

"I would not repeat that story to Lord Nobunaga. He would have the man found and have his head removed, then have a spike through it. Or have a spike put through it, then have it removed. Sometimes it's one way, sometimes the other."

"The words he said to me—what do they mean?"

"They mean there are drunkards everywhere. I'm sure you have them in Africa. I've seen with my own eyes that you have them amongst the Portuguese."

I finished saddling my horse and let the matter go.

"I would not mention it further, though," offered Ogura. "Unless you truly do want to see the man dead."

I swung up onto my horse and grunted. "If I had wanted him dead, I would have done the job myself."

"Ah yes," Ranmaru joked. "Yasuke, the feared black giant. Except no one has seen you fight for real, have they? I hope you won't turn coward when the battle starts."

"Keep talking, Ranmaru, and you'll not live to see the battle."

"Ha," scoffed Ranmaru. "No enemy will take my head, and no friend of mine will either."

"No enemy *would* take your head," I retorted. "Their master would mistake it for that of a woman's and punish them."

We laughed and spurred our horses toward the gate. Sixty thousand men waited at the bottom of the mountain or somewhere along our march to join us. Far more than would be needed if the reports of Tokugawa's success were true, but Nobunaga had a streak of showmanship in him. It also made sense to give some of the less experienced men a taste of battle here, in advance of an anticipated march west to join Toyotomi when the time came.

I'd gone to see Tomiko before leaving Azuchi. I approached her in the castle and asked if I could talk with her later. I met her at the steps at night, accompanied her on her walk down to the village.

"I'll be marching east tomorrow."

If there was any reaction from her at the news that I would be pursuing Takeda instead of Mori, I could not read it in the darkness, and I felt foolish for having thought it would matter to her.

"I wish you success," she replied. "And victory."

We continued down the path, through the town, and out toward the docks, where the shacks of the head-cleaners stood. I stood in the doorway, watching Tomiko lift the heads, carefully examining each one.

I'd let them know that they were loved.

That had been her answer when I asked what she would do if she found the heads of her brother and father amongst the dead, and with those simple words I realized the gaping wound my world had centered around. I'd been valued, even respected at times, but never loved. Not since the day I climbed out of the ore-stripped cave the final time and into the light of a different sun, my village ravaged, my mother dead, my father forever lost to me.

"My father . . ." I began slowly, talking to myself as much as to Tomiko. "I'll never see him again. I'll never know . . ."

Tomiko looked up at me, pausing the search for her father's head, and I wondered which was more difficult—knowing the worst had happened, or not knowing what happened at all.

"I would have been a miner," I said, words rushing out of me. "I never had my father's wanderlust. He loved us, but too long in the village and he would start to become distant, vacant. I yearned for people, not for places. For my family. Instead of lighting incense at the Jesuit altars, I would have brought gifts each day to lay at the base of the Msoro tree; instead of kneeling in the Jesuit pews, I would have sat with my people in the M'Mwera hut; instead of learning a false history from the Jesuit priests, I would have learned the ways of my people from the mwene. I would have married. Would have had a child to lift into the arms of my mother and father, to ask for their blessing."

Tomiko placed the head she was holding back onto the pile with reverent care, giving me her full attention. I watched her hands, dainty amongst the dead, blessing each victim with the graceful dignity of her touch, and I realized why I had sought her out. All of my separations had been sudden ones—from my family when I was taken, from the others of my village at the dock in India, from the old Lomwe-speaking slave who tried to help me, from Valignano when he sold me at Honno-ji. I looked down at my own hands, scarred and thick and dangerous. In the end, we all just want someone to say goodbye to.

OUR PASSAGE WAS SWIFT AND smooth. We crossed the flatlands outside of Azuchi, then through the low mountain passes toward Gifu Castle,

Nobunaga's former stronghold before the completion of construction at Azuchi.

We made Gifu before dusk, and even low in the mountains the air chilled quickly once the sun went down. There was a light covering of snow on the ground. Though I had seen snow before, I had seen it seldom enough that I still marveled at it. Even my father, in all his travels, had not brought back tales of snow and ice and biting cold winds.

As I had in my early days of slavery, I tried to see it through my father's eyes, then relay it to my mother in my father's words. He would have described how the cold would reach deep inside you, causing you to hunch and shiver in an attempt to expel it from your skin and blood and lungs. How you would move closer to the people around you to steal a bit of their warmth. The dry, white plume of your own breath in front of you, the air in your lungs turned to crystals hung in the air.

As a child I thought my father had seen the whole world, but I exhaled and stared, and wondered at all the small discoveries that the world still held. I wished I could share them, with both my mother and my father.

At Gifu Castle, we met up with Akechi's forces. When Akechi was presented to Nobunaga, his son-in-law Hidemitsu accompanied him. I stood behind Nobunaga and watched Hidemitsu's face, the badly broken nose flattened across his right cheek. He stood to Akechi's right. He bowed low to Nobunaga, then kept his gaze forward.

Akechi bowed his greeting to Nobunaga as well, then spared a glance at the two swords which I now wore in my sash, a new development since last he'd seen me. It was the first time I'd seen Akechi up close since my introduction to Nobunaga at the Honno-ji temple. His face was wrinkled and had the early signs of spotting. The top of his head was shaved smooth and the gray hair at the side, stretched and tied into a knot behind him, was thinning. He appraised me coolly, and met my eyes only briefly. I bowed, and he returned the bow in acknowledgment, but lowering his head only low enough that insult could not be taken and respect was not certain.

"Lord Hatano Hideharu and his family have been delivered to Azuchi Castle. They are resting comfortably in one of your guest houses. He sends his deepest gratitude. Yakami Castle is yours, my lord."

Nobunaga bowed slightly in acceptance and Akechi was dismissed, shooting another pointed glance in my direction before leaving. Hidemitsu turned and followed, never having looked my way.

From Gifu we rode quickly over easy terrain to Inuyama Castle, deep in the Oda home province of Owari. I tried to picture my lord here as a young man, riding amongst the low hills and valleys, but I could not reconcile the confident, ambitious, detail-oriented leader of the Oda clan with the irresponsible and disrespectful Fool of Owari he had claimed to have once been.

From there we turned north, crossing out of Owari, through the forests and into the foothills of the mountains. We began to see the evidence of Tokugawa's efficiency. Bodies laid alongside the road, bloated and picked at by fat crows, their satiated cawing echoing along the lower cliffs. Only a few houses still stood. The others, as well as temples and any official buildings, were left in smoldering ruins. In a few of the homes, walls torn down and open to the elements, the same scene played out—the bodies of women and children lined up neatly with their throats slashed and a man in formal robes pitched forward on a tatami mat, his forehead to the ground.

"Loyal men," Ranmaru said, riding beside me. "Takeda samurai who refused to serve Oda. Seeing so many tells of Tokugawa's reputation, they knew not to fight and chose seppuku instead."

I looked at the scenes as we rode by, the bodies dusted with snowfall, the blood frozen and near black. I could not see the short blade in the bellies of the fallen men, but I knew the rites of seppuku, plunging the knife into your bowels, then bringing it up and across if you could maintain your faculties long enough to do so. In formal settings, one committing seppuku would nominate a trusted person to serve as their second, and the second would sever their head once the sword had been plunged into the belly, a mercifully quick ending. These men had not had that luxury. They had slit the throats of their wives and children, disemboweled themselves, then died slowly and painfully with their faces on the floor.

Other than the loyal samurai and the soldiers who had clearly been cut down in battle, there were few other bodies.

"Should there be more?"

"You have a keen eye." Ranmaru winked at me. "It seems more men surrendered than fought. It's not surprising—Takeda Katsuyori has always proven a poor comparison to his father. The Oda and Takeda have a long history together, generations of feuding. Under Takeda Shingen, their clan often held the upper hand against the Oda. When Lord Shingen died, his son Katsuyori took the reins. Katsuyori sought to prove himself with a victory against the Oda, but Lord Nobunaga's forces routed the Takeda at Nagashino, and they have never recovered."

I watched Nobunaga, but there was no reaction. He stayed focused on the road ahead of us, sometimes lifting his head to look at the mountains, or squint at a treetop, but I knew that as always, he was listening. Ranmaru continued.

"Katsuyori has tried to revive his clan's fortunes with high taxes, and maintain his loosening grip on leadership with heavy punishments for even minor offenses. He has grown ever less popular amongst his own, so it is no surprise to see his people turn to us."

Almost as if summoned, we caught up to a crew of former Takeda. They'd been left under the command of one of Tokugawa's men, clearing the road ahead of us of snow and bodies, making it easier for us to pass. Tokugawa's man bowed to Nobunaga and the captives quickly did so as well, then returned to their work, largely ignoring the Oda army as they lifted and shoveled and swept.

Despite their efforts, and the presence of other such work parties further up along our path, our progress slowed. The temperature dropped even further as we climbed, and the snowfall was thicker. The horses clumped together. The road beneath us turned to muck with the melting snow and heavy traffic. Servants rode ahead to set the field tents for the night's camp, so that they would be ready when we reached them.

We camped in the evening in an opening on the mountainside. The Oda-emblemed wind-blocks that had been set up around the camp rippled and popped, and I felt for the men who had to stand outside them to serve watch. Groomsmen cleaned and fed and watered the horses by torchlight. Servants made bowls of hot soup and rice for the small company that had rode with Nobunaga; the others had to settle for cold fish and a bit of fruit.

A messenger arrived. He was greeted with a bowl of steaming soup and brought to Nobunaga's tent immediately. Nobunaga, Ranmaru, the brothers, and I, plus a half dozen of Nobunaga's trusted samurai, sat in a circle and waited for the messenger to warm himself.

"We've yet to engage Katsuyori, but we have him pinned down. He has—"

"No." Nobunaga raised a hand and the messenger immediately kneeled and put his face to the ground. "Tell me from the beginning."

The messenger lifted his head, bowed it again in a slight nod, and restarted.

"He fled immediately to Shinpu Castle. He left three thousand men at Takato Castle to cover his retreat. We considered marching past Takato altogether, but did not want to leave ourselves open to attack from the rear, or to leave our line of supply vulnerable. There is only one road into Takato Castle, the other three sides are guarded by steep cliffs . . ."

The messenger must have seen something in Nobunaga's expression, realized that he did not need to describe Takato Castle's challenges to his warlord. The messenger cleared his throat.

"A handful of men volunteered to ford the river. They took the guards at night and opened the road for our forces."

I was not familiar with Takato Castle, but I could imagine the risk involved in the mission. Waters in the narrow passes of the high canyons would be raging, and frigid. There would be no safe way across. Crossing them at night, beneath the eye of an enemy force, was a feat of extreme courage and loyalty.

"Who did the Takeda leave in command at Takato?"

"Lady Suwa. She fought bravely, but once we were inside the walls there was little they could do. Nevertheless, Tokugawa was impressed. He allowed her to take her own life."

Nobunaga nodded his approval. Ranmaru spoke up.

"I could see smoke. From Shinpu?"

"Hmm, most likely," Nobunaga said, considering. "Katsuyori depended on his mountains as a defense, not his castles. Our spies tell us Shinpu was built more for luxury than for repelling an attack. If Katsuyori received word that Takato had fallen, he would know Shinpu could not hold."

"It's true," the messenger said, clearly nervous now. "But there is something else. We've captured men from Shinpu, questioned them. Katsuyori ordered the other nobles locked inside the buildings before he burned the castle and the surrounding city."

"What kind of coward . . ." Jingorou started angrily, before holding his tongue and his rage from further expression.

The room fell silent. Tokugawa's childhood as a hostage of the Imagawa clan was not unusual. It was customary to seal alliances by sending a family member to live with another clan, much as Akechi had recently sent his mother to live with the Hatano clan in exchange for surrendering the castle. Perhaps Katsuyori was angered at the betrayals that had occurred along Tokugawa's march to his capital, but regardless, a lord of Takeda's stature would have dozens of children or wives or mothers or sisters of noble families living under his protection. Burning them alive would be an irreproachable breach.

It was a final, desperate, and deplorable act, and a sign that Takeda Katsuyori viewed defeat as inevitable. He had broken every one of his alliances, and no family, no matter how minor, would pledge fealty to him after such an act.

All eyes rested on Nobunaga, and none dared speak.

"But you know where he is now?"

"Yes, my lord."

"And there is no more hope of fleeing?"

"We have him surrounded. We are awaiting your order."

"Then tomorrow we will end the Takeda clan."

Nobunaga's face, as always, gave nothing away. He rose and left the tent, walking out into the cold of night.

WE SLEPT FOR A FEW hours, then rode in the night. We met up with Tokugawa's forces just before dawn on a ridge opposite Mount Tenmoku. In the foothills, nestled in the mountain's base, we could see a compound that had been hastily fortified—sharpened logs nailed across each other in an X pattern to form palisades in two rows, one for initial defense and one as a fall-back position; thatched shooting blinds woven tightly together, with cutouts for archers. A woefully small number of Takeda battle standards were planted out front, waving listlessly in the weak breeze.

"They ran for Iwadono."

Tokugawa's jaw settled into the fleshiness of his throat and his voice hitched with a shortness of breath that was new, but his eyes remained sharp, his aura of command undiminished.

"They were refused there. Oyamada Nobushige is lord at Iwadono, and he has come over to our side, after hearing of the burning at Shinpu. None of their other castles are within reach. We have them encircled. We can line the arquebuses here"—he pointed to a line of trees to the west of the compound—"but it will be difficult to line up rows of men to maintain a continuous volley, so once we shoot, they will charge while the men reload. If we can draw them out—"

"We won't need to." Nobunaga's eyes were on the compound, not on Tokugawa. "His vassals have turned. Those left in the compound will be the most loyal of his men, those who would gladly lay down their lives for him."

Nobunaga turned back to address the impromptu war council.

"They will know they cannot win, and that they cannot hold. They will try to punch a hole through our line for Katsuyori to flee through. It's the only thing they have left to fight for."

Nobunaga pointed to the gap between the palisades. "They'll make their stand here. It's narrow enough to reduce the advantage of our numbers, and the tree line is dense enough there to protect their flank from a cavalry charge. We'll line our arquebus in front. Two lines. Single volley each. When they charge, our cavalry will be in behind. I'd rather have them on the open field, but better to meet them here in the pass than to leave them behind their walls.

"No one other than the forward line is to advance. The men stationed around the compound are to hold their positions and ensure no one gets through. Your lines are solid?"

Tokugawa nodded. "There are no gaps, my lord. A mouse cannot escape us."

"Relay the orders."

The meeting broke, and the commanders went their separate ways. Nobunaga glanced at me.

"Are you rested?"

"I always sleep well the night before a battle. I'd rather rest my head upon stones than upon feathers."

"I'll be sure to take away your bed, then, when we return." Nobunaga smiled, then flattened the smile, looked sternly at me. "Make your name. Today, and every day forward. You are samurai. Be feared."

Though I'd often been tempted, I had resisted putting on my full armor since it had been presented to me at Masahide-ji. I had cleaned it, cared for it, inspected every tab and latch and lace, but I had not worn it. Armor was meant for battle, and the act of dressing in it now, for the first time since then, helped set the focus of my mind. While I tied the greaves and tightened everything into place, I remembered my first battle. Barely thirteen, a young slave facing off against three Ottoman soldiers in full regalia. Even then I'd been calm, once the initial bolt of panic had passed. War had never made me nervous. It was the place I was most comfortable. It was the one place where I had been every man's equal from the beginning.

The camp was nearly silent as men prepared for war. They cleaned and re-saddled their horses, inspected their arrows, dried their gunpowder in case it had become damp from the snow. They smoked their armor over low fires to rid it of lice or other insects. Busy work, to occupy their minds, or routine to assist them in focus. When the men had prepared themselves and gathered in their ordered formations, Nobunaga addressed them briefly.

"Does the Oda standard not fly in the capital? Our enemy will fall before us as our enemies always do. I began with a force of two thousand men against an army of twenty-four thousand. Now I bring a force of sixty thousand against less than a thousand. But battles are not won by the side with the most men, battles are won by the side with the most warriors! I would rather attack with six hundred brave men than sixty thousand uncertain ones. And so I tell you this—if your life is so precious to you that you are unwilling to lay it down, leave here now. If you stay, know this—whether your last breath is drawn as a young man at war or as an old man in his bed, death awaits every man. But honor and glory do not. Honor and glory await only the brave!"

The men cheered and we lined up across the pass. Our hands and feet were tight with cold and we stuck our fingers beneath our armor to keep them from stiffening before battle. Our breath curled in front of us in white mists and stopped, as if pressed against something, and disappeared. The arquebus line was sent forward.

I could feel the armor plating flex around my muscles with every slight movement—smooth and comfortable, unlike the bulky metal plates the Portuguese and other Europeans had favored. It felt like a part of me. It felt like it was meant for me. I tied my helmet on, felt the slight forward weight of the carved wooden rhinoceros horn.

I glanced at Nobunaga, encouraging the men, then to Ranmaru beside me, along with Ogura and Jingorou. I'd fought for survival, I'd fought for empires, and I'd fought for no other reason than it was what I was told to do. Never before had I fought to be a part of something.

The Takeda standards waved in the wind, and their archers came forward to the palisades, the sun glinting off their crimson-painted chest plates. I tested the grip of my sword, and the feel of it in my hand was natural. I waited for the signal.

26

The beginning of anything is sudden.

A near-synchronous series of pops from the kneeling arquebusiers, the cloud of smoke that accompanied them. Then men stood and took a step back and the second row of arquebusiers stepped forward, knelt, and fired. Two lines, single volley each. A pause.

The smoke from the rifle shot swirled in the twisting mountain winds, then parted, revealing a single Takeda soldier in bloodred armor waving a battle standard, then another, and another. A hail of arrows launched from behind the palisades and woven blinds. The arquebusiers withdrew and our horsemen drove forward. With a shout, the battle was engaged.

The Takeda arrows continued to fly, no matter that they were as likely to strike their own men as ours. Nobunaga had been right. Their goal wasn't victory, it was to create confusion. The Takeda mostly stayed behind their first-line palisades, using the long-poled yari spears to stab at our horsemen or the curved naginata to hook them and draw them to the ground. A few battle-crazed soldiers rushed out from behind their protection, blades drawn, and were swiftly cut down or simply ridden over.

My horse twitched beneath me, as eager to join the fray as I was.

"Wait." Ranmaru gestured beside me. "You are not a foot soldier. We will strike where we are needed, when we are needed."

The Takeda held but they had only a single line of defenders, while we could send wave after wave of attackers descending upon them. Divisions of men cycled through the attacks, signaled on when to attack and when to withdraw through a complicated sequence of flag-waving. The Takeda fought and held, but they were clearly tiring as the sun shifted from morning toward afternoon. Nobunaga watched from a wooden dais that had been constructed overnight for this specific purpose.

"Does he fight?" I asked Ranmaru.

"Only when necessary. But when he does, it is something to see. I hope that you will live up to his standard."

I was about to reply when the expression on Ranmaru's face suddenly changed. He pointed to the west side of the compound.

"There. They've almost breached. Come."

He checked with Nobunaga, who gave the slightest of nods, then rode, leaving myself and the rest of Nobunaga's guards to follow.

We circled to the flank and climbed. We'd left behind the mud and snow of the trail and galloped across bare rock. There were twelve of us, and Ranmaru led us through the treacherous tree-line ride as if he had memorized the placement of every branch, every stone. We came to rest a few hundred yards above the compound, on its western side.

"The downhill ride is too steep. We'll leave the horses."

We dismounted. The others pulled their face plates into place, and the men I had known and rode with were replaced by the faces of demons. Blank, soulless eyes with etched scowls and twisting brows. I had no need of one. The deep black skin of my face would look as otherworldly and supernatural to our foe as any of the meticulously detailed metal creations.

We descended as quickly as the footing would allow. The numbers here were even, with our forces being unable to shift significant numbers of men through the terrain to this location. Nevertheless, a hole had been broken open in the Takeda palisades and the fighting was fierce where our men were attempting to force their way through.

Their horses had been abandoned for the same reasons as we had abandoned our own. Some of the horses were running free along the lines, hindering both sides. Others had fallen in battle and lay on their sides with arrows and spears protruding from their stomachs. Smoke filled the air from a series of small fires.

A Takeda soldier lunged at me from the side and I grabbed his spear instinctively, then twisted my grip and snapped the pole of it in half. His eyes went wide and I drew my katana, slashing down across his chest. The blade moved through leather armor and flesh with little more resistance than a pool of water.

Ranmaru cut through soldiers with an almost supernatural ease, and Ogura and Jingorou moved in unison, alternately attacking and defending in flawless precision.

We formed a loose wedge and pushed forward. I towered over the Takeda soldiers as they rushed me, my reach with my sword almost as long as their reach with their spears and naginatas. They screamed as they fell and bled out onto the rocks and snow.

A calm came over me, as it often did in battle. A calm that comes with knowing you have a single task, that every other thing can be blocked out or is unimportant. The battle becomes the only thing, and there is something in that which has always been soothing to me.

An arrow caught underneath my shoulder plate, but didn't break the skin. Others bounced off my armor, my helmet, launched from too great a distance to pierce. I cut down men, three, four at a time. I fought like the Japanese fought—balanced, controlled, moving only with purpose. The flow came as naturally to me as the brutish rage and power had come to me before. The Takeda soldiers were boys placed in front of me in my Indian master's courtyard, faceless, nameless. Boys who died so I could live.

I stepped over bodies of the fallen until there were no more bodies to step over. The path to the veranda on the western edge of the compound was clear. As we approached, two men rushed out at us wearing kimonos and waving bamboo poles, no armor, no weapons. They were servants, not soldiers, and we stayed ourselves to let them go. We brushed them aside and stepped into the outermost chamber.

A large blue tatami mat covered most of the floor, a lit brazier set on each of its four corners. On the mat, the bodies of three children and one woman were lined up in a row, their throats cut, and one man, bowled over forward, his sword in his bowels. It mimicked the scene we had seen in the burnt-out homes along the road—kill your wife and children, then kill yourself through the ritual seppuku.

The bodies had been placed carefully, lovingly. The faces of the family, drained, were the color of bone. Their eyes were closed but they looked somehow serene. Their hands folded across their chest, the woman holding a small scrip of canvas in hers.

I teased it from her final grasp, careful not to disturb the body.

> *My black hair is disheveled,*
> *this world without end,*
> *as fragile as a chain of dew drops*
> *Returning goose,*
> *won't you carry these few words,*
> *to my old home of Sagami*

I folded the paper back up and placed it again within her still fingers.

Ranmaru lifted his face plate, no longer a demon. He stepped forward and grasped the topknot on the back of the man's head and lifted, revealing the face.

"It's Katsuyori."

None had stayed behind to serve as his second. To relieve him from a slow and agonizing death. Seppuku without a second was a prospect one would not wish on an enemy. Not just the lingering, painful fade into darkness, but the loneliness of it, and the utter totality of defeat it indicated.

Katsuyori jerked suddenly to life, gurgling and choking violently, spitting blood onto the already purpling tatami. The eyes flickered and rolled, but were unfocused.

Ranmaru released his hair and leapt backward in surprise. I acted instinctively, drawing my katana and performing the task that a loyal Takeda servant should have. Katsuyori's head rolled once, then wobbled, coming to rest with the open eyes looking up at the thatched roof of the chamber.

Ranmaru looked first at me, then at the soldiers who had gathered on the veranda behind us. He nodded at them. One of the soldiers ran out to secure the Oda flags, and to signal our victory.

The battle was over.

27

The battle had ended almost immediately, with the remaining Take-da soldiers either surrendering, or following their lord's example and committing seppuku where they stood, on the field of battle. The wounded were tended to, the healthy collected their trophies, the compound was first searched then burned.

The attendants began working on the heads immediately, cleaning and preparing them. Usually they had a day or more to work, but Nobunaga wanted to be on his way. That evening, a handful of samurai and foot soldiers lined up outside of Nobunaga's tent, carrying lacquered wooden boxes so they could make their offerings and be honored.

Nobunaga knew the head by how it was brought to him.

Katsuyori's head was in a noticeably larger box, painted blue and carried into the tent by two servants. It was an honor reserved for the daimyo—only the head of a clan leader would be carried by two people. The servants set the box on the ground before the stool Nobunaga sat on. They opened the latch and pulled the lid open, their movements carefully coordinated. The head was on a simple pine board, and the servants each grabbed one end of the board, lifting the head out of the box. A third servant set two small sakes beside the head, both in ornately patterned ceramic cups.

Nobunaga rose.

"The Takeda have fallen."

It was only a whisper, something meant not to be heard. I looked at Ranmaru, scanned the faces of the others in the room, but could read nothing. This was the Oda clan's oldest enemy, and the last of them now rested defeated in front of Nobunaga. A complex series of emotions flickered over his face, as if he were trying each of them on to see which one fit best for the moment. I flicked back and forth from Nobunaga, to Akechi Mitsuhide and his son-in-law Hidemitsu, seated against the wall, but neither of the latter two men would even glance at me.

The preparers had done their job well. They'd carefully rinsed the blood from the Takeda lord's hair, then brushed it straight and tied it tightly into a formal knot. They'd wiped his face clean, pulled the muscles of his face to set a neutral expression, then powdered his face white. They'd blackened the teeth, per custom, and left the mouth just slightly ajar. I tried to imagine Tomiko performing this task for her father and brother. Her hands delicate, each step executed with great care.

Katsuyori looked lifelike enough as if he might speak. Instead it was Nobunaga who spoke, addressing the head.

"Your father once had plans for Kyoto. To march there, to plant his flag in the capital and claim himself the ruler of all Japan. He would have to march through Owari to do it, but he saw that as a minor obstacle. Like the Imagawa before him, he'd thought the road to Kyoto would involve a swift victory over Owari along the way. A victory over my lands. Over my people."

A few of the samurai seated along the back of the tent shifted as Nobunaga's voice rose. Akechi looked disturbed, Hidemitsu beside him, uncertain. The head-viewing ceremony was meant to be civil and respectful, bordering on religious. The conquering daimyo would praise the courage of the defeated, promise to care for his people and his lands, then toast his passing with a cup of sake. Instead, Nobunaga's face had settled into a mask of rage.

"My lord . . ." Ranmaru ventured tentatively.

Nobunaga ignored him and continued, haranguing the fallen daimyo.

"When your father fell, I'm sure he harbored dreams that you would do what he could not. That you would march for Kyoto at the head of the Takeda clan, your banners flying proudly. But I am not one to be walked on. The Oda clan was never respected. Not by you, not by the Imagawa, not by any of the greater clans. You will all respect the Oda soon. And I will see to it that you make it to Kyoto, young Katsuyori. You have brought shame to all of your ancestors with your burning of Shinpu Castle. I will send your head to the capital to be displayed in front of the imperial courts. I will stuff your mouth with plum blossoms for the beetles to feed on. I will brush your eyes with honey so the flies eat them out of your skull and leave the sockets full with their maggots. Women and children will turn away. All who look upon the head of Takeda Katsuyori will be filled with revulsion. This is how you will be remembered."

Nobunaga lifted the cup of sake and threw it in the dead daimyo's face. There was perfect silence inside the tent. The servants who had brought the head in were openly horrified. The samurai, other than Ranmaru, stayed still but were visibly uncomfortable. Ranmaru stood hesitantly, halfway between reaching for Nobunaga and returning to his seat.

The syrupy sake dripped thickly off Katsuyori's face, creating a few streaks in the white paint. Though the muscles in the face had not moved, the expression of the daimyo seemed to have shifted from neutral to suitably shocked.

"Get out."

I had never witnessed a head-viewing before. My familiarity of the custom came only from what Valignano had taught me on the long voyage over, and so I alone amongst those in the room was not in some state of disbelief. I stood and turned to exit, following Nobunaga's order. My movement seemed to break the spell, and others began rising as well, suddenly eager to leave. Akechi was the last to leave, rising slowly to his feet, throwing a dangerous look in Nobunaga's direction. If Nobunaga noticed, he did not react.

As we pulled aside the flaps of the tent, the servants were called back. "Prepare the head for Kyoto. Let it be seen by everyone."

I WAS BONE-TIRED, BUT IT was still much too early for sleep. As quiet as the camp had been in the morning, it was loud now with celebrations. The other samurai were shaken by Nobunaga's behavior.

"Come," I said. "Let's join the men."

We selected one of the larger and louder campfires, and when we approached, all stopped and stood and bowed. I had started to grow accustomed to the honor, but at certain times it still affected me. A slave being shown esteem from a people who revere honor above all else.

"Relax, we're here to drink."

A cheer went up. Drinks were poured and passed.

"It is a bad omen," Jingorou mumbled as he hunched over his cup.

"Perhaps. But it is a good strategy," said Ranmaru, somewhat unconvincingly. "The people don't care who rules them, they merely want peace. They want to farm their lands without being called to fight, to sell their crops knowing their taxes will not be raised to cover the cost of war. Let the people see Takeda Katsuyori's head. Let them see that Oda Nobunaga has brought them one step closer to the end of a war that started before their grandparents were young."

"It's not the showing I object to, it's the treatment."

"Then feel free to object to Lord Nobunaga."

That seemed to bring the discussion to an end. I lifted my cup and signaled for more. I slapped one of the soldiers on the back and passed him more sake.

"If you're looking for better omens, look for them at the bottom of a cup."

The men laughed, tentatively, then more fully and naturally. They lifted their cups and cheered.

"To victory."

28

The next day we marched north, into the mountains, for Takato Castle. While I and the other members of Nobunaga's inner circle had mostly been able to sleep in vacated temples or large houses, the majority of the men had slept on the ground, with only sheaths of hastily bound hay to protect them against the cold and the wind. Nobunaga wanted to give them a night's sleep indoors before releasing them to return to Azuchi, or in the case of the soldiers who had gathered from the surrounding regions, their families and homes.

The ruins of the homes and buildings in the town at the foothills of the path to Takato were charred black and dusted with snow. The dead had mostly been cleared out and piled, but the evidence of them had not—the half-burnt walls provided a look into rooms where shelves were still decorated with paintings or family mementos, where tables were still set with frost-rimmed plates and cups that had cracked slightly in the cold.

The castle had also been cleaned, and had survived in much better condition, but if you looked closely enough you could see marks on the walls where swords had struck, or the occasional puckered divot from which an arrow had been pulled.

In the main reception room, Nobunaga's servants had carefully crafted a grand dinner. The castle had been taken swiftly, so its stores and pantries had remained fully stocked with fine delicacies. After dinner came the main business of divvying up the spoils. All nobles, generals, samurai, and men of rank were gathered in the reception room. The tables were carried out and we knelt along the side of each wall while Nobunaga called men forward to honor them.

Tokugawa was rewarded most handsomely of all, being granted control of the whole of the province of Suruga, the region south of Mount Fuji. Akechi was granted a parcel of land as well, and I tracked his movements after accepting the honor, watched him return to his men. He turned and caught me looking, stared blankly back at me until I broke the contact, nodded my head.

Others who had distinguished themselves were granted smaller fiefs and castles. As the names were called and the men accepted their gifts, Ranmaru, who himself had been granted two small fiefs to add to his others, whispered to me.

"It's said you'll be made tono soon, and granted your own fief."

I shrugged off his comment, but it was not the first I had heard of it. In Azuchi, similar rumors had started. No foreigner had ever been made a lord, granted lands to govern, but no foreigner had ever been given the rank of samurai, either. With Nobunaga, all things had become possible.

As tono, I would have troops of my own, ready to fight under Nobunaga's order. My own samurai, farmers, servants, taxes. A wife from a noble family, and heirs. A future. A home, in this place so far from the home I had been raised in as a child, so different from the home and the family and the life I had dreamed of for myself back then.

And with those thoughts, a thought that I had never entertained before—was it worth it? Taken from my village, forced into war, but now on the verge of nobility—were the horrors suffered along the way justified by the honor waiting at the end? I could not bring myself to say yes. Too many had died, some at my own hand. My family. My village. The boys in the mercenary training camp, whose names I had never known. The men I killed for the Indians. The men I killed for the Portuguese. The men I killed, now, for Nobunaga. All justified by my own survival and possibly, in a corner of my mind too distant to confess to, the thought of a return to a home that no longer existed.

The price was too high. But the price had already been paid, regardless. And now there was a chance for a true home.

The reward would mean freedom such as I had never dreamed. It meant a chance to raise children of my own who would never have to pay the same price, who would reap the same rewards or better, without knowing the pain that had come before it. The idea of a family was one I had never had cause to consider before. Would I raise them with the traditions I had been raised with? Tell them what I could about my mother and father, my people, our land? Or would I raise them only for the world they would grow up in?

They were difficult decisions, but they were not necessary yet. Something in Akechi's stare had unnerved me, kept me from fully immersing myself in the dream. There were still dangers here, and I could never allow myself to forget that.

When the dinner service was complete and the tables had been cleared and the honors ended, I crossed the room. Akechi was addressing a small handful of his men, Hidemitsu at his side.

". . . the arquebus has power, yes, but the bow is the way of a true warrior. There is no skill in the use of the Portuguese weapons, no expression of the spirit . . ."

He trailed off as I approached. I bowed deeply. Akechi dismissed his men, but Hidemitsu remained at his shoulder.

"I hope I have not interrupted, Lord Akechi."

"I see Lord Nobunaga has elevated you."

I knew little of Akechi, but I suspected that being direct was best, and I trusted that instinct.

"He has. I sense that you disapprove. If I have offended you, I offer amends."

I kept my head bowed but could still feel the weight of Akechi's stare, studying me. He sighed and I lifted my head.

"It is not you I disapprove of. You fought well today, and from what I hear, you have carried yourself well in all things since your appointment. But I do disapprove of the breaking of traditions. I disapprove of the old ways not being honored."

He hesitated for a moment, then smiled thinly and continued. "I believe it is the curse of all old men, to fight against the new. Perhaps I am the one who is wrong. Nevertheless, a man can only stand for the things he believes in, and I believe in the importance of our traditions."

"My lord." Hidemitsu stopped Akechi with a hand placed softly on his shoulder. Akechi gathered himself.

"I wish you well, young Yasuke, I truly do. But I do hope you are the end of it."

Akechi walked away without waiting for a reply. I turned to watch him go, and Hidemitsu stepped forward, face-to-face with me.

"My lord is generous. Nobunaga loves his oddities and his European exotica, but he disgraces us all by letting you wear those swords."

I felt my blood rise, not so much at Hidemitsu's words, but at the condescension with which they were spoken. I kept my voice steady, but did not mince words.

"I have hardened my body and my spirit the same as any man here. I've slept more nights on rocks than on beds. I've marched the distance of a soldier's life with my feet bare or wrapped only in cloths. I've crossed the sea without being allowed to see the sun. I've suffered wounds from spear and sword, halberd and axe and pike, and other weapons whose names I do not know, and I have killed every man who put a mark upon me. I have served, always and loyally, and I owe no man an apology that's not been given, a service that's not been rendered, or a debt that's not been paid."

Hidemitsu did not flinch. He stared back coldly, his dark eyes flickering in the light of the lanterns with a dangerous anger. He stepped even closer, and though his head came only to my chest, it took resolve to hold my position.

"And you think this makes you worthy? You talk about a lifetime, but for us, being samurai is a matter of centuries. Of lineages traced back to the early days of the land."

I started to speak, but he smiled derisively, stopping the words in my mouth. He walked past me, pausing briefly as he did so.

"A tiger in the deep woods strikes fear into the bravest of men, but a tiger in a cage will be mocked by a boy. Nobunaga has made you samurai, and so you are samurai. But we are not the same."

I WAS DEEPLY UNSETTLED BY my conversation first with Akechi, then with his son-in-law Hidemitsu, but there was nothing to do about it. It was not worth bothering Nobunaga with, nor did I know what kind of trouble that might stir. I did not want to discuss it with Ranmaru, or Ogura or Jingorou either. It seemed something that I should settle myself, but also something that should be left to cool. I did my best to let it slip from my mind. I slept, and slept well.

In the morning, the men were released. The campaign against the Takeda had come to a close. But there was one thing Nobunaga still needed to do.

"Mount Fuji is the jewel of the Japanese empire, and I have never looked upon her. Nor have I ever been this close."

The province around Mount Fuji was now under the stewardship of Tokugawa, and while Nobunaga's main force turned back for Azuchi, his inner circle pressed on alongside Tokugawa's men. Within a half day's ride we reached the mouth of the valley that opened onto the view of the snow crested mountain.

Blossoms from the cherry trees littered the valley floor, soft and pink against the clean white snow. Beyond the valley, Fuji was near perfect in its symmetry—the long, sloping sides mirrored each other as they rose toward the summit. There was a reverent silence as we looked upon it, broken eventually by Nobunaga.

"The Jōmon and other early Japanese worshipped her as a deity. They would burn incense at the mountain's base, leave offerings. Near the crest there is a cave called Hitoana where the goddess of Mount Fuji was said to live. The worshippers would come once a year to remove any fallen branches or wayward stones or other obstructions, ensuring the path was clear should she choose to descend. Do people in other lands have such legends, Yasuke?"

The words stabbed unexpectedly, and I was a boy again, sitting on the porch beside my mother. She pointed up at the mountain.

"Do you see the cave?" she asked.

I followed the line of her finger. Far up the mountain, past the fields, past the lower rocky areas where we mined for ore, and the upper reaches of the forest where I had sometimes played, hoping to catch sight of the monkeys in the treetops, or even the striped hide of a bounding gazelle. Past those, there was a rock cliff, high on the mountain's peak, and a shaded section that I assumed must be the cave my mother pointed at.

"I see it."

"That is where we come from," she said. "All of our people. The first woman and the first man. If you climb to the top of the mountain and look outside the mouth of the cave, you will see a single footprint, the footprint of the first woman who ventured out into the world. The mother of us all."

I could feel her voice more strongly than ever, like fresh honey running down my throat or the sun touching my skin after emerging from a warm swim, and I savored the memory of it.

"We have spread across the plains," she continued, "and hills and forests, but you must never forget that we all come from the same place. Our ancestors, they will be with us anywhere we go."

She slipped her arm around my neck and pressed her head to mine, laughing into my hair.

"That means I will be with you, anywhere you go, no matter how far."

I did not trust myself to look at Nobunaga, but I knew he expected an answer.

"There is a mountain near my home, called Namuli," I started, but I choked on the words. I took a deep breath, let the memory slip away, knowing now that I could recall it at any time. "I have seen many mountains, my lord, in many lands. Never have I seen one so beautiful as this."

Nobunaga smiled, watching as the sun touched its edge to the snowy plateau of Mount Fuji and started its slow descent behind it.

"The Imperial Court has already sent word. They've offered me the titles of taishogun, kampaku, or daijō-daijin. I'm to appear before them and choose which I prefer. They will acknowledge my choice."

Taishogun, great general. Kampaku, advisor to the emperor. Daijō-daijin, chancellor of the Realm.

"There is risk in this," suggested Tokugawa. "They offer you these titles because they fear you."

"Yes. I am aware of the . . . politics. And the risks. But they fear me because they have no more wealthy patrons, and no army. They fear me because I alone can protect the Imperial Court. I'll accept their titles, I'll continue to fund their palace reconstruction and their other little projects, and as long as they are allowed their tributes, they'll leave the governance of the people and the protection of the land in my hands."

"Tenka fubu," whispered Tokugawa.

"Tenka fubu," repeated Ranmaru, then from each man, "Tenka fubu, tenka fubu."

The words rippled softly through the small gathering, on the lips of each man, repeated as if something offered forward. Tenka fubu. The realm under one sword.

A gust of wind lifted a dusting of snow and a smattering of cherry blossoms and swirled them briefly at our feet then away, carrying the words with them. The warmth of my mother's voice still hummed in my chest.

I stood beside Nobunaga and we stared up at the wondrous peak of Mount Fuji, each of us thinking of our respective ancestors.

"As a child I thought them foolish, hearing the story told," Nobunaga said softly. "Now I wonder how they could do anything but worship."

I studied his expression. He looked, more than anything else, to be satisfied.

29

Upon return to Azuchi, representatives from nearly every province and clan arrived to congratulate Nobunaga on his victory, and on the new title he would soon receive from the emperor. Though he had not yet accepted or chosen a title, and not yet ascended, all recognized that it was better to offer laurels too early than too late.

In addition to Suruga, Katsuyori's death had brought pledges of loyalty from previously Takeda-controlled lands in Kai and Shinano. From his beginnings in the tiny provinces of Owari and Mino, Nobunaga now controlled twenty-eight provinces and parts of six others.

Tokugawa had remained in the field in the former Takeda provinces, quieting the small rebellions and hunting down the surviving minor members of the clan. Toyotomi remained in Mori territory, pressing westward with his armies, the hunched and crumple-faced general showing the tactical brilliance and resolve that had seen him rise up from peasantry.

Only Akechi's men were kept in reserve at Azuchi. He and the remainder of Nobunaga's samurai and vassals lined the walls of Azuchi Castle's reception hall each day, for hours on end, as the parade of supplicants bowed and smiled and offered gifts and long-winded, flowery effusives.

There were tiger skins and scarlet cloths, barrels of rare sake, boxes of dried sea cucumber and salted abalone, and in one spectacular display, twenty stunning white swans. Nobunaga would study each gift and profess his appreciation, while the rest of us murmured over the various unboxed wonders.

Servants discreetly slipped in and out of the hall, carrying gifts, removing gifts, refilling cups, and bringing fresh plates of food. I glimpsed Tomiko amongst them and watched her. She conducted her duties quietly and gracefully, her head bowed to avoid eye contact with the gathered guests, her movements calculated to draw no attention. She blended in, disappeared, and I remembered her frightened expression when Nobunaga had pointed to her that first night at Honno-ji. I thought she looked at me, once, glancing toward me while setting a small porcelain cleansing bowl in front of some lord, but it was brief enough that I could not be certain.

I had learned to fight like a samurai, but still sometimes struggled to sit like one, and Nobunaga, despite all the attentions being presented him, was always quick to recognize when I had reached the end of my comfort. He would bark out some order or minor errand for me to run, but always with a smile beneath that let me know it was for my own relief.

I limped and stumbled down the stairs of Azuchi Castle and into the strengthening spring sun. I was glad to be out of the cold of the eastern mountains. My knees ached, my hips felt locked in place, and my feet were immobile and numb.

The courtyard was bustling with activity. The traveling entourages of the lords and vassals had swelled Azuchi's numbers in the past days. The farmers and commoners from the town at the castle's base were spending more time in the castle court as well, driving heavy traffic in barter with the incoming travelers and the goods they had brought.

I paused for a moment on the castle steps and imagined myself with a small castle of my own. I had fought to hold down such thoughts ever since Ranmaru had mentioned the rumor of my being granted a fief, but occasionally I allowed my mind to wander. I'd been a little more than a full year in Japan. I'd been watchful, attentive, had absorbed all that I could, but I could not dismiss Hidemitsu's criticism that their traditions were rooted in centuries, not months. Would I be as perceptive as Nobunaga, recognizing the discomfort of one subject in a crowd of a hundred? Had I learned enough about the Japanese that I could wisely resolve disputes amongst those I governed? Would I be loved by the people, or would I be seen as an outsider, and resented?

I spotted a familiar brown frock near the guest house where Hatano Hideharu had been staying with his family since surrendering Yakami Castle to Akechi. Nobunaga had given orders that the hostage Hatano be treated comfortably, but Nobunaga had not yet called on him personally. When he was, he would be expected to offer apologies to Nobunaga for having opposed him, and to pledge his loyalty, and that of his family. He'd be given some title and task and formally align himself with the Oda clan, but for now he was to stay indoors and wait for word.

Brother Organtino stood out front of the guesthouse which Hideharu was quartered in, and while I watched, Father Valignano exited the house and joined him. They began to walk away and I hustled to catch them.

"You have business with Lord Hideharu?"

The Japanese came automatically to me now. I repeated myself in Portuguese, but the question went ignored in both languages.

Brother Organtino smiled warmly and Father Valignano placed his hand on my shoulder.

"Hello, Brother. You are a most welcome sight, as always. We are glad to see you safe. Were you in the battle?"

"Toward the end, yes, but I never felt myself in harm's way."

"I have seen you fight. I doubt you ever feel in harm's way." Valignano chuckled. "We have been through much together."

I felt a warmth of reminiscence from Valignano's hand on my shoulder, from his kind words. It had the sense of a peace offering, and yet the word "together" felt false, as if we had been equal to each other when I knew that had not been so. I took a step backward, embarrassed with myself that I had responded so easily to his merest praise. I chided myself that Valignano's every word was carefully chosen, and intended to some purpose of his own. I switched subjects.

"The construction on the church has been most impressive. I suspect you'll be done soon."

"Yes. We do have quite a congregation already, despite not yet having a roof. Our numbers will only grow, of course, once Oda Nobunaga tears down the Shinto shrine."

There was no question in the sentence, but there was in Valignano's eyes, his eyebrows arched as he watched for my reaction. The Shinto shrine where Nobunaga had made me samurai. The temple of Masahide-ji, built to honor the Oda retainer who had committed seppuku in hopes of setting Nobunaga along a more responsible path, toward leadership of the clan. To Nobunaga, it was the most cherished building in Azuchi, more so even than his castle, and he would never disrespect the memory of Masahide by destroying it.

I stayed silent and Valignano continued. The casual tone in his voice was forced, and I understood that his next words were a message that I was meant to deliver.

"I understand he has certain . . . traditions he needs to maintain for his people, but it is a new day in Japan. Nobunaga will be . . . what? Chancellor? Shogun? You will soon be a close advisor to the most powerful man in the country. It is an opportunity to bring Japan forward, into more . . . modern thinking. To stop encouraging the worship of animals and ancestors and bring the people of Japan into the light of the one true God. Do you not think so?"

Valignano's words and tone echoed the teachings of the Portuguese priests, how the Africans had to be brought into the light, led, transformed, but while my thoughts rebelled, my body betrayed me. I bowed my head in agreement. I was immediately angered at how quickly I could fall back into the old habit of obedience, but I could not find the will to raise my head or object. My legs felt like lead beneath me, and it no longer was due to the hours of kneeling.

"After all, he did the same with shrines and temples of Mount Hiei, did he not? With the priests inside? Your new benefactor's hands are as dirty as anyone else's."

"You say 'benefactor' as if you had no hand in making it so."

Valignano seemed to soften, dropped his guard for just a moment. The castle grounds were quiet, but there were still a number of people about. Behind Valignano, a servant raked fresh lines in the gravel. Another was arranging gleaming white pebbles around one of the large garden stones.

"Do you know why I chose you, so long ago? It is because you understand that sometimes distasteful things are necessary. You've served me well. Giving you away was not an easy choice, but it is one I would make again. You know I will always do what I must."

He started to leave. I burned inside at how casually he had mentioned giving me away.

"Do you remember Goa?" I called out to his back.

Valignano stopped, turned over his shoulder.

"You used to walk an hour or more out of your way so that I could avoid seeing the auctions and the slaves being brought ashore. I do that same thing now, here, to avoid your church. *The one you sold me for.*"

I'd meant to raise my voice in anger, but instead it cracked in unexpected hurt. It was the first true emotion I'd ever shown him—I'd always kept any feeling from my voice or expression around him, even on that first meeting when I was yet little more than a boy.

Valignano seemed truly shaken for a moment by my response, but he shifted quickly to anger.

"I pulled you from a life cleaning floors and kissing feet. I taught you, I lifted you, and look where you are now. Would you rather I left you in that tiny rat-infested seminary run by fools?"

"You took me because you thought I could be useful to you. Do not pretend it was for any other reason."

"I took you because I thought you could be useful to *the church!*"

A handful of people had stopped in the street to watch our exchange. Noticing this, Valignano cooled as suddenly as he had burst. He ran his hand down the front of his robe, smoothing some imagined wrinkle.

"I hope not all your memories are sour ones."

As I watched Valignano walk away, I felt Brother Organtino's hand on my forearm.

"Isaac," he began. "You must be cautious. Father Valignano has . . . reservations about Nobunaga. I cannot say more than that and I should not say even that. But you must be careful."

"If there are plans—"

"Isaac," Organtino interrupted. "You know Father Valignano better than I, maybe better than anyone. You know there are always plans, always contingencies. But it doesn't mean they will come to pass. I'll speak to him. If the shrine matters, I'm sure he can be persuaded. It means nothing to him. The port at Nagasaki, though . . . it is important to Valignano. He will not surrender it easily. If you can sway Nobunaga on this point, if there could be some . . . accommodation reached . . . it could avoid trouble."

Brother Organtino seemed strained, the ridges of his cheeks more pronounced, some of the softness of his body gone. They had planned this misdirection together. I had spent enough time with Valignano to see through his machinations. The port was what Valignano truly valued, the shrine was meant only as a lever. Organtino looked pained at playing his part. He could not look me in the eye. He started to walk away, then stopped.

"He is more fond of you than you know. And he has protected you more than you know. Be cautious, my brother. We want to see you safe."

On the evening of the fifth day of honors there was a surprising guest.

"I present Lord Hideharu, of the Hatano clan of Tanba Province."

An attendant in simple black pants and shirt made the presentation from the doorway of the main hall, then slipped from view. If Nobunaga bristled at the title of "Lord" being used for the defeated Hideharu, he did not show it.

Hideharu stepped through the doorway, alone, wearing a wide-shouldered white shirt with a sky-blue vest. His hair was pulled back and tied behind, his pate bald and shining in the flickering light of the braziers. He approached halfway toward Nobunaga and bowed, touching his head completely to the floor, then after a moment rose.

"I have not yet properly thanked my host for his generosity and his hospitality, but let me not be quite so late in congratulating him on his victory."

Something felt off. I studied Hideharu. He looked proud, not defeated, no trace of humility in his stance or voice despite the respect shown by his bow. His hands were at his side, and beneath the cuff of the long flowing shirt, I could see the slightest of tremors. I looked at Ranmaru, then at Nobunaga, but could not attract their attention and was not sure what I would try to communicate to them if I could.

Brother Organtino's words had unsettled me. In the days since his and Father Valignano's visit I had been on the lookout for conspiracy everywhere, picturing every shopkeeper and merchant and farmer as a deadly enemy. It had worn my nerves thin, and in all likelihood I was continuing now to look for something that wasn't there.

Nobunaga stood.

"You have been a most excellent guest, Hideharu."

Hideharu flinched slightly at being called by his name without title. It was not a slight Nobunaga would make accidentally.

"I trust that you and your family have felt safe here. It is my wish that all who come under my domain feel so."

"And soon all will be under your domain."

The words were congratulatory, but the interruption was pointed. Nobunaga was silent a moment.

"Soon, Japan will be at peace, yes."

"As my home province of Tanba is at peace."

The last word was said with venom, and Hideharu's comments brought whispers, quickly silenced. The hairs on my neck prickled. A challenge had been laid, in tone if not in words. The conversation could only degrade from this point, the only question was how far it would go. Nobunaga could not stand down, nor, I knew, would he have any desire to.

"Are the people at Yakami Castle not fed tonight? Their fate would have been much worse had their lord not been wise enough to surrender."

Akechi shifted noticeably, an unmistakable breach amongst the samurai who were expected to kneel silently along the walls during these audiences, and I was reminded that he had given his mother to the Hatano clan as guarantee of Hideharu's safety. Akechi's mother would be at Yakami Castle right now, surrounded by enemies in the same way Hideharu was surrounded by them here at Azuchi.

Nobunaga's words had struck a blow, and I could see he was savoring the confrontation. He paced, while Hideharu was still. My instincts screamed at me to end this, but there was no way for me to intervene without bringing extreme dishonor to myself, and to Nobunaga as well.

"A wise ruler understands when he is outmatched. Now we will be ruled by my Lord Nobunaga," Hideharu said.

There were a few short gasps from those gathered. Nobunaga stopped, suddenly seething.

"I have sometimes been criticized for allowing people to speak too freely. Perhaps I should take that criticism to heart."

"My apologies, my lord. I meant no disrespect. I have watched your rise, as has all of Japan. You have come a long way from the whelp whose behavior brought dishonor to his clan, and shame to his father. Now all of Japan bows to the Fool of Owari."

I rose, but too slowly, my feet numb and clumsy beneath me. Nobunaga took two graceful steps and lifted a naginata from a rack against the wall. I saw Akechi rise as well, then Ranmaru, slower to react. Though I had been quicker, I was not quick enough. Nobunaga rotated the long shaft of the naginata once between his fingers, then drew the blade of it across Hatano Hideharu's neck. Hideharu never moved until the blood spurted from his neck and he grasped at it, involuntarily.

He seemed to have expected Nobunaga's reaction, and accepted it.

Akechi stood horrified, unmoving.

Nobunaga dropped the bloodied blade and retired to his quarters without a word. The shock subsided, servants rushed in to remove the body, scrub clean the mat. The crowd dispersed, unsure of the proper protocols.

In the morning, I searched for Father Valignano but he was gone. I had the feeling that something had been set in motion that I could not see and could not stop.

30

The crane lifted from the marsh, the small silver fish wriggling in its beak flashing shards of reflected sunlight in all directions as it fought. The crane spread its wings broad and soared gracefully against the spring sky. Nobunaga raised his forearm slightly and the speckled gray hawk resting upon it exploded upward. The hawk flapped its wings twice, then tucked them and arrowed toward its target.

The hawk's talons tore at the outspread wing of the crane and the crane dipped, banked, and recovered. The hawk circled and dove. It struck the long neck of the crane with its beak and latched on. The crane cried out. The fish fell from its mouth, turning and glinting like a tiny star come crashing to earth. The crane twisted and lashed out with its strangely jointed legs but could not reach the hawk.

It banked and rose and shook the hawk loose, but it was already too weakened. The hawk struck the neck again, more violently this time. The neck of the crane curled around the hawk's beak and the long wings folded, and the crane crumpled and fell limply from the cool pale blue.

Nobunaga gave a satisfied sigh.

"In the old days, such a hawk could be trained to strike down messenger pigeons from the air, preventing one's enemies from getting quick word to their allies. In some battles, a single good hawk could be as valuable as twenty men."

The hawk returned to land softly on Nobunaga's deerskin glove. His hawk handler came forward to fasten the jesses to the hawk's legs, then rewarded the hawk with a morsel of duck meat.

"I think the Jesuits are planning something," I said.

Nobunaga continued to smile, pleased with his new hawk. In the sky it had been majestic, but on his wrist it looked quite ordinary. A soft white belly, ghostly gray wings spotted with faint black circles. It was one of two rare Korean hawks that had been gifted to him from a regional lord to acknowledge his upcoming ascension.

"I would be quite surprised if they weren't," he replied nonchalantly.

The handler started to unbuckle the deerskin sleeve on Nobunaga's arm, while the hawk waited, almost immobile.

"I have worked with the Jesuits for years. Many of them are harmless priests and true believers. But some of them are far from that. Some are soldiers, criminals, killers, who were offered a choice between execution and salvation. There are dangerous men amongst them."

Freed from the glove and the hawk, Nobunaga shook his arm. He accepted another piece of duck meat from the trainer so that he could feed the hawk himself.

"The hawk must learn the difference between its trainer and its master. Come, let's fetch our crane."

We circled around the marsh, our boots squelching in the mud. There would be men stationed nearby, but not near enough.

"If I may, my lord, perhaps you have become too comfortable."

Nobunaga snapped his head toward me. Though he had always welcomed free talk in private, I worried for a moment I had gone too far.

"I am not unaware of danger," he said. "The ambitions of the Jesuits. The machinations of the Imperial Court. The conquered lords who are overly extravagant with both their gifts and their praise, and the pockets of rebels and dissidents throughout the provinces. I am not reckless or foolish, Yasuke, but I also will not hide behind an army at every step."

We came across the crane in a clearing. One wing was bent beneath its body, the other wing spread wide. Its neck was stretched out like a long snake. There were two sharp gashes, and the blood marred the perfect white of the crane's feathers. One leg twitched in irregular patterns, and the crane's eye rolled lazily, scrolling the expanse of the sky it had fallen from. Nobunaga pulled a dagger from his belt and opened the crane's throat wider, quickening its end.

"When one's ambition is great, so too will be the obstacles in his way. The enemies before him. Men who don't believe themselves trusted will never be loyal. It is a risk, but a required one."

The hawk handler stepped forward with a towel. Nobunaga wiped his dagger, then his hands.

"Do you understand?"

Nobunaga looked at me, and I realized this was a lesson. The rumors of my promotion must be true. Nobunaga intended to give me land, to lead people, and to lead them well. I nodded.

"What will happen to Akechi's mother? Will her safety be traded for?"

The hawk handler set about cleaning and wrapping the body of the crane. Nobunaga crouched, studying the ground where the crane had fallen.

"Akechi has always been loyal. He understands the way of these things, the nature of war."

If Nobunaga meant to say more, he was interrupted. I heard footsteps approaching, the rustling of the long grass and the popping sound of boots releasing from the grip of the muddy trail. Three guards appeared, and bowed.

"My lord, there is a rider. Word from the western campaign."

NOBUNAGA HAD NOT BOTHERED TO change clothing, and so neither had I. I had removed my boots at the castle steps and put on a pair of sandals, my socks still wet from the marsh. Ranmaru and a half dozen pages had gathered in a small side room on the third floor of the castle when the messenger was brought in.

He bowed, touching his head to the ground, then rose and spoke quickly.

"The forces under Toyotomi remain in siege position around Takamatsu Castle. The position is secure, but Toyotomi has allowed a few messengers through, letting them believe that they had found holes in our lines. The Mori have called on their retainers, and are marching on Toyotomi's position. Toyotomi humbly requests my lord's support."

"Tell him he shall have it. Eat. Rest if you must. Get a fresh horse from the stable master. But ride as soon as you can with my word."

The messenger bowed again, and backed out of the room.

"We ride for Takamatsu?" asked Ranmaru.

Nobunaga was silent, savoring what he recognized as the cusp of victory. Toyotomi had been sent west not to conquer, but to provoke. If the Mori were finally engaging, and sending their main forces forward, then a victory for us there would be a decisive one. Only a few islands and minor provinces would remain unpledged to the Oda clan, none that would present any real challenge.

"Everyone will march for Takamatsu," he said. "Send word, muster the armies. Akechi's forces will march immediately to secure Toyotomi's flank. Tokugawa's forces will have a long march ahead of them, they will serve as our reinforcement."

"And us?" I asked

Nobunaga paused.

"We must ride for Honno-ji. The Imperial Court has waited long enough for its answer, they will not remain patient forever. I will accept their title. Our men will march for Takamatsu without us. I'll take a hundred men with me to Kyoto. We'll be able to move quickly, and we'll meet up with Toyotomi and Akechi before the battle begins."

I opened my mouth to question the wisdom of riding to Kyoto with a hundred men, but swallowed my objection. Nobunaga glanced at me and nodded, as if having read my mind, and my subsequent change of mind. All was set. Nobunaga delivered his orders.

"Get the orders to Akechi and Tokugawa. Select our men and pack up. Send word to the emperor to let him know that I seek an audience with the court. Have the temple prepared. We'll leave for Honno-ji in the morning."

31

My servants prepared food for the journey, polished my armor to a black gleam, brushed and watered my horse. A battle against the Mori could be days or could be months, and they would care for the house and the small garden during my time away. They bowed in the narrow entranceway, not raising their heads until I had toed my horse toward the castle gate.

I wondered what my parents would think if they could see me, here in this place. A samurai and a respected man, with servants and a home, but a man who had been forced into terrible things along the way. Would they be proud or ashamed? I pictured their shadows merging in the morning sun as they touched foreheads and said goodbye to each other, neither knowing it was the last time. I pictured my father as the old Lomwe-speaking slave had imagined him, putting his hand on the shoulder of every young man he came across, hoping each time they turned that the face would be mine.

I shook the thoughts and let the reins fall loose in my hands as I passed through the gate. Some of Nobunaga's servants had gone ahead to prepare, while others rode alongside us, swelling the ranks of the one hundred fighting men to a number half again that size. I looked for Tomiko amongst the servants, but did not see her. I hoped she was amongst those left behind at Azuchi, rather than with us marching first to Honno-ji, then west, to war with her ancestral clan.

We snaked our way through the streets of Kyoto, past shops and merchant carts and apothecaries. Men still looked up at my dark skin and towering stature with the same wide-eyed gape as on my last march through Kyoto, but now I rode beside Oda Nobunaga rather than foreign priests, and none dared stare long, or move closer.

The Jesuit church was lit with candles, seemingly busy despite the fact that they had transitioned mostly to the new church at Azuchi. The gate to the compound had been reinforced at some time in the past fifteen months, and I wondered if that were because of the riotous crowd that had greeted my arrival, or if they were taking precautions against some other threat.

The gate for Honno-ji was a few blocks from the church. I could not believe it had been only fifteen months since I had been here last. I felt my chest tighten, my throat as well. So much had happened. So much had changed. I had last come through these gates on foot, with Oda soldiers be-hind me ready to cut me down if I gave them cause to. Now I rode through the same gate on horseback with some of those same Oda soldiers behind me, except now they would fight to defend my life with their own, as I would for them. I came first as a prisoner, and a slave. I returned now as a free man, a samurai, and a sworn retainer to Japan's most powerful man.

I dismounted and passed the reins to a groomsman. The main reception hall, where I had first been brought before Nobunaga, was bustling with activity as the earlier-arriving servants put the final touches on food prepa-rations. Nobunaga was expected at a tea ceremony with the crown prince and a few other high-ranking court members, but an extravagant meal was prepared anyway, in case of a change in plans.

"Will you eat?" asked Ranmaru.

"I have food that was prepared for the road. I think I'll rest."

Ranmaru summoned a porter and entered the main hall. The porter lifted what little I had packed and I followed him to my quarters. The armor I carried myself. After a brief meal alone, I visited the baths.

I slid the paneled door aside and was enveloped in steam. At first I could make out only shapes, but as my eyes adjusted I could see that there were a half dozen or so soldiers already in the pools, and three times as many attendants either bathing them or waiting to be called. I set aside my robe and eased myself into the waters.

Two attendants came to me immediately, in full, flowery kimonos and white-painted faces. I had a flash of my mother sitting in a row of women, all of their faces painted white using zinc ground up into paste, preparing their drums.

So many reminders of home, in this place so far away from what should have been my home. The traditions of painted faces and carved masks, and song and dance. The beliefs that we can be guided by the spirits of our ancestors. Even the legends, of holy mountains and gods that fought over the land. All these things made me wonder if maybe men everywhere were the same.

I leaned my head back. The attendants scrubbed my back and shoulders and chest, marveling at the color of my skin, the size of my body. Their touch was much gentler than when Nobunaga had tried to scrub the black off my skin in the temple's main hall upon our first meeting, but no less exploratory and curious in its nature.

I let the steam and the touch of the attendants absorb me. I closed my eyes, and remembered what I could of the singing and dancing of my village.

They toweled me dry and I dressed, cleaned and relaxed. I exited the baths but was not yet ready for sleep. I wandered the compound. The court-yard was loud with the sounds of men on the eve of war. Sake and song, and boasts to bolster the strength of the soldiers' spirits.

Nobunaga entered the courtyard, returning from his ceremony, and he spotted me.

"Did you enjoy the baths?"

"I was thinking of the first time I was brought before you. You tried to remove my skin with a brush."

Nobunaga laughed heartily. "Yes, I thought it all some trick. I truly have never seen your like. Come, walk with me."

"You've been away for hours."

"Ah, the ceremony was much more elaborate than the simple tea we enjoyed together. I admit I am but a novice in the ways of the tea ceremony. I have much more to learn."

"There seems to be much history behind it. The same is true for all things here, though."

"Do you still find our ways strange?"

"No. I feel comfortable here, and I thank you for that. It just seems that there is so much to learn. The history and culture and etiquette. In some ways I feel like I belong, in others I fear I never shall."

"Would you like to?"

"Like to what, my lord?"

"Belong."

Nobunaga stopped and turned to look at me. The sun was setting, painting the tops of the gate and the tile roofs in purplish hues and casting long shadows across the courtyard.

"Yes. I would like to fit in here."

Nobunaga smiled, clapped me on the shoulder, and continued to walk.

"I believe men earn their way. There are many Japanese-born, even of noble blood, who I would not take on as a cleaner of latrines. And there are men like you, not born to this world, who I am honored to have by my side."

I wanted to thank him but didn't trust myself with words.

"I used to regret the foolishness of my youth," he continued. "But your youth did not provide you the opportunity to be foolish. The same is true for so many others under my command. I have come to recognize how fortunate I am to have squandered gifts and still be rewarded while others have such a narrow path they can walk. This is the lesson that Masahide gave his life to teach me, and is one I will not take for granted again. Japan will soon be one. I will need men like you beside me to remind me to rule well."

I gripped my sword and bowed my head.

"I am in your service, my lord. Now and always."

"And I am glad of it," said Nobunaga. "You have brought honor to the clan with your service. This may not be where you were born, Yasuke, but this is where you belong. You are a man of Oda. I hope you have never felt otherwise."

32

I woke to the soft thwacking sound of an arrow lodging into wood. I swept aside the sheets and grabbed my katana. The other three men I shared quarters with were still sleeping. I slid the panel door open and stepped out into the hallway. It was quiet, no one else seemed to have heard anything, or to have woken.

I moved quickly but silently onto the porch of the sleeping quarters. Sword still sheathed, but in hand. I could not see the guards' quarters from where I stood, nor the gate. I was about to step off the porch for a quick inspection when I heard the whistling of another arrow, heard the same thwack when it struck.

It had been fired into the stables, where the groomsmen were generally known to work through the night to prepare the horses for morning. I strained my eyes in the direction that the arrow had come from. At first I could not make out anything but darkness, but then another arrow came. And another. The horses neighed and bucked in their stalls.

My instinct was to charge forward, but my responsibility was to Nobunaga. I hesitated for a moment, thinking of returning for my armor, but I had no idea yet what the situation was, and I did not want to waste a moment. The groomsmen charged out of the stables toward an as-yet unseen enemy, armed with nothing but tongs and shoeing irons. I silently wished them good deaths. I sprinted for Nobunaga's quarters.

A gong was struck signaling a general alert, and I knew that someone had likely given their life to sound it. As I reached Nobunaga's quarters, men were rousing, stumbling from their rooms, their heads dulled with sleep and sake, confused but quickly becoming alert. Nobunaga's room was empty. I grabbed the long-poled naginata from its rack and continued down the hall.

Nobunaga was standing in the private garden behind his room. Ranmaru had already reached him, and both had bows in hand, a quiver of arrows slung over their shoulders.

"What is it?" he asked.

"I don't know."

"Iga?" suggested Ranmaru, but Nobunaga shot the idea down.

"If Iga sent men, they would be upon us before we woke." He turned to me. "Are they inside the walls?"

"I believe so. They've taken the stables. That's as much as I know."

"Then we'll get no messengers out."

A few other Oda samurai came through the hallway, Ogura and Jingorou amongst them, gathering around their lord. Ranmaru pointed to one of the newly arriving soldiers.

"Up to the roof."

He nodded and disappeared.

The main courtyard came alive with the sound of drums, of steel clashing against steel, of men screaming and dying. Any hope that this was some drunken skirmish gone too far was extinguished. We were under attack. Ranmaru turned to Nobunaga.

"They knew the stablemen would be awake. They likely know where you are staying. They'll focus their attack here. If we move, we can buy time."

"They are in the courtyard already," I countered. "Moving is dangerous. They'll focus their attack here, yes, but our men will focus their defense here as well. We should hold behind their line."

The two men nodded in assent.

The soldier clambered back down into the garden from the rooftop, clearly shaken.

"There are standards," he stammered.

"Whose?"

"The standards are the five-petaled bellflower. Akechi's men. There are thousands of them, outside the walls."

"Akechi's men were ordered to march west," Ranmaru stated, disbelievingly.

"How many are inside?"

Nobunaga's question was immediate, no shock or anger or emotion of any kind at the news of Akechi's betrayal, and I admired him for it. We were a hundred men, a half hundred more if you counted servants, as outnumbered here as Takeda Katsuyori had been at Tenmokuzan, but Nobunaga showed no sign of fear. The soldier shook his head and could not muster an answer. An arrow cut through the screened wall and whistled past us before sticking into the fence at the rear of the garden, fired blindly in hopes of striking something other than paper or wood.

"What's done is done," said Nobunaga. He nocked an arrow and re-entered the compound, and the rest of us followed.

A dozen Akechi soldiers had already made it into the compound. Nobunaga loosed an arrow, then nocked and loosed another, his movements smooth and almost inhumanly quick. The first two bodies fell to the floor, impeding the progress of the men behind. We charged forward, cutting them down easily in the narrow space.

In the courtyard we could hear the popping of rifles, at first sporadic, then settling into a rhythmic volley as the soldiers outside gathered themselves and became more organized, the hours and days and months of training taking over. The sounds of clashing swords and screaming men subsided, indicating that the initial wave had been pushed back.

"In your armor," ordered Nobunaga. "Grab whatever weapons you can. The lull won't last long."

Nobunaga's overnight guard, already dressed for battle, remained behind while the rest of us hurried to our quarters to prepare. We returned with quivers of arrows, bows, and spears and naginatas. We helped one another with latches and laces as we donned our armor.

"Let Akechi come within reach of my bow and I will put an arrow through his treacherous eye," Ranmaru ranted.

I thought of Valignano, exiting Hatano Hideharu's quarters at Azuchi, about Hideharu taunting Nobunaga before being struck down.

"The Hatano. They must have heard of Hideharu's death and executed Akechi's mother."

"He risked that when he traded her to them," sneered Ranmaru.

"Well, then, let us ensure that his name is remembered only with scorn."

We joined Nobunaga on the front veranda, where he was shouting out lines and formations. Ogura and Jingorou grabbed pots and chairs and anything they could find to block the top of the stairs. Quivers of arrows lined the back wall of the veranda, within easy reach. There were maybe five dozen Oda soldiers in the courtyard and another dozen on the veranda, guarding Nobunaga, but the men that had been selected to march to Honno-ji were the Oda clan's best. If we were to fall tonight, we would not fall easily.

There was a shout and another wave of Akechi men pushed through the gate, then spread wide, a mistake. A narrow column could have punctured our lines, but spread wide they made easy targets for the Oda arquebuses.

After a few volleys, the ground shook with the force of an explosion. At the far end of the compound, black smoke rose into the sky.

"It was a distraction. They've taken the armory."

Reality began to settle in. The guns were our great equalizer, but there would be no more ammunition once the men expended whatever they carried with them. We would be less than a hundred facing off against thousands.

"Tokugawa will still be mustering his men. Toyotomi's men are engaged with the Mori, even if they do receive word and break off, they are a day's ride away at least, probably two."

"Defend our lord," one soldier called.

The men in the courtyard fired until they had nothing left to fire, then drew their swords and re-formed in the courtyard below us, at the base of the stairs. The sun had started to rise, turning the sky a soft gray, and as the smoke from gunfire cleared, we got our first glimpse of the enemy.

They came forward like beetles, their armored carapaces brown and gray, with the odd speck of yellow and red, their faces hidden beneath their masks and helms. The men clashed and mixed together, the armored Akechi forces surrounding the Oda men, most of whom were still in their nighttime robes.

The handful of archers on the veranda rained down arrows on the invaders, focusing on the front of the line, hoping to slow the progress of the main force by laying bodies of their own dead in their path. Nobunaga and Ranmaru, trained in the weapon since birth, nocked, pulled, and loosed in a single rhythmic motion, repeated over and over in precisely the same manner.

The string on Nobunaga's bow snapped, and I passed him his naginata. The quivers had run low and the Akechi men had opened a gap that almost reached the base of the stairs.

"To the top of the stairs," Nobunaga ordered. "Prepare to hold."

The men gathered on the head of the stairs. I counted twenty-two of us. In the courtyard below, the Akechi were countless, and there were more waiting beyond the gate if they were required. Ranmaru seemed to sense my thoughts.

"You would have been ugly as an old man anyway."

I smiled back at him.

"Even with death at our door, you are jealous of me. You must have been the most handsome man in Japan before I arrived."

We laughed grimly and gripped our weapons and we waited.

The first men to break through at the bottom of the stairs were cut down mercilessly by our arrows, but they continued to come, behind them, over top of them. I had the longest reach and I speared the first man to the top, a wildly charging soldier, through the stomach, then lifted him and threw him down to the mass of bodies beneath, but it did not deter the next from coming, or the man after the next.

Below us, there were still pockets of Oda men engaged in fighting, but they had been separated and overwhelmed. On the stairs we stood our ground and drove the Akechi back. Behind the scattered obstacles Ogura and Jingorou had placed, we lined up in two rows—the first, to block the top of the stairs; the second, to kill any man who broke through, as well as to quickly fill any hole in the first line.

I stood shoulder to shoulder with Nobunaga and Ranmaru on the front line. We cut down the charging men, then kicked their bodies down the stairs in hopes of tripping the men below. I lost my katana in the belly of an Akechi soldier and I picked one up from one of the bodies at my feet and I continued to fight.

To my left, I felt Nobunaga sag. I spared a moment to glance over and saw he'd been struck, an arrow embedded deep in his leg. He never slowed, his naginata flashing in and out of the storm of bodies with a preternatural grace, but the blood pouring down his leg would soon weaken him. I called to the men behind me.

"Our lord is struck, get him to his quarters."

Nobunaga opened his mouth to countermand the order, but did not. He was quickly whisked away and another man came forward to take his place. It was warfare over a few feet of territory, the twenty or so stairs between the courtyard and the veranda. We held as best we could for as long as we could, but the numbers were too great.

"Fall back to the hallway," Ranmaru ordered.

We backed off the porch and into the front hallway, cutting and slashing as we moved. The Akechi men gathered on the veranda, and paused. The narrow hallway would reduce the advantage of their numbers. They would still overwhelm us eventually, but at great cost, and no soldier was eager to pay it. They eyed us through the open doorway while we relaxed our shoulders for a moment, taught ourselves to breathe again.

The morning had fully come, and early mists settled around the feet of the Akechi men outside. I saw that Jingorou had also suffered a wound and was bleeding badly from his hip.

"Disloyal dogs," Ranmaru shouted. "I will take a thousand heads today. The hands of the attendants who prepare them will bleed from the work and they will curse the name of Ranmaru for bringing them so many dead. The last head I take will be that of Akechi Mitsuhide. You know as well as I that the guards' quarters of Azuchi fill with laughter at the mention of his name. You betray your lord to follow an old coward and a dullard. Let Akechi come forward, and I will show you how he stands against a true man of Oda."

I stood behind Ranmaru, my head visible to the Akechi above his. I knew that only a few of them had ever seen me before, and that many feared me as a demon. I rose to my full height, allowing my head to scrape the wooden cross beam, my shoulders to fill the breadth of the hallway. My face was above the level of the lanterns, which would shroud it in darkness.

"My friend is too kind to you. He offers you honorable deaths, but I do not. I say that you have discarded your honor this day by turning against your lord. I will not take your heads, not first. First I will take your thumbs. Then I will cut the noses and lips from your faces. I will pull the eyes from your skulls. You will not be honored with displays in front of Lord Nobunaga. I will leave your bodies in the courtyard to rot in the sun and be pecked at by crows. I will leave your heads with no names, and no way for those who come after to give them names."

The few Akechi men we could see turned pale. I saw Ranmaru's shoulders shudder and knew he was suppressing laughter. Without turning his head he whispered, "So you do know how to boast."

I put my hand on his shoulder and leaned close to his ear. "Yes, and I have not forgotten you calling me a slayer of pigs. Fortunately for you, others are more deserving of my anger right now, but when we are through cutting down these traitors, I may yet test your sword against mine."

"It would truly be an honor. I would fight you like a brother. And I would win."

I could not see his face, but I could hear the grin in his voice. Behind us, the other Oda had picked up and started launching taunts and insults at the men on the veranda. The Akechi shifted and stirred, and looked at one another uncertainly. I heard a gravelly voice rise up from behind them. They parted, and Hidemitsu stepped into the hallway entrance, the shadows across his face exaggerating the rightward shift of his badly broken nose.

"What is this? Does Nobunaga's pet tiger poke his head from his cage to growl at us?"

I could see the smirk cross his face despite the shadows, hear the titter of laughter from the men behind him. I no longer had cause to control my rage.

"Mock if you will, Hidemitsu, but deep in your bowels you know this truth—the cage does not protect the tiger from the boy. It protects the boy from the tiger."

Hidemitsu's smirk turned to a dark look.

"Hearing you speak our language is an assault to my ears. Seeing you carry a sword in your sash and accept honors not meant for you is an insult I no longer have to swallow."

"Then come inside. If you think me undeserving, then prove your words."

He glanced around the hallway and I could see the calculations whirring in his head. The narrow hallway would negate his skill, speed, footwork, handing the advantage to my size and strength and reach. He stepped back and ordered his men forward.

There was shouting on the veranda, calls for courage, and the first wave of men raised their weapons and charged into the hallway.

"There are no better men to die with," Ranmaru whispered.

There was the clang of steel on steel, but they were foot soldiers and we were samurai. I struck men with my sword, my shoulder, my elbows and feet. Blood splashed the walls red and black, and the wooden columns splintered and cracked with the force of blows. The Akechi withdrew.

The insults and taunts began anew. In the doorway, Hidemitsu's broken face hovered over the shoulders of the heavy-breathing men. He turned and waved his arms at someone from the direction of the courtyard. A few moments later, the Akechi foot soldiers stepped aside and their archers set up in the doorway.

"To our lord's quarters," Ranmaru shouted, and we scrambled down the hallway.

Jingorou was too slow to run with his injured hip and he knew it. Ogura reached for his shoulder to drag him, but Jingorou threw him off, pushing his brother to the ground. I turned to grab Jingorou, but our eyes locked for a moment, and I saw something serene and resolved there. I grabbed Ogura instead, lifting him to his feet.

I nodded at Jingorou, but there was no time to convey anything meaningful. The Akechi archers unleashed their barrage into the narrow hallway. Jingorou thrust himself forward, threw his arms wide, blocking as many arrows as he could to cover our retreat. If Ogura cried out, I didn't hear him. I followed the others down the hallway toward Nobunaga's quarters, pulling Ogura limply behind me and hoping he had turned away from watching his brother's sacrifice.

Nobunaga was on the large tatami mat in the center of his quarters. A servant had broken off the shaft of the arrow and removed the head, and was now wrapping the wound. Nobunaga looked at our faces as we entered the room, and knew.

"Go," he told the servant. "Gather all the others and leave now, tell them you are unarmed. They will not let you pass, but if they have any honor they will not harm you."

The servant nodded and ran from the room. I looked around to see who we had lost. Our numbers had dwindled to nine men, ashen-faced and bloodied, exhausted.

"It's time," said Nobunaga.

"No, my lord, we can . . ." Ranmaru's objection sputtered and stalled. He had no answers to offer. He clenched his jaw. "What do you need?"

"Burn the temple."

"Jingorou . . ." Ogura murmured. He hung his head, mourning his lost brother for no longer than a moment, then composed himself. He raised his chin, his expression stony but his eyes afire. "They are in the hallways."

"Then we will remove them." I wiped clean the blade I had taken from a dead Akechi soldier and turned to go back to the hallway.

The others formed up behind me. Ranmaru gathered the lit braziers and handed one to each man, leaving one behind to light Nobunaga's room.

"Fast and hard," he said.

We rushed into the hallway, a battle cry on our lips. Jingorou's punctured body lay amongst the dead from both sides, but none spared a glance. The Akechi were unprepared for an attack, and retreated quickly back onto the veranda, hoping that more space would give benefit to their greater numbers.

We pushed a dozen men backward over the railing, and swung our braziers and lit the veranda ablaze. A few of their soldiers stood and fought, but most of the Akechi men scuttled down the stairs to regroup. Their archers recovered quickly and sent a volley of arrows.

I watched Ranmaru as he fell, the shaft of an arrow lodged deep into the side of his neck. I cut down two Akechi men who stood between us and raced to Ranmaru's position. He tried to speak but could not. I lifted him and carried him down the hallway to Nobunaga's quarters.

The wood and paper veranda caught quickly and there was now a wall of fire between us and the Akechi. I laid Ranmaru down in Nobunaga's room and looked at him helplessly while he sputtered and twitched. Nobunaga placed a hand on his chest and Ranmaru calmed. No words were exchanged between the two men, and none were necessary.

I listened to the clashing on the veranda and could tell by the sound that no Oda man would be returning. Nobunaga placed a hand gently on my shoulder and I rose.

He had changed into an all white robe, open to the waist. A short knife, its handle wrapped in paper, was laid out ceremoniously on the mat. His katana was still in its scabbard, and he offered it to me with both hands.

"It honors me to have you as my second," he said.

"My lord, I—"

"Please." He lifted the sword forward and I took it from him. I removed my helm.

"I will die beside you, my lord."

"No, Yasuke. Akechi must not have my head, or my sword. If he has neither to display, it will be harder for him to convince the others to follow him. I need you to fight, not to die. Use my sword. Give my body time to burn. You will be my miracle. My Divine Wind."

On the day I was made samurai, Ranmaru told me the story of Tomoe Gozen, the subject of the Noh play, the samurai who had been commanded by her lord to live, not die. When I asked Ranmaru if he would commit seppuku for Lord Nobunaga he had said yes without hesitation. When I asked if he would live, if ordered, he had not answered.

I choked back tears, nodded. "On our first march to Azuchi, Ranmaru told me that it is honorable to serve, but that one should be able to choose their own master. You are the master I would have chosen. I am forever in your debt. I will not fail you."

Nobunaga placed both his hands on my arms and smiled up at me, his expression at peace.

"Yasuke, I have never been your master."

We locked eyes for a moment, then, with a deep breath, he set about his final task.

He knelt on the mat. There was no time for a death poem, no time for ritual. He picked up the short sword and plunged it into his abdomen. His face contorted, but he retained his dignity. There was no grunt or cry. He drew the blade up and across, his arm shaking, then leaned forward.

I drew his katana and executed the cut, quick and merciful but precise, leaving a small flap of skin at the front of the neck so that my lord's head did not strike the ground. I knelt beside him. I forced my mind to blankness, my eyes to blindness, and I cut the thin flap of skin at the front of his throat while allowing no connection at all between my thoughts and my actions. I rinsed the head with oil and set my lord's expression at peace and wrapped the head in a cloth.

Dark smoke was billowing down the hallway and starting to enter the room. Outside, I could hear Hidemitsu's gravelly voice calling for sand so that they could dampen the fire and come for Nobunaga's head. I placed it beside his body. I touched the wrapped cloth and wept, but only for a moment. I could not allow the time.

I remembered kneeling in front of my people, tied up at the village hearth, my calloused hands pulling futilely at the ropes that bound them.

"I won't let them have you," I had repeated. I knew even then there was little I could do, but I could not stop myself from saying it over and over again, brushing my hand against their shoulders and faces. My words had no effect on their fear, but I continued speaking to them regardless. "I won't let them have you. I won't let them have you."

Kneeling before Nobunaga's body, I made the same promise I had made as a boy, kneeling before my captured people. One that a boy could not keep then, but a warrior now could.

"I will not let them have you."

I reached for my helm, touched the rhino horn that I had carved to perform for Nobunaga, and which he had so thoughtfully included in the design of my armor. His words, upon giving it to me, had been, "Let them see your face, and let them run from it."

Ranmaru lay dying quietly in the corner. Nobunaga's headless body lay keeled over in front of me.

"What's done is done," he had said, just hours ago when he had learned of Akechi's treachery. No regrets, or wondering about what might have been. I would follow his example. Whatever destiny I might have been born to, it ended when I was taken from my village. This was my new destiny, one which I had been set for since being sold to a mercenary for two bags of salt—to kill as many as I could. To fight and stand and hold as long as I could, to preserve the legacy of my lord Oda Nobunaga. I put on the helmet.

I ran down the hallway and over the railing of the veranda. I leapt through the flames with Nobunaga's sword in my hand, my lord's blood still dripping from it, and if the sudden fear on the face of the Akechi soldiers was to be my last pleasure in this world, it was enough.

I fought with the precision I had learned from the samurai and the rage I had learned from the mercenaries. My mind was clear and I was just the movements of my body. I pictured my father dancing in the sun, and, like when I had studied his dancing as a child, everything slowed.

My father snapped his wrist to make the dried nuts wrapped on his wrist rattle. I lifted the katana and struck first to the hands then across the chest, sending an Akechi man crumpling to the ground. My father stomped one stilt into the ground then leaned forward, shaking his shoulders. I executed a downward slice, perfectly placed to avoid the helmet but catch the face, ending another. My father dropped both knees to the ground, then popped himself up in a sharp twist. I spun and struck a rear-approaching soldier in the side of the helmet with the back of my fist, then quickly drew Nobunaga's sword across his throat. My father leaned back, thrusting his chest and throat upward to the sky. I struck down a fourth soldier, a fifth, a sixth.

I felt a spear jab into my shoulder. I grabbed the shaft of it as I twisted away, wrenching the spear from the hands of the soldier who had thrust it, before kicking him screaming into the fire. I pulled the spear from my shoulder, flipped it, and buried the head of it in the ribs of an onrushing soldier. I wrapped the shaft of the spear between my forearm and upper arm and snapped the shaft clean in half. I threw the broken end of the shaft at the closest of Akechi's men, and when he raised his arm to shield himself, I sliced deeply across his belly. I pushed his leaking body aside and continued forward.

Three soldiers came at me in a coordinated attack, naginatas raised. I slashed Nobunaga's sword with enough force to push all three spears aside, splintering the staff of the first, then finished the stunned men with three quick cuts. I saw Hidemitsu behind a crowd of men, the bone-white notch at the bridge of his nose clear in the morning sun, his eyes wide with fear. I had the satisfaction of seeing him turn and flee. Let him live with the shame of having chosen his own life. I would die here, in service to my lord. He was right—we were not the same.

Soldiers gathered around me, disorganized and afraid, and I gave them reason to feed their fear. After a lifetime of fighting for no other reason than that I'd been ordered to, I finally had a reason to fight, a belief. I slashed and struck and I was once again that young slave in the Indian courtyard, striking down every boy they placed before me, without remorse, without regard, without hesitation, but no longer without purpose. No longer without choice.

I piled the bodies of the Akechi dead in front of me. Their swords and arrows struck home, but did not slow me. I closed my eyes against the sweat and smoke and blood and tears and fought the Akechi men blind. My arms were too tired to swing a sword, my legs too heavy to move, but I forced myself to fight until the flames behind me grew hot enough to burn skin, burn bone. I pictured my father bringing his hands and knees down into the dirt, the drums gone silent, his dance completed, and only then did I give in to the exhaustion of my limbs. Only then did I succumb, and fall.

IV

Freedom

Until the lion has its own storyteller,
the hunter will have the better story.

—African proverb

33

I was holding my mother's hand on the long walk to the shore. She was dressed the way my father had described the queens and princesses of the great central African cities. Nine gold bands were wrapped around her neck, engraved with patterns of vine. She wore a gold ring in her nostril, and two gold chains linked her nose to her ear. Her eyes were covered with butterfly wings dipped in silver. Her hair was pulled into a long pleated braid running down her spine, twisted with orchids, and atop her head was the skull of an ostrich, its short gray fur combed soft, its beak jutting majestically from her forehead, its giant eye ringed with diamonds and rubies, the iris of it black and gleaming and eternal.

The sky was clear and the moon was full, our way lit almost as bright as in afternoon. Before us, the sand trembled and puffed and the beach came alive with the beaks and fins of tiny sea turtles, seeing the world for the first time and yet somehow knowing their way precisely.

They pulled themselves forward through the sand, scraping their soft underbellies against the grit, the shells on their backs not yet hardened. They moved as one, drawn to the great expanse of the sea, and one by one they slipped into the softly rolling surf and dipped beneath the surface. Where they belonged. Exchanging sand and sky for salt and the deep. Born into one world but meant for another.

I turned to my mother but she was gone, as were the sand and sea, replaced by the dusty road that led from the farmlands back to my village.

I caught a glimpse of my mother's back, running down the hill toward town, the hem of her skirt wrapped up in one arm, her laughter, free and clear, carried back to me on the wind. Around me were the baskets I'd dropped after she and her friends had stacked them in my arms, yams bouncing and rolling and coming to rest in the reddish-brown dirt.

I collected the spilled yams and carried the baskets down the hill and into my village, my mother's laughter still ringing in my ears. The buildings were intact, but empty. No smoke or ruin, but no people either, at least that I could see. There were sounds of young children chasing one another, their squeals and flapping footsteps echoing through the streets, but I saw no sign of the source.

I placed the baskets outside my front door and shook my arms out, releasing the dull ache that had built in them. I went into the backyard, pulled the cover back from the carving table. I ran my fingers along the tools, the half-carved masks, the blocks of acacia that had not yet been touched. I felt a hand on my shoulder.

I turned to see my father, grown old. His hair had gone gray and hung in short curls about his ears. His cheeks and forehead were wrinkled, the hand that had reached for me was spotted and frail and the fingers shook slightly as he pulled it away, but his eyes were alight, healthy, youthful.

"You found me."

My voice trembled, with both wonder and grief. He smiled, the wrinkles in his cheek gone smooth, his expression calm.

"No," he said. "Not yet."

I WOKE TO THE SOUND of church bells, the smell of incense.

I tried to lift myself from the small wooden cot I was lying on, but a dozen different body parts screamed their refusal. I groaned and lay back.

There were fragments of memory. Brought before Akechi, bleeding, beaten, barely conscious.

"Nobunaga's African," he spat. There were soldiers around us, but I did not know how many and could not raise my head to look.

"Any man who opposes us earns his own death," Akechi pronounced, more loudly than he needed to, speaking more to those assembled than to me. "But this is not one of ours. Nobunaga insults all of us by setting this man amongst us."

I saw blood drip onto the ground in front of me. Nobunaga's sword was through my sash but my arms were being held, and even if they had not been, I lacked the strength to swing them. Through a haze, I listened to Akechi's words, but the venom in them felt false. He had not approved of my ascension to samurai, but at the reception after Tenmokuzan he had spoken respectfully to me. Those words felt more true from him than the ones he spoke now, but I left them unchallenged, fought just to stay awake.

"He is not even human, is not worthy of death."

There was a cheer from the soldiers behind me, then Akechi's hand on my chin, bringing my face to his. His expression softened, became the same stoic look of Tenmokuzan, and I could see in his eyes that this anger was just display.

"Send this black beast back to the Jesuits."

A sudden panic gripped me and lifted me from the cot. I bolted upright despite the pain, scanned the room. There, in the corner, was Nobunaga's sword. Akechi had not recognized it as Nobunaga's, and not considered that Nobunaga could have given it to me.

"Easy, easy," called a friendly voice.

Brother Organtino entered the room, smiling, as always. I turned toward him and felt something in my ribs spasm.

"Sit back. Please."

"How long have I been here?"

"Over a week, I'm sorry to say. Some of your wounds had become quite infected. You've roused a few times here and there, and we've managed to get water into you, and a little food. But this is the first time I've seen you anything close to lucid. Are you hungry?"

At the mention of food, my stomach ached in its emptiness. I nodded and Organtino signaled to another priest in the hallway.

"We're in Kyoto?"

"Yes," Organtino replied slowly, seemingly deciding how much to tell me. "The church in Azuchi . . . is no more, I'm afraid. Nor, really, is Azuchi itself."

I swallowed hard and laid my head back, thinking of the servants that had stayed behind to look after my small home and garden. Thinking of Tomiko. I had no doubt Azuchi's defenders had fought well, but Akechi knew the castle far better than any enemy would. Whatever happened, I hoped they had escaped.

"Tell me."

"Yes." Organtino cleared his throat. "After Honno-ji, Akechi sent his men through the streets of Kyoto to root out Oda loyalists. There were executions on the temple grounds, amongst the ruins. All very . . . difficult. He also sent forces to Azuchi. The castle, as you are well aware, was left with just a token force for its defense and Akechi knows the castle as well as any man. It was overwhelmed quickly and burnt to the ground."

"Akechi rules now?" I asked the question through gritted teeth, already planning how I would get to him.

"No. Akechi gravely miscalculated. The Oda vassals did not want to be stained by Akechi's treason. They did not resist him, but did not join him either. They left him to stand or fall on his own. He also miscalculated on Toyotomi. Akechi had foolishly sent a messenger to the Mori asking them to support his claim. One of Toyotomi's men intercepted the messenger. Toyotomi negotiated a hasty peace treaty with the Mori and was marching his army back to Kyoto before Akechi had any time to consolidate power. Nobunaga has been avenged, if that means something to you."

He said this last piece softly. He was beside the bed now, wiping my face and arms with a wet cloth. I thought of Akechi's face when I was brought before him. It was the first time in all my time in Japan that someone had spoken disdainfully to me because of my skin. Akechi's anger while he insulted me and dismissed me and ordered me taken to the Jesuits was so much different than how calmly he had spoken to me after our defeat of the Takeda. Was it an act? Had he hoped that sending me back here would secure the support of the Jesuits?

"Did Akechi also miscalculate on support from Valignano?"

Brother Organtino shifted nervously, unwilling to look at me.

"Why did Father Valignano visit Hatano Hideharu at Azuchi? What did he say to Hideharu that caused him to provoke Nobunaga?"

"I did not go inside. I did not speak with them."

"But surely you know—"

"Please," he interrupted. "You no longer need to concern yourself with Japanese politics."

"Why do you say that?" I asked, but Organtino's face became so tortured in response that I let the question pass.

"Where is Father Valignano?"

"He's traveling. He's in the north, but he plans to leave Japan soon. He'll return to the port city of Nagasaki, then on to Europe." Organtino clasped his hands in front of him, looked away, hesitated. "There are early signs of . . . hostility toward our mission. From Toyotomi. Perhaps Akechi was not the only one who miscalculated."

A second priest entered the room with a platter and a bowl of broth, the steam rising off it. A fresh-looking piece of bread. My stomach stirred and I sat up a little.

I remembered Brother Organtino's words to me during our last meeting at Azuchi, speaking of Valignano. "He is more fond of you than you know. And he protects you more than you know."

"Valignano told Akechi not to kill me. That was part of the arrangement."

Organtino sucked in his breath, signaled the other priest to leave.

"Valignano is harsh, as you know, but he is not unfair. Perhaps he felt your life has been traded enough times."

Organtino stood.

"I'll let you eat and rest."

As he turned to walk out of the room, I called out to him.

"Nobunaga. Did they find his remains?"

"None that could be recognized," Organtino said gently. "He was consumed by the fire, it seems."

WHEN I WAS WELL ENOUGH, I was given chores around the church. Sweeping, cleaning, small repairs to clothing or equipment. But never outside the compound. Nevertheless, I heard rumors. Toyotomi had secured his leadership, routing the remaining Akechi forces and soliciting pledges of allegiance from Oda vassals, typically in the form of family members.

Tokugawa, his greatest rival for the position, had quietly moved from Suruga Province, which had been granted him by Nobunaga, back to his home province of Mikawa, completing a treacherous crossing of Iga Province along the way. There was peace between the two men, but an uneasy one.

"Am I being held here?" I asked one day.

Brother Organtino shuffled his hands beneath his robe and answered as honestly as he dared.

"You are the last surviving member of Nobunaga's inner circle. The wisdom of housing you here is . . . still unclear."

AFTER SEVERAL WEEKS HAD PASSED, I was called to come to the gate of the compound. I knew what that would mean, and had already made my decision. I dressed and packed a small bag, and tucked Nobunaga's sword and scabbard in a sash at my waist.

In the shadow of the church's entrance gate, Brother Organtino was receiving a small circle of priests. Front and center amongst them was Father Valignano, his beard slightly longer, his skin slightly darker, but still with the same imperious air. At his shoulder stood Brother Ambrosius, the priest who had first received us at Nagasaki, the long scar on the left of his jaw slicing through his stubbly beard. With him stood a half dozen others, all with the same hard look. The faces of soldiers in the frocks of priests. Valignano was gesturing in the way of one offering instruction.

"You're a long way from Nagasaki," I said.

Valignano turned to me, perturbed at having been interrupted.

"Yes. I've gone quite out of my way to come gather you. We're to return to Europe."

"I wish you a good journey, but I won't be joining you. I'm staying here, in Japan."

Valignano's smug smile froze in place. His face hardened, the cold expression I had seen him use on a score of junior priests. He clasped his hands in front of him, adopting his preferred stance of command.

"That's not your choice to make, Brother Isaac."

In his look I saw the nameless slaver who had dragged me to market, the Portuguese mercenary who had trained me, the Jesuit priest who told me my people were beasts. All the people I had ceded to. But I was no longer content with mere survival, nor, even, with the crumbs of occasional kindness offered by those who would look down on me. Not when Nobunaga had shown me I deserved more.

"My name is Yasuke," I said, meeting his stare. "And it is my choice to make. It always has been."

I brushed past him. He took a surprised step backward, scowling as he did so. The other men didn't move. As I walked through the gate and out into the streets of Kyoto, Brother Organtino blessed me with one last smile.

34

To live.

That had been Lord Nobunaga's final command to me, and I would honor it.

I bartered for a strong horse and rode for Azuchi. I did not rush—there was no need to. I followed the same path I had followed on my first trip to Azuchi, alongside Ranmaru and Nobunaga. There was a pang of regret when I reached the penultimate hill in the early dawn. Despite the news, I was still half expecting to see the golden pagoda of Azuchi Castle glinting in the rising sun, awaiting the emperor's visit. Instead I saw the rubble of buildings torn to the ground, the scorch marks upon the earth, the razed fields.

Some of the homes still stood and others did not. As I prodded the horse up the path to the castle gate, I could not bear to turn and look down the narrow lane that led to the home I had been given. I hoped it still stood, but I did not want to know.

As for the servants, I expected they were safe. Whatever Akechi was, he believed in honoring the old ways. Servants would not be harmed, provided they did not raise arms in the fighting.

If Toyotomi ruled now, then perhaps Tomiko was in his service, but I hoped she was not. I hoped she had been released and was riding west to Mori lands even now, to see her brother again, her father.

When I spoke to her before leaving for Tenmokuzan, when I told her how I thought my life would have been if I had not been taken, she considered it all for a moment, then replied in her quiet voice.

"You know what you would have been if your past was different. You know what you are today, what men have made you. The only thing that matters is who you will be tomorrow. And that choice is yours to make."

This was the gift Nobunaga had given me—the freedom to choose who I would be.

The stairs were all that remained of Masahide-ji. I found a rock with a sharp enough edge and started digging in front of them. When I had a hole that was long and deep enough, I placed Nobunaga's sword inside it and covered it up. I did not know how the Japanese prayed, so I offered my own words. I called out to Masahide to let him know that his sacrifice had not been in vain. That his young charge, Nobunaga, had brought honor to the Oda clan. That the Fool of Owari had become, for a time, the most powerful man in Japan.

The sun was beginning to reveal itself in full behind the mountains, turning the valley and the lake a vibrant orange. I remembered my mother and father, when they said goodbye to each other for the last time, their shadows touching foreheads one to another in the morning sun.

I looked down. Beneath me were mostly slabs of rock that had been buried and leveled to create a floor around the temple, but near the temple stairs, where I had dug, a cracked stone had left open a patch of raw dirt. In it, I had left a single, solitary footprint. Perhaps my ancestors had watched over me after all. Even in this place so far from home, I was not alone.

I was now swordless, and masterless. There were choices to be made, but none that needed to be made immediately. I stood for a moment, admiring the view. I would begin by seeing some of the land that my lord had loved. That my friend had loved. I picked a direction and mounted my horse.

AUTHOR'S NOTE

Yasuke was a man of African origin born in the sixteenth century who was taken from his home as a child by slave traders. When he was a young man, he accompanied Jesuit missionaries to Japan, where he was "given" to Oda Nobunaga, a Japanese warlord.

In writing *The African Samurai*, I have adhered as closely as possible to known facts and timelines. There are, of course, conflicting accounts regarding some of these events, but I have typically gone with the most widely accepted. There are two areas where I knowingly made alterations, but in both cases I believe I remained true to the spirit of events and was not egregious with my changes.

The first element that I reimagined involved the execution of Hatano Hideharu and the subsequent execution of Akechi's mother by the Hatano clan. Those events did occur, but they occurred a couple years prior to their presentation in the novel. I brought those events forward to make the connection to Akechi's betrayal more immediate and to avoid having to tell the details in flashback or in conversation.

The second involved the culminating events at Honno-ji. Yasuke was amongst the small party who accompanied Nobunaga to Honno-ji before he was betrayed. He was also captured by Akechi forces and brought before Akechi, who insulted him and ordered him sent back to the Jesuits. However, Yasuke was not captured at Honno-ji, as is presented here. He escaped through Akechi lines and made it to a nearby compound where one of Nobunaga's sons was staying, to provide him with a warning. Whether this was done under his own auspices or under direction from Nobunaga is debated. Regardless, the warning was too late, Akechi forces overwhelmed them, Nobunaga's son had to also commit seppuku, and Yasuke was captured there. I modified this because it would be anticlimactic unless I were to make Nobunaga's sons into major characters themselves, and I did not want to expand the cast.

Another research-related element: there is some dispute about Yasuke's origin. Some suggest he was Ethiopian, others from Sudan. Most think he was from the Makua tribe in Mozambique, and that is what I used as the basis for the African customs, legends, and so on. Because of the dispute, however, I stopped short of explicitly stating either the tribe or location. Very little is recorded about his life prior to Japan, and so the sections taking place in India, Portugal, and China are mostly speculation.

What happened to Yasuke after Akechi sent him back to the Jesuits is unclear. He may have gone back to Portugal or even to Africa, or he may have remained in Japan. There are descriptions of people who might be Yasuke, seen fighting in Kuchinotsu, the port city where he arrived, and in Korea, where Toyotomi Hideyoshi deployed armies after completing Nobunaga's push for unification. However, there are no confirmed accounts. Yasuke's post-Nobunaga life is largely unknown because there are no records produced by Yasuke himself, only records of others' observations of him. This made me think, on a larger scale, about history in general. It's often said that what we know is skewed because history books are written by victors, but I think that is overly simplistic. I think that what we know is skewed because history books are *written*, period. We are deeply familiar with the pasts of cultures that provided written histories, and largely ignorant of the pasts of those which practiced oral histories, such as Indigenous and African cultures. This is the importance of recording our stories, and of sharing them with one another. I'm grateful to have been able to share this one with you.

SELECTED BIBLIOGRAPHY

Chaplin, Danny. *Sengoku Jidai: Nobunaga, Hideyoshi, and Ieyasu: Three Unifiers of Japan*. Createspace, 2018.

Lockley, Thomas and Geoffrey Girard. *Yasuke: The True Story of the Legendary African Samurai*. Great Britain: Sphere, 2020.

Mason, R. H. P. and J. G. Caiger. *A History of Japan*. Tokyo: Tuttle, 1997.

Ota, Gyūichi. *The Chronicle of Lord Nobunaga*. Translated and edited by J. S. A. Elisonas and J. P. Lamers. Leiden: Brill, 2011.

Russel, John G. "The Other Other: The Black Presence in the Japanese Experience." *Japan's Minorities: The Illusion of Homogeneity*, edited by Michael Weiner. New York: Routledge, 2009.

Turnbull, Stephen *War in Japan 1467–1615*. Great Britain: Osprey, 2002.

Yamamoto, Tsunetomo. *Hagakure: The Way of the Samurai*, 1716.

Additional Sources

The YouTube informational series *The Shogunate*

Isaac Meyer's *History of Japan* podcast

SengokuArchives.com

The Facebook group Feudal Japanese Miniature Wargaming

The description of Yasuke's mother in chapter 33 is based on the artwork of Adeyemi Adegbesan. You can see his work at yungyemi.com.

The poem on page 213 is from *Yasuke: The True Story of the Legendary African Samurai*.

ACKNOWLEDGMENTS

Enormous gratitude and credit are owed to my editor, Janie Yoon, who knew exactly how to bring out the best in this story. I can truly say this story isn't mine, it's ours.

My agent, Chris Casuccio, has been a tireless champion for this book from the beginning, and his efforts on my behalf have been far above and beyond what was expected.

My thanks to Diane Young for her invaluable input on early drafts and her career guidance in general, and to David Oiye for his early read and comments.

With travel being curbed by the pandemic, I was left looking for alternate solutions. Fujimoto Kenji at Japan Exploration Tours came to the rescue, performing research on key sites for me, including providing live walk-throughs and video recordings.

Thank you to the Japan Foundation of Toronto and to G. Coyote at Paradise Bound for sending additional research materials.

I want to acknowledge the community at One Academy for their belief in me, and for constantly reminding me that not only is it possible to take on big challenges, it's necessary.

Last but certainly not least, I am grateful for the support that I have received from all of my family and friends. Special thanks are due to Beth Jean Evans for many "no-talk" writing get-togethers, for the playlist that accompanied me through most of the work, and for always having snacks.

THE
AFRICAN
SAMURAI

CRAIG SHREVE

This reading group guide for The African Samurai *includes an introduction and discussion questions to enhance the conversations sparked by this book. The suggested questions are intended to help your reading group find new and interesting angles and topics for your discussion. We hope that these ideas will enrich your conversation and increase your enjoyment of the book.*

INTRODUCTION

Set in late sixteenth-century Africa, India, Portugal, and Japan, *The African Samurai* is based on the true life story of Yasuke, Japan's first foreign-born samurai and the only samurai to be of African descent. Timeless and epic, the novel is a magnificent reconstruction and moving study of a lost historical figure, and a truly enthralling dramatization of the complex political machinations of the time, from which rises the most unlikely of heroes.

TOPICS & QUESTIONS
FOR DISCUSSION

1. Yasuke's first memory of his home in Africa is of seeing the turtles hatch and go to sea. What is the significance of this memory for him?

2. What are the different ways in which the idea of home is represented in the novel? What does home mean for Nobunaga? What does home mean for Yasuke?

3. When we first meet Yasuke, he is in the service of Father Valignano. Does Yasuke serve as bodyguard? Confidant? How does their relationship seem simple on the surface, but proves complicated as the novel unfolds?

4. Yasuke is given as a "gift" to Oda Nobunaga. What does it say of Nobunaga that Valignano perceives Yasuke to be the key to getting permission to build a church in Japan?

5. What is the significance of "tenka fubu"—"the realm under one sword"—in the novel? Does it refer only to Oda Nobunaga's vision and ambitions for Japan?

6. How does Nobunaga's vision for a united Japan relate to his fascination for "all things foreign"?

7. Once in the service of Nobunaga, Yasuke begins to remember, to piece together his past, in his home village in Africa, in India as a child soldier, in Portugal under the tutelage of the Jesuits. Discuss his journey and how it informs his service to Nobunaga.

8. How does Yasuke's memories of his mother and father inform his present life?

9. How does Yasuke's experience training and working as a child soldier in India shape his life's path?

10. How does the Jesuits' instruction and treatment in Portugal different from Yasuke's treatment and instruction later by Father Valignano?

11. Sumo wrestling, Noh theater, samurai, seppuku—Yasuke becomes steeped in Japanese culture and tradition. What deeper meaning and symbolism can be derived from these traditions? Why does Nobunaga introduce them to Yasuke?

12. Nobunaga is described as one who "respects tradition but is not bound by it." In what ways does he show respect for tradition, and in what ways does he show that he is not bound by it?

13. What is the significance of Nobunaga asking Yasuke to be his second when performing the ritual seppuku?

14. What does freedom ultimately mean to Yasuke?

CRAIG SHREVE was born and raised in North Buxton, Ontario, a small town that has been recognized by the Canadian government as a National Historic Site due to its former status as a popular terminus on the Underground Railroad, the system of routes and safe houses that assisted slaves escaping from the Southern states. He is a descendant of Abraham Doras Shadd, the first Black person in Canada to be elected to public office, and of his daughter Mary Ann Shadd, the pioneering abolitionist, suffragette, and newspaper editor and publisher who was inducted posthumously into the National Women's Hall of Fame in the United States. He is the author of *One Night in Mississippi*, and a graduate of the Humber School for Writers. He lives in Toronto, Ontario. Connect with him on Twitter @CG_Shreve.